The Book of Extraordinary Historical Mystery Stories

The Book of Extraordinary Historical Mystery Stories

Best New Original Mysteries

Edited by Maxim Jakubowski

Mango Publishing
CORAL GABLES

Copyright © 2019 by Maxim Jakubowski
Copyright © 2019 individual contributors stories
Published by Mango Publishing Group, a division of Mango Media Inc.
Cover & Layout Design: Jermaine Lau

Mango Publishing Group
2850 Douglas Road, 2nd Floor
Coral Gables, FL 33134 USA
info@mango.bz

For special orders, quantity sales, course adoptions and corporate sales, please email the publisher at sales@mango.bz. For trade and wholesale sales, please contact Ingram Publisher Services at customer.service@ingramcontent.com or +1.800.509.4887.

The Book of Extraordinary Historical Mystery Stories: Best New Original Mysteries
Library of Congress Cataloging
ISBN: (p) 978-1-63353-968-6 (e) 978-1-63353-969-3
Library of Congress Control Number: 2019935686
BISAC category code: FIC022060 FICTION / Mystery & Detective / Historical

Printed in the United States of America

Table of Contents

Introduction

Welcome to what we hope will become a long-lasting series of anthologies presenting the best in genre.

Crime and mystery fiction has for decades proven both popular and commercial in all its guises, from the hallowed investigations of Sherlock Holmes to the mean streets of contemporary noir, through the golden age of Agatha Christie and her traditional cohorts, the dark shadows of psychological thrillers, women detectives, private eyes, and a variety of categories that have persisted in defying the imagination and seducing readers in thinking that crime does, in fact, pay or, at any rate, royally entertain!

For our opening volume, we present fifteen brand-new stories by some of the best authors practicing the craft today, each introducing imaginative facets of crime and its subtle variations but set in the past, in periods ranging from far-flung prehistory to the murky days of World War II, and moving through medieval periods, mythical times, the somber alleys of Victorian times, and a whole variety of past years and places where the allure of mystery only serves to enhance the deviousness of the plots and their heroes and villains.

Historical mysteries are one of today's most rewarding subgenres, often characterized by the charms of Umberto Eco's *The Name of the Rose*, the Brother Cadfael tales of the late Ellis Peters, and so many other major talents of the writing world. In times without forensics and the modern tools of the detecting trade, the authors and their hardy characters must use their little gray cells and their powers of deduction with so much more diligence than the detectives and cops of today, and this often constitutes one of the greatest charms of historical mysteries (and fiction).

But, first and foremost, these are tales to exercise your imagination and set your sense of wonder free.

The next volume in the series will present a similar panorama of amateur sleuths and private eyes, and we hope you will keep this deadly appointment.

Enjoy!

—Maxim Jakubowski

The Sound of Secrecy

Martin Edwards

Jersey, 1999

I recognized her at once.

After so many years apart, I'd wondered if we might we pass each other by without even realizing. Oddly, that seemed a more dreadful prospect than that she might simply not turn up for the funeral. For all I knew, she was already cold in her grave. At our age, every day is a bonus. Yet, somehow, I knew that, if she could possibly manage it, she'd make the journey across the Channel. I felt certain she'd want to pay her last respects to Edward Le Saux. After all, she'd driven him to murder.

I slipped into the small, draughty church two minutes before the service was due to begin. The good turnout came as no surprise. By all accounts, Edward had made a success of his life. A couple of failed marriages, admittedly, but he'd earned a fortune in high finance, and in his later years he'd given a large chunk of it away to good causes. I wondered if his largesse represented conscience money, an attempt to atone for what he'd done. A killer turned philanthropist, in search of redemption.

Lina was sitting at the end of a pew, trim as ever in her black coat. The ash-blonde hair had turned gray but looked as silky as ever. The urge to touch it was almost impossible to resist, but I took a place on the other side of the aisle, right at the back. At that moment, she glanced over her shoulder, and our eyes met. Hers were an unforgettable shade of cerulean blue. I held her gaze for a few moments, and then she looked away. Did a smile of pleasure play on her lips, or was I succumbing to my old vice of wishful thinking?

As I picked up the order of service, the organ began to play. *Nimrod.* Fitting enough, given Le Saux's physique. I found myself drumming my fingers against the back of the pew in front of me, but when the elderly man next to me gave a reproachful cough, I forced myself to stop. My thoughts, as so often these days, stumbled back to the past.

Bletchley Park, 1942

The rattling of the teleprinters made me grind my teeth. Noise always bothered me, but in the long, low wooden huts, there was no escape from it. It was like listening to a horde of women knitting in a frenzy. Someone had left the door open, and I took advantage of their carelessness to stand there with my eyes fixed on Lina Wraithmell. Watching her bend over the machine as paper spewed out.

She'd arrived in January, one of half a dozen young women recruited to tackle the flood of incoming messages. At that point, BP only ran to a single teleprinter, kept under the stairs in the Hall, operated by two girls to an eight-hour shift, three shifts a day. They worked like slaves, but so did the rest of us: there was a war on. The first time I saw Lina was mid-way through a night shift, when I was summoned to a briefing in an office on the first floor of the Hall. She was taking a nap, curled up on the pile of cardboard boxes next to the machine. Even exhausted, even uncomfortable, even with those beautiful eyes shut tight, she was the most marvelous creature I'd ever seen.

Within a few months, BP acquired more than thirty teleprinters, and as one of the most experienced operators, Lina was sent to work in our hut. I couldn't believe my luck, though I didn't know how to make the most of it. I talked to her whenever the opportunity arose, but I'd never plucked up the courage to ask her out.

Heavy footsteps slapped the floor of the corridor, making the linoleum squeak in protest. Looking up, I saw Edward Le Saux heading toward me. Six feet five and fourteen stone, he had an elephant's tread. You could tell from his gait that he brimmed with confidence. His father, an offshore banker, had sent him to be educated at Westminster. Le Saux was an only child, the apple of his pater's eye, and there wasn't a school on his native island deemed good enough for him. Of course, his examination results proved to be as brilliant as his performances on the rugby field. The move to Oxford, the same transition that had transformed my life, opening my eyes to a brave new world of infinite possibilities, he'd taken pretty much for granted. He marched around the front quad at St John's as if he owned the whole college.

A crooked grin warned me that he knew exactly why I was loitering outside the teleprinter room. "Aye, keeping tabs on the lovely Lina, eh?"

At least the cacophony meant that nobody else could hear his booming voice. I felt color suffusing my cheeks. I'd always hated being teased, though God knew I'd had plenty of experience, plenty of time to harden myself to gibes. Always the odd one out at school, the stammering swot, the bespectacled boy from a drab suburb of Derby who cared more for mathematics than for the companionship of his peers.

"Just taking a break before putting my nose back to the grindstone." With Le Saux, I liked to affect a casual manner. It was as if I were experimenting with a different type of personality, trying it on like a new jacket in a tailor's shop. I don't suppose he was fooled for a minute.

He slapped me on the back with his huge left paw, jarring my spine. "If you say so, Prof. I'm off to the canteen. Fancy coming for a brew?"

I was about to say no, I'd told my oppo I'd only be gone for five minutes to meet a call of nature, when Lina pushed back her chair and got to her feet. She must have been about to take the length of tape to the translators in the next-door hut. As she turned, she saw us standing in the doorway, and mustered a weary smile. Le Saux winked and jerked his head toward the way out. She stole a quick glance at her oppo, still intent on the job in hand, before nodding in reply.

"All right," I said.

"That's the ticket!" He made as if to give me another encouraging back slap, but for once I was nimble enough to skip out of reach.

Jersey, 1999

When people began to make their way to the graveside, I lingered outside the church door. My own prayer was answered as Lina approached me. She walked slowly, but her movements betrayed no hint of stiffness, and her back wasn't in the least bowed. Not like mine. She was tall for a woman, still elegant and poised. *Soignée*, you might say.

"Wilf." She held out a gloved hand. "How wonderful to see you. It's been a long time since BP."

"Fifty-seven years." I squeezed her fingers tight, couldn't help myself. "You haven't changed."

She laughed, that unforgettably sunny sound, before withdrawing her hand. "If only. Makeup works miracles these days, thank heaven. Don't look too closely for wrinkles or age spots, will you? At least I'm not forced to wear those wretched mittens anymore."

The intense cold at Bletchley Park had caused many of the young women to wear woolen mittens. Hers were gaily patterned, I recalled, zig-zags of yellow and red. The colors, she joked, contrasted with the blue of her fingers when she left her mittens back at her billet in Gayhurst.

"I wondered if you might be here," I said.

"The same thought crossed my mind when I read that Edward had died," she said. "That you'd come to say goodbye to him, if you could. He was your friend."

Were he and I friends? I suppose that's how people regarded us. At Oxford, we'd done little more than exchange banal civilities, despite the fact that we were studying the same subject at the same college. He was two years above me and infinitely more mature, while our backgrounds could scarcely be more different: the well-heeled public schoolboy and the shy grammar school lad whose parents had both started work at fourteen. At BP, things were different; nobody cared where you came from, whether you were a civilian or in the services. Even rank hardly mattered; only the toadies wasted much time in saluting. Since Le Saux and I were already acquainted and worked in the same hut, people bracketed us together. Perhaps that perception of friendship was closer to truth than I believed at the time. I'd regarded Le Saux as a competitor for her affections, a fearsome rival in a contest never openly acknowledged. In my heart of hearts, I knew it was a battle I could never win.

My stammer had faded away at Oxford, but now I was tongue-tied in her company. I hadn't lied; it was astonishing how little she'd changed. Although she was wrapped up warmly in coat and scarf, she looked as though she'd not put on a pound in weight. I felt hapless and hopeless. The stirring conversational gambits I'd practiced fled from my mind.

"It's marvelous to see you again."

"And you, Wilf." She slipped her arm through mine. "Come on, we'd better join the rest of the mourners. Don't want to give people the wrong impression, do we?"

Bletchley Park, 1942

Hut Two was home to the canteen as well as a lending library. People liked to moan about the food and grumbled that even if second helpings had been allowed, there'd be no takers, but I had few complaints. I never had a big appetite, but was addicted to coffee, and at BP, thank the Lord, tins of the real thing from Lyons were in plentiful supply. Lina, a fussy eater, pulled a face as Le Saux helped himself to a fruit pie out of a packet.

"I don't know how you can eat those cardboard tarts. I'm sure they must be bad for your digestion."

"You're right." He never minded talking with his mouth full. "Tarts have never done me any good. I just can't help myself."

She giggled and told him he was awful. For the hundredth time I found myself envying his easy way with women. Such an ugly fellow, Le Saux, with that nose smashed into a shapeless lump on the playing fields of England, yet the fact he was far from conventionally handsome didn't affect his ability to charm the ladies. He'd enjoyed a fling with one of the Wrens, a busty and none-too-bright redhead, which had been ended by her transfer to an outstation. The powers that be, Le Saux confided in me, had concluded that her work wasn't up to snuff, although he could vouch for her skills in at least one area of human activity. Naturally, he wasn't heartbroken. Plenty more fish in the sea, he assured me. Especially at BP, where women outnumbered us three to one.

"May I join you good folks?"

The smug drawl was unmistakable. I felt myself shudder at the sound of it. Ray Bonetti was in his early thirties, a sleek, dark-haired linguist with a toothbrush moustache, whose faint resemblance to Errol Flynn had earned him the nickname Captain Blood. His mother, Le Saux had told me, was an Italian artist who had fallen in love with a London gallery owner and settled in Britain at the turn of the century. Ray's ancestry made him suspect, given that Il Duce was hand in glove with Hitler, but he'd been given the necessary clearance, worse luck. The moment he'd arrived at BP, he'd cottoned on to Lina. She must surely have found his smarminess and self-satisfaction as infuriating as Le Saux and I did, but her natural good manners meant that she never did enough to discourage him from seeking out her company.

"If you must." Le Saux's habitual grin almost robbed the words of offence, but not quite.

"How's my favorite boffin?" Bonetti demanded. "Wilf, old fellow, I'm counting on you to bring this damned war to a swift conclusion, you hear?"

I winced. Even in jest, it wasn't the done thing to allude to our work. All of us had signed the Official Secrets Act the moment we walked through the front gates. We'd taken a solemn oath, and we had to stick to it as if the slightest lapse were punishable with death. For all we knew, it would be. None of us was really sure what work anyone else here was carrying out; we knew only what we needed to know in order to do our jobs. But Bonetti was a braggart and a hard drinker—a dangerous combination. Fluent in five languages he might be, but I hoped against hope that the authorities would realize their blunder and post him elsewhere. Even though the rule at Bletchley Park was supposed to be *once in, never out.*

I took so long to frame a reply that he lost interest and turned his attention to Lina. "Hello, my dear. How are tricks?"

"Tricks are fine, Ray," Lina said calmly. "To what do we owe the honor of your company? Come to tell me you're having second thoughts about taking me to the flicks tonight?"

He smirked. "Anyone would think you didn't trust me."

Le Saux scowled at him, and seemed about to say something, before thinking better of it.

"Should I trust you?" Lina's tone was unexpectedly coquettish, and a shocking thought sprang into my head. What if she actually found him attractive? Surely it was inconceivable.

"With your life!" He chortled. "Seven o'clock at the front gate, it's a date."

"I might decide to stay in Gayhurst and wash my hair instead."

"You won't do that," Bonetti smirked. "You wouldn't want to miss James Mason, would you? Even if he isn't a patch on Errol Flynn."

Jersey, 1999

The mourners began to drift away from the graveside. Edward Le Saux had no children, and his obituary in the *Daily Telegraph* had mentioned that both his former wives were dead, but the well-preserved companion of his declining years, a woman called Marilyn, had arranged for people to go on to a hotel for refreshments.

I murmured to Lina, "You'll remember, I was never much of a one for socializing. Would you care to come for a walk with me? It would be good to talk. Catch up on old times."

She didn't hesitate. "I'd like that, Wilf. There's no one else here I know, and I imagine you're in the same boat."

I nodded. "I never met any of Le Saux's family. By the time I went up to Oxford, the war had already begun. He was stuck on the mainland, with Jersey under German occupation."

"It must have been desperately difficult for him," she said. "He was such a fierce patriot. A phrase he taught me sticks in my mind. Jersey had a unique status in the British Empire, he called it *a peculiar of the Crown*. Marvelous phrase, don't you agree? It tickled my fancy. I suppose that's why he cared so much about his work at BP, wasn't it? He was determined to save his family from Hitler's tyranny."

I raised my eyebrows. "He never spoke about it to me."

"Dear Wilf." She tugged at my arm. "Those thick-lensed glasses never cured your short-sightedness, did they? It's just as Edward said. Affectionately, mind. You always lived in a world of your own. Not seeing what was right in front of you."

I stiffened. What did she mean? Had she carried a torch for me after all? Was that what had brought her to Le Saux's funeral?

"Sorry," I mumbled. "I suppose I've always led a sheltered life. When I was young, I was extremely naive. I can't even claim to be worldly-wise in my dotage."

"Perhaps that's what made you such an expert code-breaker. That single-mindedness."

"Obsessiveness, you mean."

"Perhaps. Anyway, I'm sure you were invaluable. That's why they kept you on at BP after the balloon went up. After Edward and I were banished."

"Banished?"

She shrugged. "Moved on. Shoved out of harm's way. Come on, let's take a stroll. Don't walk too fast, will you? My tennis-playing days are long behind me, alas. But the harbor is just round the corner, and a breath of sea air will do me good."

Bletchley Park, 1942

"Enjoy the film?"

I bumped into Lina under one of the trees that fringed the lake, our paths crossing as she returned to her post after a break. For the past twenty-four hours, I'd been consumed by jealousy about her date with Bonetti, and I nursed a secret hope that he'd behaved so despicably that she'd slapped his face and resolved to have nothing more to do with him. I'd no doubt that if his hands had wandered in the darkened cinema, she'd have put him in his place.

Her vigorous nod made my heart sink. "James Mason is such a dreamboat. He plays this deranged composer, and two women are trying to find out what happened to a friend who went missing...well, I won't spoil it for you. You must go and see it for yourself. *The Night Has Eyes* is the title. It's terrific, ever so spooky."

"I'm glad," I said miserably. "I'll bear it in mind."

"You do that. Oh well, duty calls. Must dash."

Five minutes later, when I was back in the hut myself, Le Saux demanded, "What's eating you, Prof?"

I found myself muttering something about Bonetti, and Le Saux put a beefy arm around my shoulder. "Fellow's a creep. I don't trust him an inch. Not fit to lick Lina's boots."

"I hate to think of her being...messed about," I said thickly.

"Oh, don't worry your head about Miss Lina Wraithmell. Take my word for it, she can take bloody good care of herself."

"She's only nineteen."

"You may think she's only a slip of a thing, but you haven't played tennis with her. Hell of a powerful forehand. Don't forget, she's not a deb. Her uncle was a boxer, you've probably heard of him. Whirlwind Wraithmell."

I'd never come across the name. Boxing repelled me; how could men hitting each other be termed a sport? "I didn't know that."

He laughed. "There's probably a lot you don't know about young Lina. She's not only delicious to look at, she's...ah well, never mind."

"What about Bonetti?"

"I need to have a quiet word." Le Saux's expression hardened. "Friend Bonetti will get the message to keep his greasy hands off, don't you fear."

Jersey, 1999

As Lina and I strolled past the buildings that looked out onto Gorey's harbor, I almost needed to pinch myself. Over the years, I'd dreamed of spending time in her company a thousand times, but I'd feared my fantasies would never become a reality. Yet I'd booked in at my hotel in St Helier for two nights, daring to hope that, if she came to the funeral, I could persuade her to have dinner with me. After decades apart, we had so much to say to each other. Yet, now it came to the point, somehow we didn't need to keep chattering nineteen to the dozen. She was very good at companionable silences.

"Charming, isn't it?" she said, breaking into my rêverie. Her wave took in the boats bobbing on the water, the harbor wall, and on the hill above, the sturdy gray bulk of the ancient castle. "Even on a cold autumn day, it's like a picture postcard."

"And you're even more charming," I said gallantly.

"You're still awfully sweet, Wilf." She squeezed my hand. "I really was very fond of you, I'm sure you picked up on that."

My heart skipped a beat. I knew that I mustn't gush. This was the chance of a lifetime. I mustn't make a fool of myself. "So your husband died five years ago? I'm sorry."

"It was a blessed release when the end came. Graeme was the managing director of a steelworks in Newcastle for fifteen years, but then his memory failed, and the last few months were very difficult. No fun getting old, is it?" She stared out at the gray water. "What about you? Did you marry, have a family?"

It was on the tip of my tongue to say no, of course not, there could never be anyone else for me, but I had the sense to restrain myself.

"People used to say that I was married to my work." I ventured a self-deprecating laugh. "I finished up in a university. A bit of teaching, but mainly research, thank goodness. Nothing remarkable. I published a few academic books which are now years out of date."

Bletchley Park, 1942

The night in question, that never-to-be-forgotten night, I was peering at a particularly complicated piece of encryption in the dim yellow light of a small, green-shaded lamp. It suited me to lose myself in the mysteries of code-breaking. When I wrestled with a knotty problem, I was no longer conscious of the rumble and roar of the bombe machines—the sound of secrecy, people called the racket—and I no longer felt nauseous, even though the shuttered blackout windows imprisoned the fumes from the leaky coke-burning stoves and made the air foul.

A huge hand clamped my shoulder in a vise-like grip.

"Prof. Spare me a moment," Le Saux hissed in my ear.

"I'd better just—"

"*Now.*"

His voice was barely audible, but his urgency didn't brook argument. My oppo, a middle-aged don from Cambridge, was in his usual trance-like state. He seemed to favor self-hypnosis as a means of trying to interpret the Germans' latest plans. Most of the time we worked together, he seemed unaware of my existence. He didn't even look up as I followed Le Saux out of the room.

The teleprinter room was on the other side of the long corridor from ours, and close to the exit. The door was open. Lina glanced round, as if she was expecting us. Murmuring something to her oppo, she stood up and joined us. Her beautiful face was pale and drawn, but we'd stepped outside the hut and into the darkness before I realized that she was trembling.

"Is something the matter?" I asked.

"You could say that," she said in a hoarse whisper.

"You don't look well. Didn't you tell me you suffer from migraines? It might be—"

"Never mind about migraines." Le Saux spat out the words. "A problem has cropped up, and I need your help."

"What sort of problem?" I was bemused.

"There's been an accident," Lina murmured.

"What—"

"You don't need to know the details," Le Saux snapped.

"Please, Wilf," Lina said. "Just listen to Edward, then tell us if you're willing to help."

"Of course I'll help, if I can," I said. "But what is this?"

"We've very little time," Le Saux said roughly. "Ray Bonetti's dead. He's fallen in the lake and drowned. Pure accident, but we were there when it happened. Lina and me, that is, and we don't want any fuss-making. It won't bring Ray back, and it would embarrass Lina and me. Won't do anyone any good at all. So we need you to say that you were with us throughout the meal break. I'll take you through the plan in detail, but the key point is this. The two of us never left your side, not for one moment. Understand?"

I was barely able to take it all in, but I gave a feeble nod.

"You'll help us, then?" Even in the pitch-black night, there was no mistaking her tone. She was begging me. *Begging* me.

"Of course," I said. "You can rely on me."

Le Saux gripped my hand. "Stout fellow. It's for the best, believe me."

"Bless you!" Lina leaned forward and gave me a peck on the cheek.

My knees felt weak, as if at any moment they might give way. Bonetti was dead, and Lina was in my debt. It was almost impossible to believe. Whatever had happened, how could I not be delirious with joy?

Jersey, 1999

"Bonetti's death wasn't an accident, was it?" I said.

We'd walked without speaking until we reached the harbor wall. A few cars were parked on it, dangerously close to the edge, or so it seemed to me. If the brake wasn't properly applied, the low barrier was scarcely enough to prevent them from plunging into the sea.

Lina touched my arm. "No, Wilf, it was no accident."

"I was an accomplice to murder," I said. "An accessory. You may not have realized it, you may have regarded me as too innocent to be trusted, but in my heart, I always knew."

She raised her eyebrows. "Did you?"

"Oh yes. Even before the balloon went up, and I was summoned for questioning."

"You stuck to your guns," she said. "Edward wondered if you'd crack under pressure, but you stood firm."

"What else could I do?" A keen wind blowing in from the Channel made my rheumy eyes water. "I despised Bonetti. For all I knew, he was an Italian agent, or some sort of informer. Perhaps he had people back home who were being threatened..."

"The same might be said about Edward." A sharp edge entered her voice, almost as if she were minded to defend Bonetti's good name. "His parents were here, remember. Uncles, aunts, cousins. At the mercy of the occupying troops."

"Le Saux was no spy," I said. "A murderer, yes, but not a spy."

"A murderer," she repeated. "A murderer, you say?"

To my distress, tears began to trickle down her cheeks.

Bletchley Park, 1942

I climbed the oaken stairs of the big house to undergo my interrogation. The hall was a monstrosity of Victorian Gothic, all dark paneling and ornate plasterwork. Three senior officers whom I'd never seen before conducted the interview. They sat around a large table, their tea mugs standing on a map of France, and fired questions in an attempt to confuse me into self-contradiction. But I'd rehearsed my answers, and I stuck to them as doggedly as I used to work on the codes.

The discovery of Bonetti's body in the lake had prompted a hue and cry, it seemed. I suppose everyone who worked the night shift in our hut was questioned about their movements. But at Bletchley Park, even a hue and cry needed to be conducted with the utmost stealth.

"Unpopular fellow, was he?" demanded one of the officers, a square-jawed man with a parade-ground voice.

"I wouldn't say so, sir. I found Ray quite cheerful and friendly, as a matter of fact. Not that I knew him well."

"A ladies' man?"

"I wouldn't know, sir."

My interrogator shook his head dismissively, as if to say, *No, well, perhaps you wouldn't.*

"Pally with the Wraithmell girl?"

"Not especially. He passed the time of day with her once or twice when I was in her company, that's all I can say."

"So last night you spent the whole of your meal break with her and Le Saux?"

"That's right, sir."

"Quite certain about that, are you?"

"Absolutely positive, sir."

One of his colleagues, bald and bespectacled, made a few notes on a pad in front of him.

"Very well. That's all for now."

I waited until I reached the bottom of the staircase before heaving a sigh of relief. I'd done it! I'd given Le Saux an unbreakable alibi. With my help, he'd get away with murder.

Jersey, 1999

"Please don't cry," I said in desperation. "I know exactly what happened."

Those blue eyes looked straight into mine. "You do?"

"Le Saux loathed everything about Bonetti, above all the way he treated you. They quarreled, and things got out of hand. I never believed that he simply tripped over into the lake and drowned. Not even in the dark. It doesn't make sense."

Slowly, she inclined her head, but said nothing.

"Le Saux came across Bonetti misbehaving with you. I've pictured it a thousand times. He knocked Bonetti unconscious, and then pushed him into the water. A postmortem would have revealed how he died, but the inquiry couldn't be handled like a crime in peacetime. In view of the alibi you and I gave him, there was no evidence to pin guilt on Le Saux. Besides, he was good at his work. Whatever they suspected, he was too valuable to sacrifice. Winning the war was all that mattered. Perhaps I wasn't the only one who wondered about Bonetti's loyalty. Far better to write his death off to bad luck than risk blowing the gaff on the work we did at Bletchley Park. So ranks were closed, lips were buttoned. Secrecy was drummed into everyone, it became second nature. Certainly it trumped any ideas about justice in an individual case. And quite right too."

"You think so?" Lina bowed her head. "I've spent the whole of my life wondering about that."

"I didn't lie for Le Saux's sake." I took a breath. Time for me to tell her how I felt. Even if her health was poor, we might still spend precious months together. "I did it for you, because I loved you. And you felt guilty because Le Saux killed Bonetti for you. So you were desperate for me to help get him off the hook, to dodge a charge of murder."

Lina closed her eyes. "Oh, Wilf, all these years, you believed that..."

"I squared it with my conscience, because I hoped that you...that is, before we could even talk about what had happened, you were whisked away."

"I was sorry I wasn't even able to say goodbye," she said in a muffled voice. "But I was sent back to Gaythorne and told to pack my bags. They sent me straight off to the outstation at Eastcote."

"I didn't know," I said. "As far as Bletchley Park was concerned, you simply vanished off the face of the earth. Like Edward Le Saux. Everyone was so wretchedly discreet. I didn't find out anything about what had happened to either of you until after the war. By which time I learned you were married. Later, I found that Le Saux returned home after the Channel Islands were liberated."

"For the rest of the war, he worked in Whitehall," she said. "They could keep an eye on him there. He and I stayed in touch, but before long, I met someone else. Edward took it quite well, considering what he'd done for me. He'd saved me."

"By killing Bonetti."

"No, no," she said, betraying a touch of impatience. "That's why I prayed we'd get the chance to talk. I didn't want to go to my grave without thanking you and telling you the truth. It's the least you deserved."

"I'm not—" I began, but she put up a gloved hand to silence me.

"Of course, I guessed you had a bit of a pash on me, Wilf. You weren't the first, and you weren't the last. I was only nineteen, and I suppose I enjoyed the attention. But I made a terrible mistake with Bonetti. I reckoned I could handle him, but he was vile. A predator. When he took me for a stroll by the lake that night, he pushed me up against a tree, and tried to...well, I fought him off, and picked up a stone."

I stared at her, open-mouthed. She gave me another smile that was, I realized, a smile of pity.

"Did I mean to kill him? I don't know, perhaps. I wanted to stop him mauling me, and I banged the stone against his temple. A forehand smash, it was worthy of Wimbledon. Then I panicked and heaved him into the lake. I don't think he was dead, but I've never been sure. I hope he was. It was all over in less than a minute. Then Edward found me. He'd stalked us from the hut, he was sick with jealousy, but he lost us in the darkness. Neither he nor I carried a torch. I was panic-stricken, but he pleaded with me to calm down. He said he'd make sure you gave us both an alibi."

"And I did," I said slowly.

"And you did." She hesitated. "As a result, I've had a good life. I didn't want it to end without saying thank you."

And then she blew me a kiss, and, very deliberately, stepped off the harbor wall.

The Temple's Coin

Lavie Tidhar

1.

The money train had traveled a long way to finally come here, a stone's throw from the holy city of Jerusalem. Now hundreds of fires burned on the plain below the Hills of Judea, and the smoke rose into the darkening skies. The locals enjoyed a brisk trade with the thousands of pilgrims who had come this far, from the diaspora in Babylon and Damascus. They came to pay witness to something extraordinary, the rebuilding of the Second Holy Temple by the king.

They had raised money and paid the tax. The king's tax collectors went far and wide, to all corners of the empire where Jews now lived. They raised the Tyrian half-shekel that was due from each. In Egypt, in Greece, in Rome itself. And as they did, the chests of money grew heavy and many, and as they did more and more pilgrims joined the money train, until thousands traveled together to Judea, protecting the temple's coin.

The five men who had come to steal the money watched from the hills above. They had laid certain plans and made certain arrangements, and now they merely watched this remarkable phenomenon, this traveling festival, which had accrued upon itself its own crowd of camp followers—small traders, mercenaries, prostitutes, priests, slaves, and cooks.

The wine merchants did a roaring trade.

In the center of this commotion stood the great tents holding the money chests. They were surrounded by thousands of people, people who had given everything they had toward this great project of Herod the king.

He was not much liked. Some whispered that he wasn't truly Jewish—the son of an Edomite convert and a princess of the Nabateans. But he was king. And what king, when all is said and done, is truly liked? A king is like the weather; he just is.

The men watched, then made their way around the footpaths of the hills, past the money train encampment to a nearby valley, where the sounds of revelry and prayer weren't heard, and no fires burned. The men moved softly through the dark; they cast no light, and their swords were drawn. They were used to operating in the night.

There in that nearby valley stood three black tents, all but invisible in the dark. Arnulf, the German, rose behind a guard and neatly cut his throat with a *pugio*. He held the body as it dropped and laid it down gently.

They moved fast and with lethal force. The guards here were well-trained, grizzled veterans of the legions, of wars in Hispania and Nabatea, but they had not expected trouble, not expected to be *known*. The battle was short, near-silent, and brutal. Of the five men carrying out the job, only one, Achillas, the Egyptian, took a *gladius* to the neck, and the others left him where he fell.

When the guards were dead, the four men entered the central tent. Aran, the Judean, gave a low whistle. Arnulf said, "Rabbel, you get the chariot."

The Nabatean, eyed fixed on the chests inside the tent, said, "Get it yourself."

"You're the…" The German gave up.

"I want to see it first," Rabbel said. "Just see if it's true."

Aran grinned. He broke the latch and opened one of the chests.

The men, as one, drew a breath.

"So that's what all those shekels amount to," Gaius, the Roman, said.

"Half-shekels," Aran said.

"Who cares," Gaius said.

Rabbel said, "I'll get the chariot."

He left almost at a run.

"Gaius, go with him," Arnulf said.

The small Roman grinned and vanished after the charioteer.

Aran and Arnulf remained, staring at the contents of the chest.

"They wouldn't even *know*," Aran said. "All those fools, out there on the plain."

"*Someone* would know," Arnulf said. "But that won't be our problem."

"How much do you think is in there?"

"Not enough to build a temple," the German said.

"Yes, but it's only one shipment," Aran said.

"Only," the German said.

They heard the sound of horses, coming fast.

Gaius reappeared, gave Arnulf a nod.

"Ready?"

"Ready."

The carried the first of the chests outside and loaded it onto the chariot, then loaded the others. The chests were surprisingly light.

"Portable assets," Gaius said, like he was quoting someone. The others stared at him.

"What?" he said. "I used to do security for a Greek banker."

They followed Rabbel and the chariot on foot until they reached the other horses, secluded on the far side of the valley. They were fresh and watered. The men mounted the horses.

"There's one extra horse," Aran said.

"So?"

"Shame about the Egyptian."

"More shame to leave the horse. It's a good horse."

"Who cares about the horse? You could buy yourself a new one. Buy a stable."

"I'm taking the horse."

"Leave the horse."

They stared at each other until Aran gave up.

They spurred their horses on. The chariot shot ahead, and the three men followed. They vanished into the Judean Hills. The whole operation took *pars minuta prima*, only the first small part of an hour.

The festivities on the plain below Jerusalem continued unabated for most of the night.

2.

The sound of construction was everywhere. A foreman shouted at a group of bare-chested laborers who were struggling with the pulleys ferrying the large stones to the unbuilt wall. The sun beat down and tempers ran high. An Egyptian architect in the shade of a palm tree consulted with his minions. Herod had imported architects from all across the empire, from Rome and Babylon and Greece, and they seldom, if ever, agreed with one another.

A slave materialized by my side. Phoenician. A runty little thing. God alone knew where they found him.

"You're Josephus?" he panted.

"Depends," I said. "Who are you?"

"The priest wants to see you." He looked at me accusingly. "You're late."

"Priests are always in such a hurry," I said. "I was taking in the sights."

"Ain't much to see, is there," he said. "It's just another damn construction site."

"You're free with your tongue," I said.

"Look, mister, are you coming or not? I ain't got time for chitchat."

"Important, are you?"

"I work for an important man. I work for an important office."

Slaves got like that sometimes. This one no doubt figured if only he worked hard enough the priest would finally release him from bondage, make him a real somebody. It was not unheard of. Still. Unless he converted, he would never amount to much in this particular setting. This might have been Herod's kingdom, but it sure as shit was the priests' temple. And don't anyone dare forget it.

I let him lead on. What did I care? I'd been back in Judea for just over a year, and I liked Jerusalem about as much as I liked getting a spear in the side. Still. There was a shitload of money floating around in the capital, and sometimes some of it even fell my way. I still took on the occasional job. Bodyguard stuff, mostly, for rich local merchants or wealthy out-of-towners. Never a priest, though. They were usually as tight with their money as a whore was with her time.

God knew there were plenty of both in the city.

He led me past the emerging walls and the subterranean caverns and the grand hall where the Sanhedrin would meet in full assembly each day to pass down judgement. It was unfinished, and the Sanhedrin, all seventy-one of the old bastards, were forced to inhabit temporary accommodation in a part of the old temple. They didn't like it much.

Why Herod—who was not exactly the most pious of men, to put it mildly—decided to rebuild the temple in such grand a fashion was anyone's guess. The man was into architecture like other men are into dice. He just kept building: the new port in Caesarea Maritima, the fortress of Masada, the temple...it was like a vice with him.

There were workers all around us, but the slave led me down to the foundations and into quiet corridors where it was cool and the workmanship, I was forced to admit, exquisite. At last he ushered me into a room and closed the door.

It was simply furnished, and occupied by a solitary man dressed in the robes of the priesthood. He looked up from his desk and gestured for me to come forward.

"Be with you in a moment," he said, scratching busily, almost angrily, on the sheaf of papyrus before him.

"So many accounts," he muttered. "So much paperwork. It would be a miracle if I get any time to pray today."

He applied a seal carefully, then put the papyrus away and looked up at me.

"You are Joseph, the informer?"

"I go by Josephus, mostly," I said.

His mouth turned in a moue of distaste.

"How very Roman of you."

"When in Rome," I said, "do as the Romans do, and all that."

"You're not in Rome anymore, *Josephus*. This is Jerusalem. We do things differently here."

I shrugged. "Not *that* different," I said.

"I am Yehuda, the priest," he said, letting it go—for now, at least. He was not the High Priest. But he was pretty high up all the same.

"Yes," I said.

"Leave us, Itthobaal."

The little slave's shoulders sagged.

"Yes, my lord," he said.

"And don't make that face."

"Yes, my lord."

"And bring us water, please." He turned to me. "You have not tried the water of the temple, have you, Josephus? You are in for a treat. It is as sweet and clear as the voice of the Lord."

"It would taste even better mixed in with wine," I said.

He frowned again. "*Water*," he said. "Itthobaal?"

"My lord?"

"Why are you still here?"

The little slave practically ran for the door. Then there were just the two of us.

"You come highly recommended," the priest said. I wished I could say the same about him, but I held my tongue. He leafed through papyrus.

"You served under Augustus in Parthia?" he said.

"Octavian, we called him then."

"You knew him?"

"I was only a foot soldier," I said. The truth was I had met Octavian a couple of times. He was an odd bird even for a Roman, but a strict commander and an able administrator all the same.

"Trained in the legions?"

"Yes."

"Liked it?"

"Not really," I said. "But the pay was good and I got to see a bit of the world."

"What happened then?"

"Not much," I said. "I was wounded, recovered, followed the Emperor to Rome, but then he decided there were too many of us and released us back into civilian life. There isn't much of a pension, so..."

"So?"

"So I take on work, when I can find it."

"As it happens," he said, "I do have a job for you. Ah, Itthobaal, thank you." The little slave reappeared with the water. He handed me a cup and I took a sip. It really was very good.

"Leave us, Itthobaal."

"But lord..."

"Go!"

He vanished again.

The priest took a sip from his own water and smacked his lips in exaggerated appreciation. The water wasn't *that* good. He said, "What I have to tell you cannot leave this room."

"Alright."

"Can I trust you?"

I shrugged. "Sure."

He looked at me hard. It was clear he didn't much like me. It was also clear he was desperate. I couldn't decide whether he looked angry or afraid.

"You know of the temple tax," he said.

"Hey, I already paid," I said.

"That's good," he said.

"I do my part."

"Well, this concerns more than a half-shekel," he said.

"Go on."

"There was a shipment of tax from the diaspora. It's gone missing."

"How could it go missing?"

He rubbed the bridge of his nose.

"It was hijacked," he said.

"*How*? So many coins, it would weigh... Oh."

I should have realized.

The tax was a half-shekel coin. Not locally minted. The Romans would not allow obviously Jewish coins to be minted here, so Herod co-opted for use the Tyrian shekels, ironically carrying the face of that old enemy of Israel, the god Ba'al. This is why, outside the temple, there were literally hundreds of money changers. With all the pilgrims flooding into Jerusalem, all with their own currencies, there was always need for a ready supply of coins.

But.

Not *that* many.

"They converted the shekels into something more portable *before* departing," I said.

He nodded.

"Gold? Precious stones?"

He nodded.

"And they'd be carried *separately*," I said. "While all the main convoy carried was a decoy."

"A few legitimate chests," he said. "The coins *are* useful. But yes. The majority would be valuables, or simply letters of credit from the Roman bankers."

"Smart," I said.

"I'd like to think so."

"Only it wasn't that smart if they got hijacked."

"That," he said stiffly, "was unfortunate."

"Clean job?"

"Very."

"Professionals?"

"It would seem that way."

"I see why you want to keep it quiet."

"What I *want*," he said, "is to get it sorted. Of the men, one was killed during the attack. We were lucky—someone was able to identify his body. Achillas, an Egyptian. Fought with Marc Antony in Egypt. He'd been hanging around Jerusalem for a couple of years now, doing odd jobs."

"Any known associates?"

"I was hoping to leave that to you," he said.

"Alright. So you want me to do what, exactly? Recover the money?"

I had the feeling he wasn't quite on the level and that I wouldn't much like the job.

"If you can," he said. "But not...mainly, no. This can't come out. And it can't be allowed to happen again. A message needs to be sent."

"What sort of message?"

"The sort of message God gave the Philistines." He smiled.

"Spell it out," I said.

"Oh, for..." He sighed. "Find them," he said. "Kill them all."

I smiled. "I just wanted to hear you say it."

"You can keep a tenth of what you find," he said. "And I will cover reasonable expenses. There'll be a bonus, too. Here." He tossed me a papyrus. It was a letter of credit.

"Alright," I said.

I went to the door and pulled it open. The little slave, Itthobaal, tumbled in. He gave me a wounded look.

"I'll see myself out," I said.

3.

"Let go of me!" she said. "I don't know nothing!"

"I've heard that too many times before, sweetheart," I said.

"Well, can you hear this?" she said, and kicked me in the balls.

I doubled over in pain. She stood over me, a fiery little Parthian dressed the way Eve was before the snake ruined everything, and glared.

"Let's...start...again..." I said.

"Get out!"

"Tell me who Achillas rode with."

"Achillas was a *shit!*" She kicked me again, I think for emphasis.

"Enough!" I straightened up and showed her my dagger, but it didn't much faze her. I guess she'd seen bigger.

"Get out."

I crawled out of there. Two drunk laborers went past me with a girl between them and vanished into another room. Vashti's was not exactly an upmarket establishment.

When I got to reception, the brothel owner regarded me askance.

"Had fun?"

"I want...my money back."

"Get out or my men will throw you out."

She had two burly Reubenites behind her, flexing their muscles.

"I'll...show myself...out."

I staggered out into the fading sunshine.

That could have gone better, I thought.

4.

I sat outside drinking watered wine and watching the entrance to Vashti's. It was near the city walls, and attracted a steady stream of customers. I was across the road in a Roman-style *popina*, keeping my eyes open and myself out of sight. This Ishtar was the closest thing the dead Egyptian, Achillas, had had to a girlfriend. That much I'd found out quickly. I'd found out a bit more from my sources, but I wanted to see what a visit to Ishtar would bring me.

So far, only pain.

It was late by the time Ishtar came out. It gets cold in Jerusalem, and she was wrapped up warm and walking fast. I paid my tab and rose and followed her, discreetly. Jerusalem's a city of narrow twisting streets that have little logic to them. A couple of times I thought I'd lost her, but then she turned up ahead and I kept up the pursuit. She came to a place near the Pool of Siloam. It was the sort of place ex-legionnaires and Sadducees hung out in, a mixture of the disgruntled, the rebellious, and the plain criminal. Ishtar slipped in and I followed.

It was dark inside the *popina*. I saw her lean over a figure in the shadows and whisper something. The figure rose. They walked to the entrance together and separated. I hesitated, then followed the new arrival. I had followed him down to the pool when he turned and I saw the glint of a dagger.

I came in low and fast. The wind was knocked out of him, and then I was on top of him and my own *pugio* was in my hand and at his throat. He stopped fighting and lay still, staring up at me with bright feverish eyes.

"The money," I said.

"Take it!" he said. "I don't have much."

"The temple tax job," I said. "That was you."

His eyes widened. "Is that what this is about? But we followed the plan."

"Where is the money?" I said.

He started to laugh. "There is no money," he said.

"Give me something," I said. "And do it fast or my hand might slip."

"Screw you."

I cut him, just a little. He didn't like it at all.

"Where is the money?"

"I told you, we followed the plan. You've got it all wrong—"

I cut him some more.

"Arnulf! Arnulf's the one you want!"

"Give me names. Make it fast."

He pushed, recklessly. The knife sunk into his skin and blood sprayed my face. He gurgled, then the light in his eyes faded and he lay there like a child's doll. I searched his body, then rolled him into the water and the Pool of Siloam took him. I washed my face and hands as best I could, and then I got out of there.

5.

They found the corpse the next day, and someone identified him as Aran, a Judean. Some farmer's boy from the Galilee who had fought in the war with the Nabateans.

These guys all had military training, that was for sure. Now I was two names down, Achillas and Aran.

I went to find a money-changer.

"Where did you *find* this?" he said.

"What is it?" I said.

"It's an eight-Aurei gold medallion," he said. "Minted in Rome in the time of Maxentius. That's him on the reverse. Handsome fellow, wasn't he. I wish my barber could style a beard like that."

"Worth anything?"

"Are you kidding? I don't even think I could cover it."

"Seen any more of these around?" I said.

He glanced side to side and lowered his voice. "Word is there's some fellow been asking around for a deal. Trying to offload some high-denomination coinage, fast. Not everyone has the kind of inventory that can cover that. And of course you want to make sure it's *kasher*. No one wants to run afoul of the king."

"Stolen?"

"Man, I don't know. I don't like to cast aspersions."

"You mean you don't want to lose out on the deal."

"Look," he said, eager by now to be rid of me. "There's a place not far from here, by the North Gate. Lots of pilgrims, lots of their personal bodyguards and such-like."

"I know it," I said. "So?"

"So ask there. I don't know any more."

"Sure?" I said. "You can keep the coin."

He stared at me in avaricious suspicion, then palmed the gold quicker than you could say the Shema.

"Gaius," he said. "Gaius the Roman. That's all I know. Now go!"

"Pleasure doing business with you," I said.

I left him there, still counting his money.

6.

They found me before I found them. It was an ambush, they had fed the old money changer the line and he'd fed it to me flawlessly, like a fisherman on the Sea of Galilee. I'd swallowed it whole.

A fist sank into my stomach and I doubled over and said, "Oof!"

"Kill him now, Rabbel! Kill him!"

"Let's...talk it over," I said.

I saw the flash of a nasty Nabatean blade. I grabbed his leg and he lost his balance and fell. I head-butted him and grabbed the knife. My head bloomed with pain. I stuck the knife in his side and fell back just as his companion came at me with the sword.

"Die!" he screamed.

The sword came at me with the pointy end, fast. It was the sort of pointy end that settles arguments. Then something smashed him on the back of the head and he fell on top of me, and I could smell his blood.

"What's going on here, then?" a voice said.

I looked up. Some giant Judean yokel with official robes stood over me smiling, holding a bloodied brick.

"There's no fighting and no open blades near the temple," he said.

"Listen," I said, "you don't understand. I work for the prie—"

"Save it," he said. "I don't care. You two can work it out in the ring."

"Are you insane? I'm telling you I—"

That brick came down.

That was the last thing I saw for a while.

7.

"What the—?" the other man said.

I groaned and rubbed my head. Looked at him.

"You look like I feel," I said.

"I should kill you," he said.

"There'll be time for that, I think."

He looked confused, and he shouldn't have been.

"Roman?" I said.

"Yeah."

"You must be Gaius. I've been looking for you."

"Well, you found me. You also killed my friend."

"Supposed to kill all of you lot, on account of the missing shekels and all."

"Listen," he said, "we ain't got it. We should have split the city long ago, but it all went as wrong as Adam and Eve after they tasted the fruit."

"They gained knowledge?"

"They got shafted," he said.

"Is that what happened?"

"I don't *know* what happened! And Arnulf's disappeared. You're the one killed Aran, right?"

"Yeah."

"And you killed Rabbel. He was a nice guy, for a Nabatean."

"Sorry for your loss."

"So now there's just me and Arnulf," he said. "Listen. We could team up, you and me. Recover the money. I'll cut you in for thirty."

"Fifty," I said.

"Deal," he said.

"Time to go, sleepyheads," a voice said.

I did not like the sound of that voice.

I did not like the smell of our cell.

I did not like the clink of metal chains much, either.

"Go where?" Gaius said. But I could see that he finally twigged.

"Move it," the big brute said. "Ain't got all day."

The cell door opened. He stood there grinning at us with big square teeth. City guard, taking a little personal time. I shuffled out after Gaius and into the ring.

8.

Herod had built everything magnificently, but this Coliseum was both old and small, more like a Judean amphitheatre than a proper ring. I knew it; it was on the outskirts of town, toward the Gehenna Valley, where the butchers plied their trade. As far as I knew it wasn't even operating, but I guessed they'd had a special show in mind today.

There were a few spectators on the stands, all waiting for us. I saw money change hands—a lot of money. The big brute tossed a trident and a sword on the ground.

"Get to it, then," he said.

"Sure."

Gaius and I moved together. He grabbed the trident and I got the sword, and we both went at the big guy together. The trident got him in the belly and the sword in the neck and he fell like a whale, but no Jonah came out of there, only his innards. I thought he must have been a little bit slow in the head.

The people in the stands cheered.

I turned back to the gate, but it was shut.

And now the gate on the far end opened.

I heard a sound I really didn't like.

I stared as it came gliding out. Not hurrying. Staring at us like it was staring at its dinner.

It was a desert leopard.

"Come *on!*" I said.

"Majestic animal," Gaius said. "I would hate to kill it."

"I would hate to die!"

"Everybody dies," he said. He hefted up the trident. The gate was still open on the far end, but the animal was between us and the gate.

I didn't dare run for it. You can't outrun a Negev leopard.

"Who hired you for the job?" I said. "How did you know where the real cargo was?"

He shrugged. "Arnulf handled all that."

"Only he's missing?"

"You can't trust a German," he said.

The leopard came at us then.

Gaius threw the trident.

I ran.

9.

The leopard was still feeding when I left through the gate. Someone came and clapped me on the back. Someone else shoved coins into my hands. I guess they'd all gotten the show they'd hoped for.

Jerusalem, I thought. Shit. All that money and all those people looking to be entertained.

All that money...

I walked all the way back to the city. I ran through the names in my mind.

Achillas, the Egyptian. Dead on the job.

Aran, the Judean. Floating in the Pool of Siloam.

Rabbel, the Nabatean. Knifed by the North Gate.

Gaius, the Roman. Death by leopard.

Which left me only Arnulf, the German.

I went back to Vashti's. I paid to get in and asked for Ishtar. She was in the same room as before, and she wasn't wearing even a fig leaf.

"Oh, it's you," she said.

"Heard your boyfriend's dead."

She shrugged. "He wasn't my boyfriend."

"I figured," I said. "So who is?"

"Listen," she said, "you're stubborn, I'll give you that. Like dog shit stuck to a sandal. But I don't have any answers for you. I'm just a girl trying to make a living. If I had a big heap of cash, do you think I'd be working in this dump?"

"Girl like you," I said, "you could be working anyone."

She flashed me a smile.

"Sit down," she said. "You already paid, anyway."

She came and sat close to me. Her skin pressed against mine. She was warm and inviting. Her lips were soft as she kissed my bruises.

"I could never resist a legionnaire..." she whispered and stuck her tongue in my ear.

She was laying it on thicker than honey, and this was a milk-and-honey sort of land. It wasn't long before we were fooling around on the bed. I never could resist the lure of troublesome dames.

She had her hand round my sword, as it were, ready to swing it into action when the door burst open and a man came through with a sword that was bigger than mine. Ishtar laughed and released me, stepping away on light feet. I felt very exposed and very alone just then.

"You could have let me finish at least."

"What'd be the fun in that?" she said.

"Shut up and cover yourself," the man said. He sat down on a chair and pointed the sword at me. I did as he said.

"You must be Arnulf, the German."

"And you're that nosy informer, Josephus. Yeah, I've heard about you. They say you're good, and you must be to have killed my guys, but, if you'll excuse me saying it, you don't look so shit hot right now."

"You should have seen me earlier," I said, and Ishtar smirked.

"Look," I said. "It doesn't have to go down this way. I just want the money. You can ride off into the sunset for all I care. Take a boat to Cyprus or up the Nile, or follow the King's Road to Damascus. Just get away from here."

"*You* look," he said, "I don't *have* it." The sword didn't waver, but I could see in his eyes he was desperate. "What a mess."

"What happened?" I said.

"The job went flawlessly," he said. "The plan was to deliver the shipment, take our cut, and vanish. You think I wanted to get stuck in Jerusalem? If I have to hear any more Hebrew, I think I'll scream. And that temple! Gods. It's as gaudy as a Babylonian brothel."

"So what happened?"

"Nah," he said. "I think I'm just going to kill you. You're one complication I don't need."

I couldn't fight him and he knew it.

"I can pay you," I said, looking over his shoulder. He didn't notice my glance.

"Pay *me*?" he said. He started to laugh. The sword came at me. Then it wavered and fell from his hand and he pitched forward, the blood spurting from his neck, over my face, the bed, and the wall.

Ishtar stood there with the bloodied blade in her hands, regarding me thoughtfully.

"You better," she said.

I stared at the mess in the room and I stared at her.

So that was that, I thought.

10.

"You did an acceptable job," the priest said reluctantly. "I just wish you hadn't made so much of a mess."

"I didn't recover any money," I said.

He shrugged. "I'm sure it will turn up, and if not there's always more."

I didn't like the priest, but I took his money all the same.

The little slave, Itthobaal, escorted me out.

"So how did it work?" I said.

"Excuse me?"

"Your little scam. Robbing your own temple tax. What happened? You hired Arnulf and his lot and then changed your mind about cutting them in on the money?"

"I'm sure I don't know what you're talking about," he said.

"That's all right," I said. I held his arm. "They do."

He tried to wriggle out, but I held him strong. Then the king's German guards showed up, and the little slave slackened in my grasp. The guards had been a present to Herod from Augustus.

The little slave watched as the guards went into the priest's room and brought him out. The priest looked up and saw me and his eyes were full of hate, but he said nothing.

They took him away, but not before they said something to the little slave. He nodded reluctantly.

"Come along, then," he said.

"Where are we going?"

He ignored me. I followed him, out of the subterranean section and into the bright sunshine.

Standing by the uncompleted western wall of the temple was the king. He was consulting with the architect and gesturing, his guards around him. They parted to let us into the presence. The king waved the architect away and turned his attention to us.

"You are Josephus, the informer?"

"Yes, my king."

"I am glad you brought this matter to my attention. And for your discretion."

"Yes, my king."

He turned his gaze on the slave.

"Itthobaal," he said. "This is an unfortunate business."

"Yes, my king," the slave said.

"We had an understanding."

The slave said nothing and neither did I.

"Centuries from now, when you and I and everyone—kings, slaves, informers, and all—are dead and in the ground," Herod said, "do you know what will still stand?"

"The temple, my king?"

"The temple," he said. "*My* temple. And they will remember *me*, King Herod, Herod the Great!"

"Yes, my king."

"When I die," he said conversationally, "I have ordered that a great number of important people be massacred."

"My king?" I said, startled.

"So that the people will truly mourn," he said. "As befits a great king."

I felt a chill at his words then but kept my face impassive.

"The priests do not understand," he said. "They think the money belongs to the temple. But it is mine. It is *all* mine. Itthobaal, make sure that there are no problems such as this on the next shipment."

"Yes, my king," the little slave said.

The king tossed me a small bag of coins. They clinked in the cloth.

"There will always be more," Herod said, complacently. Then he seemed to lose interest in us and went back to examining his wall; the guards closed around him, and we were pushed politely away.

"The *king*?" I said.

"Hush, Josephus," the little slave said. "Do not speak treason. Some thoughts are best left unsaid."

He left it at that, and I did not inquire further.

As I rode out of the city, she was waiting by the gate. She was already mounted, and we rode away from the city together. I tossed her the bag of coins and she smiled, just the once, and put it away. By dusk we came to the edge of the Judean Hills.

Down in the valley below, the pilgrims' fires were already burning as another money train came in.

Another Body

O'Neil De Noux

Another body. This one lay on a small bed in a rear room of a two-story Creole townhouse at the corner of Orleans Avenue and Burgundy Street. Detective Jacques Dugas nodded at Officer Rigby guarding the room's door. Rigby removed his bowler helmet and ran a hand through his red hair. Perspiration streaked his sky-blue New Orleans police uniform shirt with its silver star-and-crescent badge pinned to his chest. At six feet, Dugas stood over Rigby, who topped off at five feet eight. While the uniformed copper was clean-shaven, Dugas sported a trim moustache, his dark brown hair parted down the center.

Rigby stepped aside and said, "Boarding house lady found her at a quarter 'til eight, when the girl did not go down to breakfast. Said the door was unlocked."

Dugas carefully crossed the room, checked both windows before opening them, saw there was no rear balcony. A wide magnolia tree dominated the brick patio below. The light scents of flowers flowed into the stuffy room that smelled of mildew. He turned to the body, took out his notebook and pencil, and drew a quick diagram before beginning his notes:

Wednesday, June 28, 1899

He put down the time he was notified: *8:32 a.m.*

Arrived: 8:58 a.m.

"What's the boarding house lady's name?"

Rigby gave him the name and the spelling.

Body found: 7:45 a.m. by Rita Skiffle.

He looked at the victim as he wrote.

White female.

Dark brown hair.

Brown eyes.

About twenty years old.

About five feet two and ninety pounds.

Wearing light blue nightgown.

He examined the knife sticking out of her chest over her heart. Blood had pooled around the knife and rolled down her left side to the bed. Worn places on the wooden handle showed the knife's age.

She wore no jewelry, was barefoot, and the bottoms of her feet were clean. Dugas touched her arm. Cold. He checked the stiffness of her neck, her jaw, found the beginning of postmortem rigidity. Rigor mortis. She'd been dead between four and six hours. He leaned over, catching a light scent of cologne, and studied her face. Masked in the dull, unfocused look of death, eyes half-open, pupils fixed, her full lips stood out, her round face was pixie-like and pretty.

"What's her name?"

Rigby checked his notes. "Eleanor Harrison. From Missouri. Been in town six months, according to Mrs. Skiffle. Works at Kite's Antiques on Royal Street."

Dugas motioned the coroner's men to come in with the stretcher to take Eleanor away, and watched them load her and cover her with a sheet before carrying her out. He examined the bed carefully, the neat covers, the pillow.

Her purse sat on the small dresser. Inside Dugas found nine one-dollar bills and seventy-five cents in coins, along with a white handkerchief, an Orleans Parish public library card, a black comb, a pencil, a black notebook with five addresses listed (two Harrisons in Hannibal, Missouri, the address of the boarding house, Kite's Antiques, and the library). He found several names listed: Rita Skiffle, Bruno with an X next to it, Lizzy with a check next to it, Peter Quarry, and Tommy, with a star next to his name. At the bottom of the purse he found a small bottle of *Michelle* cologne, the same scent she had on her body.

Two library books lay on the dresser: Mark Twain's *Tom Sawyer* and Charlotte Bronte's *Jane Eyre*. Wasn't Twain from Hannibal, Missouri? Dugas checked the drawers and chifforobe and under the bed and found nothing of value. He checked the windows again. No indication of forced entry, and they had been locked before he opened them.

Rigby reminded Dugas the residents were assembled downstairs. Dugas knocked on the doors of the other two rooms on the second floor. No answer. He went down to the living room, where Rigby's partner stood outside the door. Rigby assured the detective he had checked the boarding house's front and back doors. No sign of forced entry.

Dugas sent Rigby's partner to canvass the houses on both sides of the street in case anyone had seen or heard anything. He tapped Rigby's shoulder and asked him to stay.

As the three people in the living room named themselves, Dugas realized all three names were in Eleanor's notebook: Rita, Lizzy, and Bruno. Dugas asked Officer Rigby to take two of them into the hall so he could interview these people separately. The big man huffed and nodded.

The boarding house owner, Rita Skiffle, was sixty-eight, a small, thin woman with gray hair streaked with white.

"I make sure the doors are locked every night. Front and back, before I go to bed at ten o'clock."

"Who has keys to the doors, besides you and the residents?"

"No one. Those are new locks. Changed last year." She went on. "I last saw Eleanor when she went up after supper." She wiped her eyes with a handkerchief. Nine questions later, Dugas asked for Lizzy to come in. Neither woman knew much about Eleanor, other than that she was such a sweet, quiet girl. Lizzy Desmont lived in the room across the hall from Eleanor.

"Desmont is French, like your name," Lizzy said, which Dugas knew.

"Why did Eleanor put a check by your name in her notebook?" Dugas showed it to the thick-set thirty-two-year-old woman with orangeish-red hair, who worked at the Louisiana Gas Company on Baronne Street. Lizzy shrugged and said, "I can figure why she put an X next to Bruno's name."

"Yes?"

Lizzy leaned close. "He is obnoxious. Rarely bathes. Grunts when he eats. Like a hog."

"Did he ever threaten anyone?"

"Oh, no. He is just scary."

He'd asked Rita, and now asked Lizzy, if she knew anyone who would harm Eleanor and whether she'd seen or heard anything last night. Both answered, "No."

Bruno Kosch stood six feet four, weighed about 280 pounds, and wore work clothes. He hadn't shaved in a few days. He kept his hands in his trouser pockets and answered the questions with short, curt sentences. He barely knew Eleanor. Never been near her room. Went to bed around nine p.m., heard and saw nothing last night. Had no idea who would hurt the girl. He complained that he was late for work.

Dugas stared at him for a long moment.

"Any reason why Eleanor marked an X next to your name in her notebook?"

The man's eyes grew wide.

He took a step closer to Dugas. "I am not what you call a friendly person. I know it. Been that way all my life. The kids called me a bully at school when I was just being loud." The big man's voice came low. "I just ain't social. But you check at work. I'm the best bricklayer at the Pelican Construction. My boss is a widow woman and she'll tell you. I would not hurt a fly." He took his hands out of his pockets. Dugas saw they were huge and uninjured. Knifers sometimes nick themselves.

"That ain't accurate," Bruno added. "I kill insects. Roaches 'specially."

The detective nodded, told the big man he could go to work now.

Dugas looked at his notes again. No one knew if Eleanor had friends or a boyfriend. He found Rita Skiffle in the kitchen at the rear of the place, asked her to check if she had a knife missing, saw her look through two drawers. None of her knives were worn, all had black wooden handles.

"All my knives are here."

"You and Bruno Kosch occupy the two downstairs rooms?"

"Correct."

"Eleanor and Lizzy are upstairs." He looked up from his notes. "Who is in the last room upstairs? The one next to the bathroom?"

"Peter. Peter Quarry. He works two doors down at White's Bakery. Leaves for work at three in the morning."

Rita Skittle looked at the two Hannibal addresses in Dugas's notes. She pointed to the second Harrison address from Eleanor's notebook.

"That's her parents."

***

Detective Dugas stepped into White's Bakery, his nostrils filling with the wonderful scents of sugar and bread baking. He eased past three customers in line to a counter where a large woman was serving two loaves of French bread to a small woman. Dugas caught the large woman's eye, opened his coat to show his gold detective's badge, and asked for Peter Quarry.

The woman pulled her hands to her lower back, rolled her shoulders and said, "In back."

Dugas moved around the counter into a large rear room where two men worked behind a long table in front of three ovens. Dugas showed his badge, focused on the younger man who stood stiffly.

"Are you Peter Quarry?"

The young man nodded, and Dugas led him through the open rear door into a small patio behind the building.

Maybe five feet five and thin, Peter Quarry's blond hair was close-cropped, a faint moustache above his wide mouth.

"Eleanor? Dead?" Quarry closed his eyes and took in long breaths. Tears rolled from his eyes when he opened them. He stepped backward and sat on a wooden bench. He sat up straight, like the nuns in school tried to get all their students to do, including Jacques Dugas.

"When did you last see Eleanor?"

"At supper."

Quarry's hands gripped the bench as he answered the questions put to him. He had left for work a few minutes before three that morning and did not know Eleanor well, except that she was a Yankee.

"I barely knew her." He sat up even straighter and added, "I saw someone in the hall."

"Go on."

"I got up at two-thirty to get ready for work and heard a noise in the hall, so I cracked open my door and saw a figure turn down the stairs at the end of the hall. Just a flash."

"A man or a woman?"

Quarry shook his head.

"I thought it was Bruno, but..." Quarry wiped his eyes. "Now that I think on it, it was not him. Not big enough. Bruno Kosch is a big man. Bigger than you."

Dugas asked about the X next to Bruno's name, and Quarry said no one liked Bruno.

"Who is Tommy?"

Quarry shook his head, just as the others had when Dugas asked about Tommy. So far, no one knew who Tommy was.

Neither did the owners of Kite's Antiques on Royal Street, where Eleanor had worked. Anna and Robert Kite, both short and portly with gray hair, composed themselves after Dugas told them about their lone employee Eleanor Harrison. Mr. Kite noted, as they spoke in hesitant voices, he knew nothing of the dead girl's personal life. Neither did Mrs. Kite, and nothing at work helped Detective Dugas in the investigation.

"She was such a quiet and demure girl," added Mrs. Kite.

***

At six o'clock the next morning, Detective Jacques Dugas and Detective Sergeant Patrick Shannon stepped into the autopsy room of the Orleans Parish Coroner's Office, a fifty-foot-square room with three high windows always cracked open for ventilation, no matter the weather. The twenty-foot ceiling helped dilute the rancid smells of decaying flesh, dried blood, glacial acetic acid, and formaldehyde.

Both detectives wore gray suits, both standing a shade over six feet, although Shannon was stouter, 230-pounds easily. Both men were twenty-nine years old. Shannon's carrot-red hair, handlebar moustache, and mutton chops needed trimming.

Eleanor Harrison lay on her back atop the nearest steel autopsy table, her pink-white body illuminated beneath the harsh glare of the new electric lights. A morgue attendant stepped away with her clothing to stack it on a wooden chair. The attendant's blue-black skin shone with perspiration, and the detectives took off their suit coats to hang them on the coat rack by the door.

Dugas returned to the body, his gaze moving from her feet—delicate feet with no calluses—up her slim legs and shapely thighs to her dark bush, and up her flat stomach to breasts large for such a small woman, to her long neck and the fine lines of her face. Human death was never pleasant to see, but the death of someone young always brought a sadness to Dugas and anger when it was homicide.

Doctor Richard Malcolm stepped into the room, acknowledged the detectives with a glance, picked up a clipboard and pencil, and moved to the body. Also about six feet tall, the lanky doctor had his salt-and-pepper hair cut short and wore a light gray physician's smock. He was in his early sixties, a retired US Army doctor who had told Dugas and Shannon many stories of attending to the dying on battlefields, Gettysburg and the Wilderness, Petersburg, and the final battle at Appomattox Court House on the morning Robert E. Lee surrendered to Ulysses S. Grant.

After a quick examination of the cadaver, Dr. Malcolm found no defensive wounds or bruises on the victim's hands, arms, legs, or feet. He carefully removed the knife and passed it to Dugas who saw no marking on the nine-inch blade of the carving knife, which he placed in a paper bag.

A stale smell filled the room when the doctor laid open the girl's chest cavity. He used a metal rod to show the path of the knife, which had slipped between her ribs, straight through her left ventricle.

"Death was immediate," said the doctor. The angle of the wound showed she was prone when the knife was plunged into her. When the doctor moved to check whether she had been violated, Dugas turned away. The doctor concluded she had not been sexually assaulted.

Before leaving the coroner's office, Dugas left the addresses in Hannibal, Missouri, so they could notify Eleanor's family that their daughter had been murdered down in New Orleans.

When the two walked into police headquarters a few minutes later, the desk sergeant behind the tall counter called out to Dugas.

"Got a note for you."

The note was folded into a square, a sheet of tablet paper with lines, writing in pencil, flowing script. Catholic school educated, like Dugas. Nuns in every school in the city used rulers on knuckles for students who did not write in the same flowing script.

Det. Dugas,

I want to help you solve the mystery. The key may be Eleanor's quiet personality. She seemed ripe for exploitation by a man of bad scruples. She seemed lonely. Never met my eyes. She read a

lot. I will work to discover if she had drawn a man's unwanted attention. An intimate.

Sincerely,

Peter William Quarry

Odd, thought Dugas. *Didn't Quarry claim he barely knew Eleanor?*

He reread the note when he got to his desk at the rear of the Detective Bureau. Eleanor's quiet personality. Quarry could have picked that up at meals. Lonely? Maybe that too. Maybe she'd mentioned that she read a lot. He read the note a third time and paused at "a man of bad scruples," then at "drawn a man's unwanted attention. An intimate."

It was not unusual for friends, associates, even relatives to inject themselves into investigations, try to help. It was not Quarry's help that bothered Dugas. It was the wording in the note.

He slipped a sheet of carbon paper between two sheets of typing paper and rolled it into his Underwood typewriter to type out a daily on the postmortem before heading back out, because murders were never solved while sitting in the office. The solution was out there on the street. All Dugas had to do was find it.

Downstairs, the same desk sergeant waved at Dugas and pointed.

"Detective Dugas. You got a visitor."

Mr. Kite rose from a chair across the wide room. He held his hat in front of him.

"A boy named Tommy Stuart came by this morning, asking for Eleanor. He works at a café across the street from us. We told him what happened. He started sobbing."

***

Molly's Café stood across Royal Street, a half block from Kite's Antiques. The place had a nice crowd; only one of the dozen tables stood empty, two stools at the counter unoccupied. Dugas stepped to the middle-aged woman behind the cash register, showed his badge, asked for Tommy Stuart.

"Is he in trouble?"

"No, ma'am. I just need to speak with him."

"I don't know." She frowned at him.

"I can step outside, summon the man on the beat who will fetch more cops, and we will file in. See how your customers like it."

The woman leaned back and called out, "Willie. Willleeee."

A burly man wearing a soiled white apron came through a door on the far side of the café. He walked over and Dugas showed him the badge, asked for Tommy. The man was almost Dugas's height but stockier and ten, maybe fifteen years older.

"He's in back."

"Show me."

"What's this about?"

"It's about I need to speak with him." Dugas looked around. "While you're at it, bring me your latest health certificate."

The man's shoulders sank and Dugas pulled out his notebook and pencil.

"I'm Detective Jacques Dugas. What's your name?"

The man sucked in a breath, said, "Willie Little. William Little."

Dugas noted it. "Okay, Mr. Little. Take me to Tommy Stuart."

Several customers gave Dugas evil looks as he followed Willie back through the door the burly man had come through. A dishwasher looked up from a long sink.

"Tommy. This cop's here to see you."

Tommy Stuart pulled his hands out of sudsy water, lifted his apron to wipe them, then grabbed a gray towel off the shelf above the sink to wipe his face. He stood about five feet nine, thin, with light brown hair and even features, including deep-set brown eyes. A red mark on his left jaw was puffy and his right eye was blackened with a bruise. Two scratches scored the right side of his neck.

"Is it about Eleanor?" Tommy's eyes begin to fill.

Dugas nodded and spotted the back door open and a tree-covered patio out back.

"Let's talk outside."

"Hey, man," William Little stepped in front of Dugas. "I got a business to run. He's got dishes to wash."

"Get out of my way or I'll move you."

"Oh. The coppers are telling me to wash my own dishes."

"No. I'm telling you to get out of my way."

William Little eased aside slowly. "You're so damn important, are ya?"

The tall detective leaned his face close to the other man's.

"This is a murder investigation. Nothing's more important."

On their way out, Dugas asked William Little to check and see if he was missing a kitchen knife. Tommy moved to the long wooden bench, sat, and buried his face in his hands. Dugas stood next to him, taking in the scents of cooking meat from the kitchen and roses on the bushes of the small patio. A breeze flowed across them, mixing the aromas and cooling the drops of perspiration on the detective's neck.

Dugas looked at the young man, maybe twenty years old, his shoulders moving up and down as he cried. A good detective knows if you can get the perpetrator to cry, he will confess. Then again, the innocent cry as well.

Tommy's sobbing subsided somewhat, and he looked at Dugas.

"What happened to your face?"

"Got into a scuffle." Tommy started crying again. "I...I...was supposed...to see Eleanor Tuesday night, but I got into a fight. Got thrown in jail."

"Where?"

"Here in the Quarter."

He wiped his eyes and looked at Dugas. "If I had seen her...she wouldn't have been..."

Dugas waited through more crying. Tommy finally gasped his way out of it, looked up at Dugas again, and said, "She was my honey pie."

"How did you get into a fight?"

"Got jumped by two men next to Jackson Square. Cops broke us up and put us all in jail. They didn't believe me. We all had liquor on our breath. I only had one beer."

"How long had you known Eleanor?"

Tommy Stuart first saw Eleanor Harrison passing on the street on the first warm day in March. The second time, he followed her to Kite's Antiques. The third time, he intercepted her, showed her where he worked, and invited her to dine there. She refused his first invitation and the second. The third time, she accepted.

"Did you ever visit her room?"

Tommy nodded. "She let me in through the back door." The dishwasher shook his head, began to tear up again.

"All right." Dugas put his notepad and pencil away. "Come along to headquarters so I can take your statement." And make sure Tommy Stuart had been in jail at the time of the murder.

On their way out, Dugas checked with William Little. No knives were missing.

***

Dugas pulled his latest daily report from the typewriter and felt his stomach rumble. Hunger pangs. He put the daily aside and picked up Tommy Stuart's statement, focused on one section.

"She disliked both men in the boarding house. She was afraid of the big one. He was unfriendly, glared at her, and the other was creepy, watched her all the time. Said inappropriate things."

"Like what?" Dugas had asked.

"About her body and her lips."

"Lips?"

"He said her lips looked like they wanted to be kissed all the time."

Dugas looked at the clock on the wall. 8:10 p.m. He started packing up his notes, heard footsteps crossing the nearly empty Detective Bureau.

"You ever go home, Boyo?"

Patrick Shannon approached, carrying two bottles of beer and a brown paper bag.

"Get your newspaper."

Shannon put the beers on Dugas's desk, reached into the bag, and pulled out two sandwiches wrapped in white butcher paper. Dugas spread out the morning's paper.

"Oh, man, that smells great."

Each detective opened the wrapping and separated the halves of his sandwich before lifting a half and taking a large bite of crisp French bread filled with roast beef slathered in dark brown gravy, with mayonnaise, lettuce, tomatoes, and pickles.. Gravy rolled down the sides of their mouths and onto the newspaper. Dugas managed to swallow before he began laughing.

Shannon gobbled, managed to ask, "What's so funny?"

Dugas shook his head. "You. You still taking care of your little brother."

"You was me rookie, Boyo. I made you the detective you are today."

Dugas nodded, and both forced themselves to slow down. Chew their food. Between bites and sips of beer, Dugas updated his sergeant on the case, concluding with, "I have two suspects. Big guy and creepy guy. Unless someone was let into the building."

He went over what was in today's daily report, which Shannon would eventually read.

"Not much to go on," Shannon said.

Dugas picked up the note from Quarry and read it aloud.

Dugas picked up the note from Quarry and read it aloud. "Detective Dugas, I want to help you solve the mystery. The key may be Eleanor's quiet personality. She seemed ripe for exploitation by a man of bad scruples. She seemed lonely. Never met my eyes. She read a lot. I will work to discover if she had drawn a man's unwanted attention. An intimate. Sincerely, Peter William Quarry."

"So?"

"So, Quarry claimed he barely knew the victim."

"Jesus, Mary, and Joseph. That's your best lead?"

Dugas grinned, gravy oozing out of his mouth.

"I know the chief calls you the smart one and you tend to solve every case you work, but this one might be your undoing."

"I doubt it," said Dugas.

"Cocky. I like that."

They finished their sandwiches, and Shannon left his junior officer to clean up.

Loud voices from below drew Dugas's attention as he descended the stairs. Two groups stood in front of the high counter—men and women, yelling in Italian, separated by uniformed cops. Dugas tried to ease past, heard his name called out.

The desk sergeant waved, cupped a hand next to his mouth. "I was about to send up for you. Ya got another visitor." He pointed to the chairs lining the far wall.

Peter Quarry, in a white dress shirt and black trousers, rose from a chair and walked toward Dugas. The small man's blond hair was neatly combed, his faint moustache gone now, and he looked pale.

"Did you talk with her boyfriend?"

"Let's go upstairs to talk."

Three detectives from the evening shift were at their desks, none of them near Dugas's desk, so he pulled a wooden chair over and patted it for Quarry to sit. Dugas did not want the desk between them. No barrier. He took out his case notes, a fresh pencil, and tablet and sat, putting his hands behind his head.

Quarry sat straight, hands in his lap. He looked at Dugas for a few seconds, then looked around the squad room.

"This is different than I thought it would be."

"Would you like some coffee?" Dugas stood, pulled his coffee mug from a side drawer. "Come along. We can talk while I fix a pot. How is this different than you thought?"

Quarry followed, stood a few feet from Dugas and folded his arms, tapped a foot as he looked around again. "You call each other bulls, don't you? Detectives, I mean."

"Yep."

"So, this is the bullpen, like they say in the papers. It's bigger than I thought it would be."

As the coffee brewed, Dugas asked, "Where did you go to grammar school?"

"Huh? Oh, Saint Prudence on Carrollton."

"What sisters taught you there?"

"Sisters? Oh. Marianites."

"That's why you have good penmanship. Sisters of Charity taught me. Same company. Different division." Dugas smiled.

He filled his mug with strong coffee-and-chicory, stirred in two heaping spoonfuls of sugar, filled another mug for Quarry.

"Sugar?"

Quarry nodded, and Dugas added two spoonfuls. They took their coffee back to his desk and sat.

"What were we talking about?" Dugas asked. "Yeah, you asked if we found her boyfriend. We found one of them."

"She had more than one?" Quarry's face reddened.

More? Interesting.

"Girls like her often do."

"Girls like her?"

"I mean all girls, all women. They flirt, and then..."

"You said, 'girls like her.'"

Dugas continued down the unpleasant path of getting this man to like him.

"They seem lonely sometimes, but a pretty girl cannot be lonely." Dugas had trouble swallowing after making such a stupid statement.

"I know. They act demure, but they are not." Quarry sat up straighter, took a sip of coffee.

"Some of the prettier ones won't even meet your eye." Dugas fed Quarry his words from the note.

"Yes. Yes."

"Pretty girls should know they can draw the attention of any man, especially a man of bad scruples." Dugas felt the coffee churn in his stomach.

"That is what I say."

"Her boyfriend says she never liked you."

Quarry sat back, color rising in his face.

"I think she let a man into her room."

"When?"

"A couple times."

"Did you see him?"

Quarry shook his head.

Dugas opened his notebook, found his notes on Quarry's original statement.

"You said you barely knew her."

Quarry nodded.

"How did you know she was a reader? She read books."

"Uh. Uh." He shrugged.

Quarry's mug shook when he raised it, so he used both hands. Not looking at Dugas now.

"She was sneaky pretty, wasn't she?" said Dugas.

"Huh?"

"The closer I looked at her, the prettier she became."

Quarry sipped his coffee, his eyes locked on Dugas's now.

"She had a symmetrical face, lovely from the left and from the right. And those lips."

The mug shivered as Quarry put it down with one hand.

Dugas went on. "Sensuous lips. I studied them, did you?"

Quarry continued staring into Dugas's eyes.

"Would draw a man's attention. She drew yours, just like she drew her boyfriend's?"

The small man's chest rose, and he fought to control his breathing.

"She was having sex with her boyfriend."

Quarry's face stiffened.

"Did she lure you?"

The man looked away, his breathing a little heavier now.

"Those lips made you want to kiss them, didn't they?"

Dugas stared into the Quarry's eyes when the man looked back, and neither blinked.

"How many women have you had sex with, Peter?"

Quarry tried picking up his coffee, put it down immediately. He blinked, and a tear rolled down his left cheek.

"You came to talk with me, Peter."

Quarry nodded, another tear rolling down his cheek.

They stared at one another for long seconds, Quarry's chest rising and falling.

Dugas dropped his voice. "Where did you get the knife?"

Quarry tightened his grip on the coffee mug, tears on both cheeks now. He looked down.

Two detectives passed to get coffee. Dugas put a finger over his lips and they took a different path between the desks.

Peter Quarry put his hands over his face and cried.

Dugas waved one of the bulls over. He asked Detective Artie Desmond to summon the night-shift stenographer.

***

Four years earlier, Officer Jessie Martin had been shot in the back by an armed robber. Martin lived but was confined to a rolling chair, which he pulled up to the desk to use Dugas's typewriter. Martin was the night-shift stenographer.

Dugas pulled his chair around to sit next to Peter Quarry, closing the distance, chairs touching. Detective Jacques Dugas, as he had done many times before, befriended a murderer to get a confession. In a hushed voice, Quarry told him what had happened.

It was a rage. Quarry had killed Eleanor in a rage. Heard her come out of the bathroom at the end of the hall, opened his door, and asked if he could speak with her. She would not look at him, and by the time she reached her door, he was on her, shoving her in and toward her bed.

He tried to kiss her, tried to kiss those luscious lips, but she pulled away. She did not see the knife, a knife Quarry had found on the street on a rainy day. The knife had probably fallen from a wagon, he guessed.

He said, "You never know when you might need a knife."

When the statement concluded, Jessie Martin passed the four pages to Quarry. Dugas gave the man a red pencil.

"You find any errors, circle and correct and put your initials next to each."

Typically, Martin would mistype a word on each page, so the confessor would correct and put his initials next to each; that way, his defense lawyer could not say he had signed the bottom of the page without reading it.

As Quarry read and corrected the sheet, Dugas reminded himself he would have to tell Shannon the old cliché ("Murders are never solved while sitting in the office,") hadn't held true this time. He took out his new Waterman fountain pen with Prussian blue ink and handed it to Peter Quarry to sign and date the bottom of each page before Dugas and Martin signed each.

"You don't need to handcuff me."

"Yes, I do. Regulations."

Dugas led Quarry down the steep back stairs. Uncooperative suspects often fell down these stairs, to be taken back up to try again. They went around to Orleans Parish Prison to book Quarry for the murder of Eleanor Harrison.

"How did you figure it out?" Quarry asked.

"Saw it in your eyes first time we met."

"You did?"

Let him spread that around Parish Prison.

"You are smarter than I thought," Quarry said.

It was more of a gut feeling. But I'm not saying it.

Dugas came back around the front of headquarters to type his final daily report on the murder of Eleanor Harrison. His legs burned. His back ached from the long day. The desk sergeant hailed Dugas on the way in.

"The ninth precinct just called. They got a murder on Short Street, just down from the precinct house."

"Any of the midnight shift upstairs?"

The sergeant picked up his phone receiver. "I was about to call up."

"I'll tell them."

Dugas started up the wide staircase to go tell the bulls there was another body.

The Secret of Flight

Kate Ellis

I can fly. That's what they believe, and I can't prove it isn't so. Not now. Not here. I cannot plead that flight is not in my nature, for they would say I was lying because my master, Satan, is the father of lies.

Many others have been brought here, to this dreadful prison they call the Malefiz House, but I had thought myself untouchable. My husband, Hans, is a friend to the powerful, so I believed his wealth would protect me from suspicion. In the normal course of things, it is the poor who are accused. That is how the world runs.

My name is Anna Walter, wife of Hans Walter, one of Bamberg's wealthiest merchants. I am a woman of standing in the town, and we have a fine house on the Lange Gasse and many servants. I told my inquisitors that I must have been accused by someone who envies my wealth, for jealousy is a powerful and corrosive poison. Then I named the one who wishes me dead. Although it seems they have taken no heed.

As I await my fate, I ponder the events that led me to this terrible place. In the year of Our Lord sixteen hundred and twenty-three, a new Prince Bishop was appointed to rule over the town, a man so zealous in the faith that he uses any means at his disposal to punish the sinful. For years now, darkness, cold and rain have caused the crops to fail, and our Prince Bishop told the town that witches had cursed our land—witches who had to be hunted down to prevent the frost returning. At first, we rejoiced that he was taking action to protect us, until the zeal of those hunts put all in fear for their lives.

I imagined I had no reason to fear Prince Bishop von Dorheim, for everybody knows me as a God-fearing woman who hates the Devil and all his works. It took me an age to realize that wickedness had crept into my own household as a worm creeps into a wholesome apple.

I came to Bamberg from Forchheim as a bride, and for many years I prayed that I would give my husband a child. Yet my prayers went unanswered. I would walk the streets of the town in my fine clothes, with my servants following behind, and see so many poor women with babes at their breast while their ragged offspring played at their feet. Each time I witnessed such a sight, I felt a gnawing ache within my very heart. I thought often of what had happened in Forchheim, before my marriage, and wondered whether the sin I committed then had brought a curse upon me that no amount of pious prayer could remove.

My husband's business dealings always thrived, even through the years of bad harvests, for wealth protects like a shield against the vagaries of nature. Hans is many years my senior, and in the early days of our marriage he played the devoted husband. Then, as I grew older and proved unable to give him the son he longed for, his manner became distant, and I began to hear tales of his infidelity with women of the town. But I stayed silent as a good wife should—as my mother had told me I must.

My reflection in the looking glass told me that I was no longer the young woman Hans had once desired. And my despair deepened when I noticed him watching my maidservant, Margaretha, his gaze filled with lust, which is one of the deadly sins the Prince Bishop rails against.

Margaretha is plump and comely, with hair like shining gold beneath her linen cap and a face like the statue of Our Lady in the cathedral. Her mother was my father's servant, so I have known her from her childhood, and I had come to love her. Until I discovered her betrayal.

It is said that many in this town consort with the Devil, and a woman of my acquaintance was accused by a neighbor and brought to this dreadful place where I now lie. I heard say that they tormented her with instruments of such a fearsome nature that it pains me to name them, and even though she confessed nothing, they kept her fettered and starving until they burned her to death. Now I fear I will meet the same fate, and I know it is Margaretha who has brought me to it. How sweet looks deceive.

When I began to suspect Hans's lust for her, I watched them closely. I saw his hand touch hers as she served his wine and I noted the longing looks he gave her. Then later I saw her belly swelling beneath her gown, and I knew that Margaretha was about to give my husband what I had failed to give him—a child.

Once I was sure my suspicions about Margaretha had substance, she and her child filled my thoughts day and night, disturbing my sleep. Whenever she left the house, I would leave too, holding my cloak close round me, following at a distance with my hood raised so I would not be recognized. I followed Margaretha everywhere: to the market and the clockmaker, to the cobbler and to the candle maker. Each errand she ran for my household, I was there, standing unseen outside every place, pretending to study the items on display in the windows and on the adjacent stalls. I was sure at the time that she did not know I was there—although I wonder now whether she was aware of my deception and said nothing, amusing herself with my discomfort.

I confess to jealousy. I confess to coveting the thing growing in Margaretha's womb. I confess to wishing her dead, so I could steal her child. But I will not confess to the dark deeds of which I now stand accused. For, if I did, I know my life would end in the flames.

I now realize that my actions were foolish, but so fierce was my envy that I needed to know each thing she did, day and night. I tormented myself, and yet if I had stopped, I would never have discovered the truth. For one day I witnessed something that told me Margaretha was deceiving us all.

To my knowledge, she had no male admirers apart from my faithless husband. Then, one morning in October, I followed her across the bridge, through the arch of the town hall and up to the cathedral, where I saw her dip her fingers into the holy water and make the sign of the cross before hurrying up the aisle toward the Chapel of the Nail to the left of the high altar. Her manner seemed most furtive, and, when she looked around, I slipped behind the great tomb of the saintly Emperor and Empress to conceal my presence.

After a while I heard soft footsteps walking up the aisle toward the chapel. Then I heard whispers, stealthy as the breeze in the branches of a dying tree, and I stepped forward to peep around the side of the tomb, ready to withdraw should the speakers look in my direction. I could see Margaretha by the chapel entrance, quite unaware of my presence. Her back was against a pillar, and the man she was with leaned toward her, his intentions quite clear even in that holy place. He was dressed all in black, and he was tall and handsome with a pointed beard that the Devil himself might have coveted.

Fearing discovery, I hid myself again until Margaretha hurried out, the man following a few minutes after. She had not seen me. But later I was to discover that the danger was far from over.

***

What was I? An ageing wife who had failed in my duty and had been supplanted by a younger woman. And yet what I had witnessed in the cathedral had given me a sliver of hope, a hope that was rekindled when I received a letter from my mother in Forchheim saying she wished to visit me. How I rejoiced that I would be able to share my fears with her and seek her wise advice.

So it was that five days later, her carriage arrived, and I welcomed her with kisses and much relief. Margaretha too came out of the house to greet her, her eyes lowered modestly as she bobbed her curtsy. My mother asked her how she was, and she answered that she was well. There was no note of shame in her voice, and at that moment I wished her nothing but ill.

When my mother took my arm and led me indoors, she whispered in my ear as though she feared being overheard.

"They say there is much witchcraft in this town and that many have been accused—even people of the better sort."

"Our Prince Bishop has vowed to purge the town of all Satan's followers," I answered. Witchcraft, I thought then, was like a plague tearing through the town, a plague which had to be stopped. "He will not stand by while sorcerers and witches destroy our crops, and Herr Forner, his Vicar General, will rid Bamberg of evil, no matter where it is found."

I know now that my words must have sounded mealy mouthed and foolish to my mother. But at that time, I believed what the town had been told. It is only now that I know the truth.

My mother said nothing more on the subject that evening, but the next day she came to my chamber when I was alone.

"Something troubles you, my child." She put her hand on my shoulder, and I saw nothing but love in her eyes. It was a long time since anybody had looked upon me with such affection, and I felt close to tears.

I composed myself and went to the door of my chamber to check for eavesdroppers, because servants can be curious creatures when it comes to their betters. Once I was satisfied we could not be overheard, I sat down beside her, and she put her arm around me.

"Otto is growing to be a fine young man," she said as I leaned my head on her shoulder. "You would be proud of your...brother."

Only Otto wasn't my brother. He was my son, but my mother had claimed him as her own, deceiving the world into thinking her with child as I hid away in shame. I was but sixteen, and his father was my dancing master—a handsome young man who had seduced an innocent young girl, as I was then.

My marriage to Hans was arranged soon after Otto's birth, but there were to be no children from the union. Hans had been wed twice before, but his first two wives had also failed to give him an heir. At first, I wondered why God had never blessed them, whether they were at fault in some way. But after a few years of marriage I began to entertain the possibility that Hans could never father a child, and, if this was the case, it meant that he could not be the father of Margaretha's babe. I thought of the man I'd glimpsed in the cathedral and how they'd whispered together. It had looked like a meeting of lovers.

"How is Margaretha?" my mother asked, interrupting my thoughts.

"I think she is with child." I hesitated. "And I think she will claim my husband is the father."

It was painful to voice the truth, but I needed to confide in somebody.

For a while my mother said nothing. Then she spoke in a soft whisper. "If that is what she claims, she is lying. For it is well-known that Hans cannot father a child. His first two wives..."

"It was not well-known to me when I married him," I said, angry that this important fact had been kept from me.

"I saw how you suffered giving birth to Otto, so I thought it a good thing that you would never have to undergo that ordeal again."

At that moment, I was furious with my mother because she had made a decision for me that I would not have made for myself. Yet she looked at me with so much love that my heart soon softened. "I think Margaretha and my husband are lovers."

"That may be so, Anna, but if she is with child, it means she has taken another lover and thinks to play on Hans's vanity for her own enrichment. She was ever a sly child."

"I can make no complaint against her because she knows my own secret. If Hans found out about Otto..."

My mother nodded slowly. "You are right. There are some secrets that must be kept for the welfare of all. Otto must believe you are his big sister and I am his mother, so you must say nothing openly against Margaretha. I advise that you pray for strength."

"I could come to Forchheim to visit you. A lengthy visit to my own mother? Hans can hardly object to that."

"We will see, my dear. But first you must ensure that your place in your household is not usurped. Have it put about that Margaretha has a young man. People love to gossip; it is human nature. Make Hans doubt her. It is the only way."

But I knew a different way. One that would rid me of Margaretha for good.

***

They say God punishes the schemer and ill-wisher, but I did not believe this applied in my case. I was a pious and honest woman, respected in all Bamberg. I attended Mass regularly and showed a blameless face to my neighbors, whereas Margaretha was a fornicator and an adulteress, a lowly maidservant who deserved punishment.

And another possibility nagged at the back of my mind, tempting me until I could resist it no longer. Should Margaretha be convicted of sorcery, what would then become of her child? If I could claim it as my own when it was born, I would become a mother at last—for I had never been allowed to be a true mother to Otto. This temptation grew inside me as Margaretha's child grew within her, until at last I was resolved on my path. Once Margaretha's child was born, I would denounce her as a witch and she would meet the fate she deserved. But I had to bide my time until the child was safely born.

When my mother returned to Forchheim, I longed to go with her, tempted by the prospect of seeing Otto again. Yet I knew my son would greet me as a sister, and my heart would break as I resisted the desire to tell him the truth about his birth. So I stayed in Bamberg, watching and waiting, as Margaretha's belly grew larger and my husband became ever more attentive toward her, barely able to conceal his delight that he had fathered a child at last.

In Margaretha's seventh month, she began to neglect her duties in the household, leaving me to dress myself or allotting the task to one of the other maids. Perhaps her conscience made her unwilling to look me in the face, or perhaps she now imagined the work was beneath her. My husband barely spoke to me over those months, and at times I wished I had returned to Forchheim with my mother. My vengeance, however, needed to be perfectly timed, and I didn't wish to miss my opportunity.

The whole town was talking of witchcraft as the arrests continued apace. The witchcraft commission demanded that each suspect name a hundred accomplices, and the witch hunters were held in such high regard that their actions were never questioned. What had begun as a necessity when the crops failed was now causing terror among our neighbors, for many wealthy men, along with their entire families, had already been executed and their property forfeit. I heard that some have petitioned the Emperor himself, but still the trials continue behind closed doors and the fires consume the guilty. Even our mayor met his death, convicted of congress with the Devil, who came to him in the form of a fair maid who later took the form of a goat and demanded that he reject Almighty God.

Either Satan was truly stalking Bamberg, or the town had been flooded by a form of madness. I do not know the truth of it, but I do know that I have never encountered the Devil in any form. Yet, as I thought of what I saw that day in the cathedral, I could not say the same of Margaretha and her meeting with the handsome man in black garments.

Although my husband rarely spoke to me, I sensed his increasing fear. What if one of our accused neighbors named him to the commission? What if they came to our house to take him...or myself? As Margaretha's time drew nearer, I knew I had to act before any suspicion fell upon us. What could be more believable than an upright citizen reporting wrongdoing in her own household to the authorities? If I were involved in the worship of Satan, I would surely stay silent. Only the truly innocent would come forward. Or at least that's what I believed then, in my naivety.

Margaretha was growing large and lazy, and I told myself my moment of triumph was imminent. Soon I would have a child, and I made plans to hire a wet nurse for my little son—for I was sure it would be a son—who would never know the woman who gave him birth. My heart leapt at the prospect. It would only take a word. A whisper. In this town, whispers are like lightning and strike more dead.

So it was that two days after Margaretha had been safely delivered of a fine son, I called at the cathedral to hear Mass. But instead of going home after the service, I went to the house of the Vicar General and asked to speak with him. I was shown into a room paneled in dark wood; what little light there was trickled through a small, north-facing window to my right. The air was stale and, all of a sudden, I found it hard to breathe. At the end of the room, behind a large oak table, sat a gaunt man with a long face, dressed in black, with eyes that seemed to see into my very soul. It was said in the town that he was a learned man and as I approached, I felt a sense of power, so strong it made me tremble. But I was not to be diverted from my purpose.

"Sir, I greatly fear that my maidservant has had dealings with the Devil, and I know not what to do." I stood before him like a supplicant, certain that playing the helpless innocent would help my cause.

He stared at me for what seemed like a long time, taking in my every feature, while I stood, fearing he could hear the pounding of my heart. Then he spoke in a voice so low and soft that I strained to hear him. "What is her name?" He dipped his quill into the ink pot at his elbow, and as he began to write I could hear the scratch of his pen against the parchment.

"Margaretha Gottfried. It grieves me that she has come to this, for I have known her since she was a child. I fear she has been led astray by wickedness and, as a good Catholic, I felt I had to inform you, sir."

"Your name?"

"Anna Walter. Wife of Hans Walter, the merchant."

He nodded, as though he knew my husband's name, and made a note in his book.

"Margaretha has just given birth to a child and I fear that she has had congress with the Devil or one of his servants, although she claims the child is my husband's." I bowed my head as though the words pained me.

"Thank you, Frau Walter. The maid will be taken to the Malefiz House to be questioned, then brought before the commission. You need not fear. Her guilt will be proved."

He looked down, and I knew it was time to leave, so I turned and walked from the room, aware of his eyes on my back. It had been done. Now all I had to do was wait.

***

When no callers arrived at our house, I began to wonder whether Herr Forner was as formidable as his reputation. Surely the report of a potential witch would not go unheeded. And yet for three days no men arrived to take Margaretha to the Malefiz House and still she drifted around the house with her babe in her arms, enjoying my husband's admiring glances. Whenever I caught them together, he was gazing at the child with wonder, his hand placed lovingly on her still-swollen belly; they made no attempt to spring apart, and fury rose within me like bile.

I went to bed that night in the chamber where I had slept alone since the early days of my marriage and lay restless until the early hours. I could hear the child crying, and my heart broke that all my planning had been in vain.

At sunrise, I heard a loud pounding on the front door, and I confess that I smiled to myself, thinking they had come for Margaretha at last. Then, to my surprise, my own chamber door burst open, and, as I struggled to sit up, I saw three men standing at the foot of my bed. One took out his sword and pointed it at me.

"Frau Anna Walter. You will come with us."

There was something familiar about the man but just then I couldn't place where I'd seen him before.

"Why? What is this outrage? I will call for my husband." Shock had made my voice feeble, but I did my best to sound indignant.

"Your husband will not help you, for you have been denounced as a witch. You have been seen flying at night to meet your fellow witches, and you have been fornicating with the Devil. We do not tolerate your kind in Bamberg."

It was then that I screamed.

***

I could not believe it had come to this: I, Anna Walter, had been accused, while Margaretha was still free. The Malefiz House is a terrible place, and even when I covered my ears to block out the cries of the tortured, their screams of torment still rang through my head. I begged for a priest to visit me, but my jailers refused, saying I could receive no visitors until I had confessed and given my accusers the names of my fellow witches who flew with me at night. I was told that if I did not readily confess, I would be shown the dreadful instruments.

I could do nothing but shed hot tears as I contemplated the ordeal that might lie before me. I was helpless as a beast in a slaughterhouse, and all I could do was pray.

On the third day of my incarceration, I was surprised when a visitor was admitted to my cell. She wore a fine cloak trimmed with fur and her hood was pulled down over her face so that at first I did not know her. Then, when she pushed back the hood, I was amazed to see it was Margaretha, standing with a smile of satisfaction on her lips.

"You had thought to be rid of me," she said, with the confidence of a mistress rather than a servant. "You made a bad mistake."

"I saw you with the Devil...and I knew the child you carried could not be my husband's."

She put her hand in the small of her back, as though it pained her, and sat down slowly on the little wooden stool, the only piece of furniture apart from the filthy pallet where I squatted, my arms tied with ropes to a ring fixed in the wall. "You are right. The child is not Hans's, although he thinks it is. He has acknowledged it as his own and when you are dead I shall be mistress of your house. I shall enjoy Hans's riches."

She stood up unsteadily and was about to leave when I spoke again. "Who is the father of your child?"

"You told Herr Forner I consorted with the Devil, but that is not the truth. My lover sits on the witch commission, and that is how I knew of your accusation. He has promised to make sure no harm comes to me or his child. He is married, but when Hans and I are man and wife, we will remain lovers. It is an arrangement that will suit everyone. I have given Hans what he thinks is his son, and I will have his wealth while my lover enjoys my body and guarantees my safety." She paused. "They say death by burning is painful. But I cannot help that. Your death will be for the greater good...Anna."

If I had not been bound to the wall, I would have struck her. When she had gone, I cried helpless tears. Then I shouted for the guard. I needed to denounce my husband. His whole property would be confiscated if he was taken, which meant I could at least thwart Margaretha's plan to enjoy his wealth.

The guard came at my bidding and said he would pass on my accusation to Herr Forner. It comforted me to know that I would have some small revenge.

***

I am due to be questioned this afternoon, and I've been told the instruments will be used if I do not readily make my confession. No food has been brought to me, and hunger gnaws at my stomach like a burrowing rat. I am weak, and yet I know I have to act before my tormentors begin their work. Once I have suffered the thumb screws and leg screws that I have been shown, I will lack the power to move, so the matter is urgent. There is a stone protruding from the wall, just within my reach, and with great patience I have been able to rub my rope bonds against it. A few moments ago, the rope frayed and finally broke, so now I am free—but I have to move swiftly.

To my surprise, I find the door to my cell unlocked. Perhaps they think it is enough that I am tethered like a beast. I open the door slowly, thankful that it makes no noise, and I sneak out, listening for any sound that might herald the arrival of my guards. But it seems they are busy, for I can hear the harrowing screams of the tortured as I search for a way to escape this dreadful place.

At the end of a long passage, I see a flight of stairs and allow myself to hope that I can flee Bamberg to take refuge with my mother in Forchheim. But I have no time for hopes and dreams. I must get away.

I hear a sound behind me, so I slip through a door to my right that has been left ajar, my only hope of safety. I find myself in a chamber where a cheerful fire burns in the grate, and I realize this is the domain of the tormentors rather than the tormented, so I close the door carefully. There are no bars on the windows here, and I rush over to the casement and push it open. Then I lean out of the window and see a long drop to the ground.

As I climb up onto a chair, I hear a scraping sound behind me. The door to the chamber is opening, so I have to seize my chance. Freedom is but a leap away.

I launch myself from the window and, to my delight, my skirts billow out and slow my journey to the ground. I can fly. That's what they believe, and I have proved it to be true.

Fair Trade

Ashley Lister

Jack Whittaker stared into the open packing crate. He cast his gaze over the walnut stocks and iron barrels of the rifled muskets and nodded encouraging approval, as though he knew what he was looking at. The box held twenty Enfield P53s, each one looking glossy and dangerously attractive. He could smell the scent of muzzle oil on the black barrels, the fragrance reminding him of overripe bananas, underscored by a suggestion of mint. The scent was more powerful than the earthy stink of the surrounding barn or the rank stench of dirt and sweat coming from General George Edward Johnson.

"How much do you want?" Johnson asked.

He could have been an imposing figure. There was a feather in his slouch hat and he wore thigh-high riding boots. His gray frock coat was open, exposing an ornate waistcoat on a broad chest decorated with rows of delicate gold buttons that complemented the stars on his collar. But the man and his clothes looked a little too lived-in to be properly imposing. There was dust, dirt, and horse shit on his boots. His slouch hat had endured one too many thunderstorms to remain rigid, and there were ominous dark spatters on the breast of his coat. His posture was stoop-shouldered and wearied. Instead of looking imposing, with his swarthy unwashed complexion and long, bedraggled beard, Johnson came across as someone who had survived hardship through being mean and low, like a rat or a cockroach.

"How much?" Johnson snapped.

The repeated words were like a slap, dragging Jack back from his reverie.

"The price has been agreed," Jack said. "I've not come all this way to haggle with you."

"What if I want to renegotiate the price?" Johnson pressed.

Jack slammed the lid of the case closed. He drew a sharp breath to cover his impatience. He could feel his stomach tightening with apprehension. The need to empty his bowels was beginning to feel like an imperative. He had been nervous about this transaction before it began, and now he could sense it was not going to go as smoothly as he had hoped. "Renegotiation isn't going to happen," Jack said crossly. "This deal was made before I left England. I was bringing eleven boxes of these guns to help arm your soldiers. In return, you were going to fill my cargo hold with cotton."

Johnson's smile was an unpleasant display of yellowing teeth. There was no suggestion of amusement reaching his dark, furtive eyes. Again, Jack found the man reminiscent of dangerous vermin.

"There's been a change of plans since that agreement was made," Johnson said carefully. "Circumstances have altered."

"Are you trying to swindle me?"

"Not at all."

"What circumstances have altered?"

"Didn't y'all hear Lincoln's emancipation proclamation?"

Jack rubbed his forehead. He knew Lincoln was America's president, but the other words were spat in Johnson's southern drawl, full of long vowel sounds and unfamiliar consonant clusters. The words sounded too long for Jack to fully understand their meaning. "I've been out at sea for the past six weeks," he said quietly. "And I've never been a big one for following the news."

"Lincoln has freed the negro slaves," Johnson explained. He said the words as though it meant the devastating end of an era. He spoke as though Jack were unaware of something as obvious and life-changing as the eruption of a volcano or the impact of a comet. "The ape of Illinois has freed the negroes," Johnson whispered.

"So?" Jack returned. To his mind, this did not sound like the worst thing in the world. He didn't follow international news and, although he had heard many people suggest slavery was the main reason that America was embroiled in a civil war, he had thought it seemed old-fashioned for the country to have such a barbaric and archaic system of forced labor. "What have your freed negroes got to do with our bargain?"

"We have no one to pick the cotton," Johnson explained. "Therefore, whilst I'd dearly love to load your cargo hold with as much cotton as I can pack in there, the reality is, most of the cotton hasn't been harvested. It can't be harvested. There's no one to harvest it."

Jack took a moment to digest this and tried to come to terms with what he was hearing. He did not consider himself particularly obtuse, but he thought he was being told that there was no cotton because the American president had made a proclamation. He wasn't sure that made sense and, instead of trying to comprehend the finer details of the general's message, he found his thoughts going back to the ominous warning his brother had muttered before Jack set sail on this journey: "You can't trust any fucker," Terry had said dourly. "You can't trust anyone."

"If there's no one to harvest your cotton," Jack began doubtfully, "how are you going to pay me?"

Johnson averted his gaze. It was a late February evening in a barn lit by a single tin candle lantern that housed a weak and guttering flame. Visibility was close to non-existent. But it was bright enough for Jack to read the feral expression on Johnson's face.

"You're trying to slance me?" Jack exploded.

His hands had tightened into fists. He'd been two months traveling over land and sea since he last shaved, and his face was hidden behind a thick, grizzled beard. Wearing an over-large privateer coat, with its bulky cut and padded body making him appear formidably broad, he didn't doubt he looked like a menacing adversary to Johnson. "You're trying to fucking slance me?"

Johnson shook his head and raised a placating hand. "No one's slancing you," he said quickly. "We have money. We'll pay a fair price."

"I don't want your worthless money. I want cotton."

"We have gold."

"I used gold to pay for these bloody guns," Jack said stiffly. His voice was rising with mounting frustration. Terry had said, "You can't trust any of these fuckers," and Jack was angry to think that his brother had been so right in his skepticism, while he had been so wrong with his stupid naivety and misplaced faith in human nature. It was galling to think that he, the sensible and well-respected member of the family, was now going to look foolish and unworldly while Terry, the family's black sheep, was going to look like someone blessed with the acumen, insight, and forethought of a shrewd businessman. The idea made Jack blush until his features were an unhealthy purple and his head pounded with the threat of an explosive headache.

Glaring dourly at Johnson, and speaking with a soft simplicity so that he could get his point across, Jack said, "I don't need gold. I just need cotton."

Johnson's laughter was mocking. "I've never met a man before who didn't need gold."

"Well, you've met one now."

"You won't be getting your cotton from any plantation in this state," Johnson said coldly. His yellow smile resurfaced and, this time, the expression sparkled softly in his eyes. "And," Johnson went on, "whether you like it or not, when I leave this barn, I will be taking those Enfields from you."

"Over my dead body," Jack assured him.

"If that's necessary," Johnson agreed.

Lazily, he pulled a pistol from the holster on his belt and waved the barrel in Jack's direction. There wasn't enough light for Jack to see what type of gun was being pointed at him, but he didn't doubt it would be an effective weapon. His bowels, already feeling painfully loose, threatened to give out on him completely.

"I can take them over your dead body," Johnson went on, "or I could simply wound you and let you die a miserable, lingering death here in this barn."

Snarling, Jack took a reluctant step back, away from the case of Enfields.

Johnson stepped closer to the crate and pulled the lid open to examine the contents. His eyes shone with greed, and he moved a greasy tongue over his lips as though he was about to devour a feast. The glint of avarice was still in his eyes when Terry stepped from the shadows behind him and cold-cocked the general with the butt of his heavy Tranter revolver.

Johnson fell to the floor as though his strings had been cut.

"Didn't I say that you couldn't trust these fuckers?" Terry growled.

"Yes," Jack agreed, unable to keep the sharp note of reproach from his voice. "You did say that."

"Then why in the name of blazes didn't you listen?"

"I did listen," Jack returned. "But I didn't have any other options. In case it's slipped your attention, there's a cotton famine back in Burntwick. I had no option except to take matters into my own hands, mortgage everything I owned, and try to rebuild the mill's business."

Terry continued to sneer. "And getting robbed by this wandought was a viable option, was it?"

Jack shook his head and drew a deep breath. If Johnson had shot him, he suspected the pain would have been bad. But he didn't think a gunshot would have hurt as badly as saying the words that he now had to utter.

"You were right, Terry. You were right."

It had been a long year for Jack, and he silently prayed his bad fortune was soon going to come to an end. He came from Burntwick, a once-thriving mill town in the heart of Lancashire. The only reason Burntwick had ever been a thriving mill town, Jack knew, was because of the Whittaker family mill. The mill had been bequeathed solely to Jack in the late 1850s, with an addendum to his father's will suggesting that, if the management of Whittaker's were given to Terry, Jack's elder brother, he would likely squander the profits and resources on gambling, liquor, and loose women. Most people who knew of this addendum to the will believed the late Mr. Whittaker's comment was likely true, and that included Terry.

As the proprietor of the Whittaker family mill, Jack had found his life was beginning to become successful. Aside from the newfound wealth and the status of living in the largest mansion in Burntwick, he also found himself betrothed to the beautiful Isabella Turing, the daughter of Lord and Lady Turing, Burntwick's highly respected gentry. For the first time in his life, Jack had power, wealth, influence, and a potential companion.

And then the war between the states had begun in America, and everything had started to fall apart.

Because his mills worked exclusively with long-staple cotton, Jack had worried the war might have a negative impact on his fortunes. However, to his surprise, prospects initially looked more promising than ever. Delegates from the newly formed confederacy had contacted him to negotiate special arrangements between the Whittaker family mill and a handful of the plantation owners in the southern states of America. Jack had been happy to secure a deal with these sources, particularly when they came with the assurance of a keen price and a promise of high-quality long-staple cotton.

Terry, perennial pessimist that he was, had mumbled his usual warning: "You can't trust any of these fuckers."

But, for the first year of the war, Jack had proved Terry wrong.

The mill had continued to thrive, producing record amounts of cotton of a quality superior to anything produced by their competitors. Sales were strong, and his workforce was happy and prosperous.

It was only when the Southern ports were blockaded by the North that circumstances began to change, and the Whittaker mill was struck by the impact of Lancashire's cotton drought. A year later there was no sign of the blockade being lifted, no other supplier able to offer long-staple cotton, and the cotton drought had turned into a cotton famine.

Of course there were people offering to help him, but always for a price. And it was fortunate, although he would never admit it aloud, that Terry's perpetual advice was always at the back of his thoughts: don't trust anyone. Rather than handing over cash he couldn't spare to dubious intermediaries, who claimed they could source new suppliers or forge pathways that would defy the boundaries put in place by the war, Jack had decided to take a proactive approach to the situation and deal with importation on his own terms.

After remortgaging the family home, and remortgaging the mill and its contents, he invested as much capital as he could muster into the hiring of a schooner, the *Remus*, and purchasing as many brand-new rifles as he could afford.

Admittedly, there had been sacrifices.

His workforce at the mill was depleted to a skeleton staff.

Worse, when Isabella heard that he was intending to supply arms to the Confederates in exchange for cotton, she begged him to reconsider. Selling arms was immoral, she explained. It was a diabolical practice. By selling arms to slave-owners, he would be helping those who wanted to maintain a hateful and iniquitous institution. The minister of her local church was one of those who had cultivated sympathies with the slaves throughout the heart of Lancashire.

Jack had argued that, by selling guns, he would be helping those who wanted to make cotton cloth in his mills and provide for their Lancashire families. He could have gone on to say that he would have happily just paid cash to purchase the raw cotton, if such an arrangement had been available, and that he had no desire to trade in guns and didn't condone slavery. But, by that point, he didn't have a fiancée, and he knew that such discussion would be moot. All he had was a smarting handprint across his cheek and a returned ring that had once pledged his troth.

Even his brother, the one person whom Jack had thought would support the excitement of an adventure sailing across the seas and dodging ships blockading ports, had cautioned him against the deal he had struck with the southern plantation owner. They had argued bitterly about the situation, and Terry had expressed his usual doubts.

Jack had scoffed at the notion of not being able to trust General George Edward Johnson. "He's a military commander," Jack explained. "He's a gentleman, and our company has been doing business with him and his estate for the past fifty years."

"Aye," Terry agreed. "And you're a fool if you trust a man who keeps other men as human chattel. More than that, remember, this is a man who's prepared to fight for the right to own others."

Those words came back to Jack as he stood in the barn and stared down at Johnson's motionless form.

Terry kicked the fallen general hard in the ribs. He then bent down and began to try to remove the man's clothing.

"What are you doing, Terry?" Jack demanded.

"What does it look like? I'm taking his jacket."

"Why?"

"Because we didn't come all this way to be beaten, did we?" Terry wrenched the jacket from Johnson's back and then put it on himself. It was too narrow a fit to go across his broad chest. "Shit," he grumbled. "You're going to have to do this."

"Do what?" Jack asked doubtfully.

Terry was down on his knees and stripping the waistcoat from Johnson's body. He made light work of the act, and Jack wondered what nefarious dealings his brother had been involved with since being shunned from the family mill so that he was now adept at stripping unconscious bodies. He supposed that was a question he didn't really want to have answered.

"You're going to have to go out there," Terry said, nodding toward the barn door. "You're going to have to pretend to be a visiting confederate general, and you'll have to get Johnson's waiting soldiers to load up our boat with whatever cotton they can find in local stores."

"He said there was no cotton," Jack reminded Terry.

"He was lying through his teeth," Terry scoffed. He threw the waistcoat and jacket at Jack and said, "Now put those on and go outside and tell this fucker's second-in-command to get your schooner stocked."

Jack only hesitated for half a second before punching his arms into the sleeves and squeezing the buttons closed. He didn't like the idea of impersonating a southern military commander, but he had traveled to this country with every intention of returning home with cotton, and he wasn't going to fall at this, or any other hurdle.

"What will you be doing whilst I'm getting arrested and shot for impersonating a general?"

Terry had removed Johnson's boots and tossed them at Jack's feet. He stood up, holding Johnson by the ankles, and began dragging him to a darkened corner of the barn. "I'm going to bind this bastard," he explained. "Then I'm going to gag him and hide him in a dark corner of this barn. After that, I'll be down at the dock, getting my cutter ready to sail and helping to make sure we get the proper supply of cotton."

Jack nodded. The *Romulus*, Terry's cutter, had proved a useful diversion. It had allowed Jack to get through the blockade with his larger schooner and he suspected it would provide an equally useful distraction for the return journey.

"What do we do about the guns?" Jack asked.

Terry shrugged. "We can leave them here, if you want, as fair payment for the cotton. Personally, I'd be happier if I could have them put on board the *Romulus*, because I think I have a northern buyer who could help me get a decent return on our investment." He paused before adding, "But I know you like to do things fairly and properly, so I suspect you'll want to leave them here."

Jack didn't need to think about the matter. "Johnson was going to steal those guns. He'd reneged on our agreement, and I could see he would have been keen to shoot me if the urge had taken him. Take the guns and sell them where you see fit."

"Very good," Terry said. He grinned slyly and added, "You're learning that it's a better life when you don't trust anyone, aren't you?"

Jack refused to acknowledge his brother's nihilism, although the words kept coming back to him as the night progressed. He pulled on Johnson's boots and hat to complete the uniform of a confederate general. Then, feeling as though he was suitably dressed for the deception, he stormed out of the barn and started barking orders at the first soldier he could find sporting the three collar stripes of a confederate captain. He could see the reluctance to obey in the man's eyes, and the threat of disobedience lurking in the set of his shoulders. But the authority of Jack's stolen uniform was enough to vanquish whatever argument he wanted to make. By the time Jack had started shouting the same orders at a convenient lieutenant, he had a platoon of soldiers rushing to ransack local stores, barns, and warehouses in their haste to fill the holds of the *Remus*. "You'll regret trusting me," he thought sourly, as he saw the soldiers stumbling to obey. But he tried not to let himself dwell on that thought.

He ordered a pair of privateers to take the boxed Enfields from the *Remus* onto his brother's cutter. And again he found himself pitying the way they blindly obeyed his instructions and put their trust in his stolen uniform.

Before dawn could crack the sky, a captain came rushing from the gangplank of the *Remus* and said, "The hold won't take any more, General."

Jack nodded and thanked him.

"With respect, sir," the captain continued, "what's this exercise been about?"

Jack smiled, relieved that the man hadn't completely decided to trust him. "I've just negotiated an arms deal," he explained. "The cotton you've just put aboard that schooner is payment for two hundred and fifty P53 Enfields."

The captain's eyes widened beneath the brim of his kepi.

"Enfields? Where are they?"

Jack nodded inland. "That barn on the hill," he explained. "You should find them in there."

It was not, technically, a lie, Jack thought. If Johnson had not tried to renege on their agreement, then the captain *should* have found the weaponry there.

"Take a unit," Jack commanded. "Go and secure the barn and make sure the weaponry is properly distributed amongst those troops that need them," he explained.

"Very good, sir."

"I'm going to inspect this cargo hold one final time before I send this crew on their merry way."

He didn't wait for the exchange to continue. He could see that Terry was already aboard the *Romulus*, and the swift little cutter was making its way out of the harbor and slicing through the waters between a pair of blockading frigates. The cutter wore its masts high, taking advantage of a light morning wind and, despite the darkness, showing itself as a highly visible spectacle.

A pair of US Navy frigates began to slowly turn in the direction of the cutter.

"Let's take advantage of the distraction," Jack told his pilot.

Without hesitating, the pilot took the schooner out of the harbor. As the frigates pursued the *Romulus* on a northeasterly path, the pilot took the *Remus*, slipped out of the port, and headed southwards. The schooner was painted gunmetal gray and, with its hold laden with cargo, its sides sat close to the water. With their sails lowered, Jack knew they would be all but invisible to any of the blockading ships, should the crew of any frigate decide to glance in his direction.

He smiled, pleased with himself and content that he would soon be returning home with the cargo he had needed. Perhaps there wasn't enough to end the cotton famine, or even turn the situation back to being a mere drought. However, he thought there was enough to keep the mill going for a few months so that he could tell himself his father had been right to entrust the fate of the Whittaker mill to his hands.

He stood in the wheelhouse, alongside the schooner's pilot, and trained his telescope on his brother's cutter. Dawn light was finally beginning to creep over the horizon, and Jack could see Terry's boat was being slowed by a pair of Union Navy frigates. It was a shame to see his brother facing arrest and whatever punishment the Union thought necessary, but Jack reasoned it was the result that Terry had been striving toward throughout his life.

The pilot saw Jack studying the *Remus* and nodded gruff approval. "He's a curious character, is that one," the pilot said.

Jack's internal smile broadened. From the way the pilot said "that one," it seemed clear he didn't know Terry was Jack's brother. "Curious?" Jack repeated. "How so?"

"Look at him giving himself up to the American navy," the pilot laughed. "You'd think he was the real heroic type, sacrificing himself as a diversion for the likes of us."

"I'd say that was pretty heroic," Jack admitted.

"Aye," the pilot admitted. "But they say he's far from being a hero. He's a blackguard."

"A blackguard?"

"Apparently, he's recently stolen his brother's fiancée, got her to jilt him because of some unethical business he was involved in, and now he's planning to elope with the woman and set up a new life far away from the mill town where he comes from. Maybe even get her to shack up with him here in America."

"Nonsense," Jack said, forcing himself to dismiss the pilot's chatter as idle gossip. He pushed the telescope back to his eye and tried to make out details and features on the figures aboard the *Romulus*. "That makes no sense. How on earth would he be able to afford to migrate to America?"

The pilot shrugged and said, "I don't know. Someone suggested he might profit from gun-running, selling stolen Enfields to either the Confederates or the northerners. They said he'd be good at such negotiations because he's a cautious blackguard and he always says you shouldn't trust anyone."

Staring through the telescope and seeing a female figure that looked very much like his beloved Isabella, Jack thought, "I should have listened to your advice, Terry. It seems true that you can't trust anyone."

Murder on the Sacred Mountain

Rhys Hughes

The snowy mountains of distant Tibet shimmered before him as Jaspers plodded down the insufferably long Dereham Road, but when he turned the corner into Livingstone Street they vanished, hidden by the mass of rusty brown houses on the west side.

But no, those weren't real mountains and he knew it, merely clumps of oddly shaped cumulus clouds that resembled exotic peaks, perhaps as big as the mountains they mimicked but of quite a different texture, fists of vapor clenched by an exotic god.

Jaspers was daydreaming. What is an exotic god anyway? Anything at all can become familiar and lose its allure, he had learned during his short but mentally active life. Yet he was content enough here in Norwich, on a Sunday morning, heading to his club.

His club was an unusual institution. Unlike the ponderous and official societies based in elegant buildings nearer the center of the city, it was an ordinary terraced house constructed from brick, notable in no way, grimy on the outside, barely furnished within.

But it was good enough for the members of the Reconstruction Club, a name chosen by Rufus and not Jaspers, who yet respected it sufficiently to straighten his back proudly as he opened a tiny gate and crunched over a few yards of gravel to the front door.

Everything was small on Livingstone Street, but it was quiet, cozy, and thus a perfect location for an impromptu association of men of all classes, but chiefly from the lower middle, who were interested in unsolved crime and liked debating the latest mysteries.

Debating them in hope of solving them, that is, and solving them in a most practical manner. Not for the members of this club were purely cerebral methods much valued. The theorists of other armchairs might reasonably claim to be the superior amateurs, but here the ideals were far removed from any such adoration of abstraction.

Above the front door, a metal plate had been fixed to a brick, and on its surface was engraved an equal sign. There was no other indication of the status of the building. Something shall be the same as another thing. That was the motto of the Reconstruction Club.

Jaspers sighed, for no special reason, and used his own key to enter the house. Every member had a key. The house had been left to Rufus by an aunt and, instead of selling or living in it, Rufus had decided to maintain it as it was, sparse and hollow, a russet husk.

The aunt had never owned much furniture. A few chairs, one table, a sofa of dubious merit. She was one of those eccentrics whose families enjoy being related to them only after they are dead. Jaspers shrugged, went into the larger of the two downstairs rooms. If he found nobody here, he would try upstairs. The staircase was horribly steep.

But there was no need for that. Rufus was sitting on the sofa, reading a newspaper in his habitual manner, one leg crossed high over the other, the patterns of luxury socks exposed, and without glancing at Jaspers, he said from a corner of his mouth, "Just me."

Rufus always had a pipe clenched between his lips, but it was never lit and rarely packed with tobacco, and his voice sometimes emerged from its wide bowl as if from a small cave mouth or a defective megaphone. In his everyday life, Rufus was a shipping clerk.

Jasper made a bleak face.

"Pollard and Gertie haven't been here for months."

"Nor have Chunder or Diggs."

"And I don't recall seeing Beastly for a long time."

Rufus lowered his newspaper.

"Now, don't get yourself worried, dear boy," he said, "about the health of the club and its viability. It will endure, for crime always endures." He frowned at the ceiling. "Maybe they've all been murdered. That would be a rum business. Ironic somewhat."

"Rather." Jaspers took a wooden chair.

It was considered uncouth for two men to sit next to each other on the sagging sofa. Knees might run the risk of touching. Those reckless days belonged to the turn of the century and were gone forever. The world had been through war, through epidemic.

It was a time to be serious now, solemn.

"Anything doing?" Jaspers nodded at the newspaper.

"Yes, as it happens! A marvel."

"Unexpected on such a sedate Sunday."

"Nothing in Norwich, dear boy. This occurred far away."

"How far? In Scotland perhaps?"

"My friend, the world is wide. Let me explain. Do you remember all that fuss about Bowman last year? Of course you do! How could anyone forget?

He sneaked across the border into Tibet. Wanted to climb one of the sacred mountains with just a couple of porters. He was caught on his way to the base of the peak and walled up alive in some remote spot and forced to become a monk and meditate."

"And our government still haven't succeeded in getting him back. It's not easy to threaten a landlocked country with gunboats. Funnily enough, on my way here, the clouds in the west looked just like mountains. Which mountain was it that Bowman climbed?"

"He didn't manage to climb any of them, dear boy."

"He went for Mount Kailash?"

"Yes, the most sacred of all the sacred heights."

"The world is wide," said Jaspers.

"That reminds you of something?" pressed Rufus.

Jaspers pulled a book from a pocket.

"Housman's brought out a second collection of poems. Only quarter of a century after his first. It's just as brilliant and gloomy and curiously uplifting as his earlier poems. In fact, they were written at the same time, but he withheld publication, who knows why? 'Wide's the world, to rest or roam, with change abroad and cheer at home.' I will have them all by heart soon. But this is quite irrelevant."

"Nothing is that," said Rufus, "not ultimately."

"Therefore we are talking about Bowman for a good reason? I await enlightenment on this Tibetan episode."

"That was almost an excruciating witticism."

"But not quite. Never quite."

Rufus had placed the newspaper on the vacant sofa seat beside him. Now he slapped it with his open palm.

"Supple has only gone and done the exact same thing."

"Reginald Supple! But how?"

"Yes, that blasted gentleman, with his countless mistresses and waxed moustaches and aristocratic manner. We all know he was born in a barn on a farm and never could remember to shut a door tight ever after, but a rich uncle in the Americas left him an inheritance most unexpectedly and he bought his way into the gentry."

"He is a genuine sportsman too, let us admit."

"*Was* one, you mean..."

"Dead? Killed in an avalanche?"

"No, he was murdered, and no effort at all was made to hide the fact. It is a baffling case, one absolutely appropriate for an investigation by us. In fact, I've already started preparations."

"That's certainly efficient. What did you do?"

"I jotted a list of items to purchase. But let me inquire what you know of Tibet. Is your knowledge accurate?"

"I know about the Lamas and their monasteries, and that the Potala is a palace of vast volume, the biggest building in the world. I know that souls are reincarnated in their religion and that a bad man might be reborn as an awfully wriggly worm. That's about it."

"Not enough, dear boy! Tibet is a very large country. The western part is not like the eastern. Mount Kailash is nowhere near Everest and all her famous brood of peaks. It stands in a region so isolated that even denizens of Lhasa, that's the capital where the Dalai Lama dwells, find it a struggle to travel there and arrive safely, yet many of them make the attempt every year because it's a place of pilgrimage."

"You have been reading encyclopaedias clandestinely while at work? Well, that's not much of a sin, I guess."

Rufus uncrossed his legs, leaned forward, and rested his head in large hands, his elbows propped on his knees.

"I did plenty of research after Bowman's misadventure, and I recall an inordinate amount of what I learned back then. Something about Kailash seemed to resonate profoundly with me."

"I understand," said Jaspers.

"For instance, I learned that the western portion of Tibet was once the site of the ancient kingdom of Guge and that its capital city of Tsaparang was sacked by an invasion of militants from Ladakh in 1630. An assault prompted by a religious crisis. They take religion seriously over there, as I suppose most of us did back then, too. Mount Kailash is prominent and strange and shaped like a pyramid."

"I guess our own occultists are wild for it?"

"Not yet, dear boy. They haven't really had time. They are still stuck on Atlantis, or one of those sunken old things. Kailash is too obscure for the Western dabblers, despite its importance to the holy minds of the East. It's sacred to four different faiths, and pilgrims aim to tramp a full circuit around it, a distance of thirty-two miles."

"Tough going even on smooth paths, but at high altitude and on rough ground? I wouldn't care for that."

"Nor did Reginald Supple. But he wanted to do something else, which is to reach the summit of the peak, and he planned a secret expedition and it has all ended in disaster. They say that anyone who climbs Kailash is a blasphemer and that the gods must punish him. That seems to be what has actually happened. He was stabbed."

Jaspers glanced at the newspaper but made no motion toward it. "How is that considered the act of a god?"

Rufus grinned, and his cheeks flushed crimson. He was in his element, teasing Jaspers and clearly committed to a plan of action that he wouldn't reveal in its entirety for quite some time.

"He gained the top and stood on the summit. There was space for one man only. He was climbing with Hooper, who was balanced on crampons on the slope a few yards below, and they were roped together. A flurry of snowflakes blocked Hooper's vision for a few seconds. When it cleared, a dreadful sight met his gaze. Supple was still standing, but now he had the handle of a knife protruding from his head. He swayed, collapsed, and slid over the side. Hooper had to act fast."

"He cut the rope connecting them, I take it?"

"Why be pulled to his death?"

"Of course! He did the right thing, but who stabbed Supple? They had porters as part of the team, I guess?"

Rufus stood, his pipe swung to the other side of his mouth. "Dear boy, I don't think you appreciate the import of what I said. On the tip of a peak where there is no room for two, Reginald Supple was stabbed *from above* by a blade that penetrated his skull."

"That's not such an easy thing to do, is it?"

"We were both in the war."

"I don't recall having to use knives."

"Did you never see flechettes being dropped by our aeroplanes on the enemy trenches? Heavy steel bolts shaped like short arrows. They picked up speed as they plummeted and could puncture helmets and heads. I saw this happen once, and it wasn't nice."

"No, I never witnessed that, but you are right."

"Supple was a fool. He went to a remote land and trampled on ancient beliefs and customs. A typical blustering oaf, full of contempt, he violated the sanctity of Mount Kailash."

"Yes, his arrogance was somewhat irksome."

"His death is welcome."

"Steady on, Rufus! He was a British chap, after all."

"Insufficient cause for pity."

Jaspers digested this.

"Well, he's dead now, so it makes no difference. But what is our next proper move as club members?"

"A reconstruction," Rufus smirked.

"Of course. What else? But I foresee severe difficulties in attempting an imitation of the climbing of Mount Kailash. I know that ingenuity and careful planning has kept down costs with other unusual reconstructions, but this one seems too outré even for our talents. Unless you have already had an inspiration? Ah, so that's it."

"I made a shopping list. The rest will follow."

"Do you want me to get in contact with Pollard, Gertie, Chunder, and the others? I can send telegrams."

"No need, dear boy, because when Supple tackled the mountain, he did it with Hooper and no one else. They did try to secure porters. They went first to the ruins of Tsaparang, where the descendants of the folk of Guge still reside, a people poor now, malnourished and shrunken in stature, but capable of great endurance, and they asked for help and offered good payment, but only one answered the call. They interviewed him, decided he was good enough, so they took him on, but that very night he vanished and they had to depart Tsaparang alone."

"Hooper reported this when he returned from Tibet?"

"He left that country in a hurry."

"I can imagine. Without Supple's body, too."

"That was probably in no fit state to be brought home anyway, after a fall of such a great distance. But he saw a knife sticking out of the crown of the head, or maybe it was a piton; he agreed that it could have been one of those spikes mountaineers use."

"Then I wonder how reliable a witness he is."

"This is the Reconstruction Club. For the time being, we shall assume he is utterly reliable. We will proceed to recreate the crime of the climb and base our conclusions on the result."

"As always. Very well. I look forward to developments."

Rufus extended his right hand.

Jaspers grasped and shook it while intoning, "Something shall be the same as another thing." Rufus laughed, then he consulted his watch, nodded at Jaspers, and left the house.

Alone in Number 21 Livingstone Street, Jaspers momentarily gave in to an urge to sit on the sofa, but the sensation bored him within moments, and he had no desire to read the newspaper. There was nothing else to do here, so he followed the example of Rufus and went out. At the corner of Dereham Road he paused and squinted.

Across the highway, down which passed only the occasional motor or omnibus, the railings of an enormous cemetery glinted in the late autumn light. How many of the bodies resting there had been murdered by killers as yet uncaught? It was a dreadful idea.

But he consoled himself. Decent people could fight back against evil, horror, and savagery, and they were doing so right now. He was a part of the resistance. The Reconstruction Club was a moral organization, and the wide world was better for its existence.

"One day, we'll start solving local crimes too," he muttered, yet there was something unconvincing in these words. Norwich was a fine city, but it lacked the allure of those places he had read about but never visited. If only he could save money to go traveling! His job as a bicycle mechanic in a garage wasn't rewarding enough.

No matter. Rufus had a trick or two up his sleeve.

Wait and see, he told himself.

He began the walk back in the direction of the center of the city, with the spire of the imposing cathedral a useful landmark. For the first time, it occurred to him that it was a sort of mountain itself, a holy peak that men shouldn't climb, and that soon enough snow would dust its slopes too. It was near the end of October and chilly.

Jaspers patted the book in his pocket and decided to find a warm place to read his Housman. His home life was dull and lonely. The club was the highlight of his life—yes, this was true—and, as this thought passed through his mind, the 'high' and 'light' made him smile bitterly as an image of the detestable yet daring Supple took over.

He saw him perched precariously on the apex of that mass of ice and rock, and the magical hand abruptly descending from a cloud to strike the fatal blow. The hand was like his own.

So he lifted his hand and gazed at it. He had forgotten his gloves, and the fingers were red and wrinkly. He thrust it back into the pocket of his coat where the book already nestled. Might the knife have been dropped from a balloon onto Supple's head? Could it have been fired in a parabola from a cannon on the other side of the mountain? Might a bird have been trained to carry out the assassination?

All the options that occurred to him were absurd.

He needed to be more patient.

Rufus had found a promising avenue of investigation. They would go up that path together, for better or for worse. No theories in an armchair could compare with physically embodying an incident, thinking it back to life with one's entire body, being it.

The remainder of his day was uneventful, and the warmer place turned out to be a bench sheltered by the remains of the city wall. Twilight fell, a gust of wind blew damp leaves in his face like a flurry of little wet female slaps, and he got up feeling chastened.

The following morning he rose late, dressed for work, sipped a cup of tea without milk or sugar for health reasons, and left the house. It was ten minutes by foot to the garage. He passed a row of small shops on the way and paused briefly by the door of one.

It was the toy shop run by Mrs Busker, the widow, who always spoke politely to him. The door was open and she was lingering on the threshold with a crooked smile for the uncaring world. When he tipped his hat, she wiped her hands unnecessarily on her skirt in answer and said, "Morning to you. Off to a good start today."

"Do you mean me or your business?" he asked.

"The latter. Customer came in to make a special purchase just half an hour ago. Don't think he was foreign, but I never saw him before. Bought the most expensive item in stock."

"I'm happy for you, quite. Now I am late for work, so I'll be bidding a good day to you, madam," he said.

And he passed on, feeling less certain that he ought one day to pursue her romantically. She seemed awfully self-absorbed. But then, she was in business, so what could he expect?

He reached the garage and unlocked the ponderous doors. There were six bicycles inside, waiting to be repaired before the end of the day. It was something he enjoyed doing, working with his hands, and in the evenings he relished the authentic quality of his exhaustion. Physical work was the only worthwhile kind, he felt, the same way that reconstruction is the sole effectual way to appreciate a crime.

He didn't hear from Rufus again until Friday.

It was just after four o'clock on a relatively mild afternoon that Rufus came into the garage unannounced.

He had done this in the past once or twice.

"Have they let you out early?" Jaspers raised an eyebrow.

"Had the day off, dear boy."

"You spent it without wastage, I hope?"

"Yes indeed. I've been seeking a suitable place for our reconstruction and I have found one, a perfect spot and very delightful, in an unexpected location, almost under our very noses."

Jaspers straightened his back and wiped his oil-smeared fingers on an old towel. "I hope you aren't going to say that the abominably steep flight of steps in that Livingstone Street house will be a substitute for the slopes of Mount Kailash? I often feel like a mountaineer when going up them. It ought to be somewhere outdoors."

"It is, have no fear, with plenty of atmosphere."

"Tell me where it is then!"

Rufus shook his head. "Even better, I'll take you there now. I've been thinking a lot about that murder and I want to test my speculations. In this bag I have the equipment we'll need."

Jaspers shrugged, collected his coat and hat from a hook on the wall, went onto the street, and locked the doors. Jaspers carried the gabardine bag slung over a shoulder by one strap like a tramp, its other strap hung loose. Jaspers remarked casually:

"Long way to Tibet."

"We can make it, one step at a time."

He led them along the street, and they turned a few corners until they emerged in Earlham Road, heading in the direction of Norwich's other cathedral, the far less graceful Cathedral of St John the Baptist, massive and oppressive and almost ugly.

"We're not going up that on the outside?"

Rufus laughed. "I'm not climbing anything, dear boy. That's entirely your task. No, what I have in mind is considerably lower in altitude and much more aesthetically pleasing."

Before they reached the cathedral, Rufus went down a path to the side that Jaspers had never noticed before. The path undulated and disgorged them in a wonderful space, a secret garden in a hollow cut into the earth, full of flowerbeds and trees and enclosed by ornate walls. At the far end, a set of stone steps rose to a pavilion.

"I had no idea," said Jaspers.

"Most people don't. Even those who have lived in Norwich all their lives are surprised by this place. It was a quarry, which explains the deep declivity, then about fifty years ago it was bought by an enthusiast, turned into a little paradise and opened to the public, but the public don't realize the fact. It's called Plantation Garden."

"How remarkable. But I don't see what any of it has to do with Mount Kailash. It looks nothing like Tibet."

"Follow me." Rufus led him between bushes into a cleared area in the center of which stood a tall stone fountain, Gothic in style, a series of tiers that ascended from a wide base to a sharp pinnacle. It trickled rather than gushed, the whole a mossy delight.

"That's our Mount Kailash?" Jaspers cried.

"Yes. I have everything we need, ropes and proper boots for you. You are Supple and I'll be Hooper."

"You are going to rope yourself to me?"

"Of course, that's how it was when it really happened. But I won't be climbing. I'm staying down here. It's a matter of altering perspectives as it becomes necessary to do so. First, we look at this fountain and try to see a magnificent distant mountain. Later, when you are at the top, we regard this structure as just the tip of the summit. I suspect that the distance from Supple to Hooper when the assault occurred was no greater than that from the base of the fountain to its apex."

Jaspers nodded. He felt numb, yet an enthusiasm for the project grew rapidly within him. He understood that Rufus actually had a clear notion as to what had happened to Supple on that fateful day, and he too wanted to know it, but one can't just share words and expect to be satisfied with that. It's not enough. Words always leave doubts behind. They had to *be* Supple and Hooper, even in such an imperfect way, in order for certainty to bless them, to reward their efforts.

Rufus gave Jaspers the boots he had obtained. They fitted well. Then he attached the rope and helped Jaspers on with the ungainly rucksack. A muffled ticking came from its interior.

"And what's that?"

"Barometer, dear boy, to measure altitude."

"Did they carry one?"

"All mountaineers do on expeditions."

"Do barometers tick?"

"It's a scientific barometer. Now I want you to start climbing. I have a pocket watch here, and you must be standing on the tip of the fountain on the stroke of five, not a second late."

"Would you care to explain why?" asked Jaspers.

"No, just trust me. Please."

"Very well. What have I got to lose?"

Gripping the mossy stone with his bare hands, Jaspers pulled himself onto the first tier. He found the climbing relatively easy at this stage, but he knew that psychology would be a powerful factor nearer the top. This fountain might count as a very modest mountain indeed, but it was quite high enough to induce vertigo, and a tumble would certainly hurt, perhaps even lead to serious injury or death.

He concentrated on placing his hands and feet on secure holds. Damp moss isn't the safest climbing surface. Water splashed his face and it was cold, but he didn't flinch. His curiosity was stronger than his aversion. He was Supple, his death a question that was about to be answered, a puzzle on the verge of a solution. He was halfway to the top now and Rufus was urging him on, calling encouragement.

"But I want you to remember something," he added from base camp, where squirrels scurried. "When you are standing at the very top, expect the unexpected. Keep your balance!"

Jaspers frowned at this advice, unsure of how to process it. The sack on his back tugged annoyingly at his shoulders, a conspiracy with gravity, and that infernal ticking irritated his ears. The barometer story suddenly seemed ludicrous. The object in the sack, whatever it was, had the shape of a large cube. It shifted as he climbed to the next tier, and a sharp edge jabbed his spine. He winced and cried:

"I'm almost there!"

"Don't look down, not yet anyway."

"What's the time?"

"Two minutes until five o'clock."

Abruptly he was on the penultimate tier and staring over the top of the fountain. Now came the trickiest part, the true summit. He bent his arms, pressed his palms down on the tiny flat surface at the top, pushed with all his strength with both arms, rose up.

His right leg came over, took the place of his right hand. Then his left leg. It was clumsy but it worked.

He straightened his knees, stood erect, wobbled.

"Good show, dear boy."

Slowly Jaspers shuffled around so that he was able to look down at his companion standing on the grass. It seemed a tremendous distance, yards transformed into miles. The rope was taut between them. Rufus had been most conscientious with his estimates.

"No need to panic, just remain calm and balanced."

Rufus held up his wristwatch.

But Jaspers couldn't hear it ticking. What he heard came from within his rucksack. Then Rufus shouted:

"Any moment now!"

And Jaspers seemed to forget what world he was in. His vision white, ears burning with wind, a feeling that he had transgressed against a faith, a people, the gods, hurt his soul. It was like depression but more acute. I have made a mistake, he thought.

But he was Supple now, not himself.

The conqueror of a mountain that was forbidden.

Violator, trespasser, blasphemer.

And the ticking stopped...

Something exploded behind him. His first thought was that there was nothing behind him, not up here, then he remembered the rucksack. The straps had come apart and the flap had slapped the nape of his neck with considerable force. Something inside was emerging. He turned his head to look and his body twisted too.

A little man was perched above him.

Some sort of hobgoblin.

A grotesque grin, a hand that clutched a knife.

Jaspers began to totter.

The knife descended and entered the crown of his head with exquisite ease and smoothness. He felt no pain.

"Keep your balance!"

But the words of Rufus were in vain.

Jaspers sagged and fell.

He didn't care at what angle he hit the ground, he was dead anyway, a knife lodged in his brain. The slack of the rope snaked past him as if in a race. He bounced on the turf, rolled down an incline into a flowerbed, and plugged his mouth with rich soil.

And that was that. No more fears or worries.

Just flurries of eternal snow...

And it kept snowing, filling the universe.

He blinked, groaned, ached all over. The snowfields were sheets on an iron-framed bed. He was in hospital. Rufus was sitting on a chair, his pipe still unlit, his frown a champion one.

When he noticed Jaspers looking at him, he shook his head. "Best not to even try to speak," he advised.

Jaspers sagged, felt the weight of the flimsy sheets.

Rufus was back in control.

"It's going to take weeks, dear boy, before you can get out of here. I
suggest you be grateful you aren't resting six feet under. I advised you to
keep a cool head, didn't I? Anyway, the fact that you fell definitely settles the
question in my mind. That's how it happened. In Tsaparang, that fellow they
hired didn't really disappear. No, he concealed himself in Supple's rucksack
after removing most of its contents. The weight was exactly the same and
Supple didn't notice."

He removed his pipe, stared at it, and returned it to his mouth. "It may
seem extraordinary that the little man remained successfully hidden until
the top of Kailash," he continued, "but Supple had his own way of doing
things, as we both know. His idea was to use only Hooper's supplies on
the way there, and his own on the way back. In Tsaparang he must have
explained this oddity to the assassin when hiring him. Supple was rather
proud of his logistical innovations."

A nurse passed in the corridor, and Rufus gazed at her like a man who
feels many pangs of desire but none of conscience. He resumed speaking
after her footsteps had gone too.

"Of course, when Supple fell, the assassin went with him, but life is a
price worth paying to punish a transgressor on Mount Kailash. No doubt the
little man believed the gods were acting through his agency. Perhaps they
were. Some force is surely protecting that mountain. Can you guess what all
the journalists are saying now? That Hooper is lying, his account is a fable,
the result of a delirium."

He held up a daily newspaper as evidence.

"Yes," he added, sombrely, "they are taking the government line and
discrediting him for solid diplomatic reasons. Kailash must remain holy,
an unclimbed mountain, therefore Supple's secret expedition never took
place and he died in an accident somewhere else. Hooper, meanwhile, is the
victim of this obligatory conspiracy. The Tibetan authorities must be kept
calm. We have strategic interests in that part of the world. You see that our
reconstruction has value to us alone. But the murder is solved. I can assure
you of that. Well now!"

Jaspers groaned faintly and Rufus stood up.

"You want to know more?"

Jaspers was unable to nod, but his expression was that of a man who is
nodding, and Rufus replied:

"There's no mystery at all. It was very simple and it went without a flaw.
A jack-in-the-box, obtained from a toy shop that caught my eye one day. It
was in the window. A pleasant woman served me. I went home, fitted it with

a clockwork timer. I also glued a joke knife into its hand, a rubber blade that retracts into a rubber handle. A few more adjustments, then my little assassin was ready."

At the door of the ward, he paused and turned.

"Broken in the fall, that amusing toy. But it served its function. I am not a mechanic by trade, as you are, but I think I did a fair job. When you are on your feet again, you might want to fix it. Could be used to adorn a bare room in the club, like a trophy. Don't know why none of us thought of that before. Trophy room upstairs."

Then he smiled thinly, waved, and was gone.

Jaspers was left behind, surrounded by endless snow, like a monk who is walled up in a remote region, unable to move any part of his body, and this was his punishment for climbing the sacred mountain. He accepted it and began his first day of meditation.

Run Rabbit Run

Sally Spedding

"Run rabbit, run rabbit, run, run, run
Bang, bang, bang, bang goes the farmer's gun..."

—Noel Gay and Ralph Butler, 1939

Monday, March 15, 1965, 7:30 p.m.

At almost forty years old, it's time to begin this diary and finish as soon as possible. Why? Not only to dredge my patchy, guilt-strewn memory but also because I could be the next to die before my time.

I'm writing in English (having learned it at the *lycée* in Saint-Géry-sur-Mer) so this won't need translating. Besides, my late father spoke it fluently, encouraging me to persevere. Now, here in Wales, there's also Welsh which is harder to grasp with few Latin roots and all its consonants, but which—thanks to weekly classes over in Gilwern—I'm beginning to master. It will also, of necessity, erase all trace of my French accent.

Whoever finds this when I'm gone will realize how trauma and tragedy left me with occasional memory loss, also fear and suspicion.

Time, then, to open this black, leather-bound notebook I bought at Abergavenny market last week. Attached is a matching black ballpoint pen which the seller said was "immortal." Would never run dry. I'd not smiled like that for ages.

Friday, July 31, 1942

I, Myriam Naomi Horowitz, was born in Saint-Géry-sur-Mer in Roussillon, France, on April 2, 1925. Benjamin, my *papa*, ran a chemist's shop, and Sarah, my equally dear *maman*, was a geography teacher. Both were hard-working, contributing to society. However, each week they'd grown more uneasy at the gradual withdrawal of Jewish rights in the more northerly, occupied zone. Changes were small at first—with access to certain parks banned, then bank accounts closed—and spread south to the reassuringly named Free Zone. We'd heard of eminent Jewish writers and musicians already fled to America,

England and elsewhere, and I'd urged my parents to get us Nansen passports for stateless refugees, just in case. But no. Being secular Jews with French citizenship who'd never attended Synagogue or read the Torah, they believed we were safe.

I'd even shouted at them during dinner. The only real argument we'd had, but Papa, especially, was resolute.

"We've ID cards," he'd argued. "That's enough."

As if to smooth things over, he then gave me fifty francs to spend on myself.

However, early the next day, with the Tramontane gale blowing our street's palm trees every which way, came three loud knocks on our front door. Three armed, uniformed young men, one of whom I'd known at our *lycée*, gave us ten minutes to leave what had been our home for twelve happy years.

Saturday, August 15, 1942

I'll never forget that killing Mediterranean heat which either boiled the blood and burned the bare soles of those daring to flee the Rivesaltes Internment Camp or forced its victims into cooler, more foul-smelling darkness, like rats in a cellar where even the smallest space became precious, to be fought over.

Accidentally separated from my parents, I'd found sanctuary in one of its huts where luckier prisoners had found chairs. Not me, standing in the darker far corner, hungry, and listening so hard for the siren announcing lunch, I neither saw nor heard eighteen-year-old Daniel Klein suddenly appear. He pinned me against the wooden wall before tearing off my knickers, forcing himself between my legs, painfully bringing blood.

"Goddess," he said afterward, smiling while buttoning himself up. "Back for more tomorrow..."

Only as he disappeared, leaving me hurt and confused, did I notice a pretty girl with curly brown hair moving away from the hut's only window. A *voyeur*, who must have seen everything.

That tomorrow in the terrible *Sahara du Midi* never came. Fate had other plans. Those of us not yet nineteen were to be transferred to what the Commandant had described as "safe houses" in the area until reunited with our parents. Vichy officials' reasons for our move were safety, sunstroke, and dysentery, each costing money. That night, with no chance to say *au revoir* to my parents, I and at least seventy others, including my rapist and the witness, were driven away to the Pyrénean foothills.

Monday, March 15, 1965, 8:00 p.m.

Wendy stares out of her cottage window at the deepening dusk veiling Llangynidr Mountain's wild ponies, roaming sheep, and predatory crows awaiting the last crop of lambs for their eyes. When darkness falls, she swiftly closes her thick brown curtains before switching on the desk light to hopefully finish her diary before her borrowed life is over. Before it's too late.

She chose her new name years ago, because *Peter Pan* was always her favorite fairy story. Also, it would be a good fit for rural Wales, where "incomers"—especially foreigners—can be too conspicuous. Her experiences in war-torn France had taught her that much. Also how real freedom, even for a thirty-nine-year-old, might never be hers. Stormy nights, hiding other sounds, were the worst. Even in this beautiful, unviolated part of the Brecon Beacons, she knew, deep in her damaged heart, that he who'd so fiercely stolen her innocence had also been a betrayer of another kind.

Sunday, August 29, 1942

Until my last breath, I'll also never forget how that handsome heartthrob Daniel Klein made sure most of those delivered to *La Maison Verte* on that beautiful starlit night were doomed. Our "safe house"—a former *Maison de Repos* bordering the tumbling River Aude, where wild boar roamed and nervous black trout were netted for the pot—was just another trap.

The following afternoon, I confided in two older staff members that I'd overheard him talking to a senior police officer near the gates before handing over what was most certainly a list of our names. The women chuckled, saying I had too much imagination, but my mind was made up. Later, while everyone in our first-floor bedroom was fast asleep, I climbed out of its rear window and slid down the nearest drainpipe, carrying just one change of clothes, my ID card with JUIVE printed in big red letters, and Papa's fifty francs.

I'd considered taking a few others with me, but never Anna Berg, that curly-haired girl who'd seen too much. Who seemed besotted with Klein, following him everywhere, tempting him with cakes and fruit sneaked from the kitchen, while giving me dirty looks. Not him, though. His were quite different.

Wednesday, September 1, 1942. May not be quite correct.

With dawn rising over the Pays d'Aillons' vast ridges of limestone rock, I found a route over the Col de Chioula near the almost deserted village of

Montaillou, home to earlier terrors by rabid Dominicans. Somewhere to visit in future, perhaps, but how to trust France ever again?

My long journey seemed endless. The only sounds were cowbells from the high pastures and bleating flocks of sheep feasting on their summer grass, their fate at least unknown, while that recurring, too-vivid memory of my parents' utter bewilderment before we were separated made me stumble several times.

***

Ax-les-Thermes at last, where clanging church bells filled the air as I followed groups of other escapees, mostly from Germany and Austria, aiming for Spain or some safe passage to anywhere else. All adults except me, I noticed, knowing why. Just a grim focus driving them on. Léon Bloch, a thirty-one-year-old violinist who'd worked in Munich, wishing me well. Also, my absent parents.

"Bad enough leaving my dog behind, and my apartment. As French-born citizens, it's scandalous how we're treated like aliens."

Feeling more lost than ever, I watched him stride away, his violin case strapped to his back, until a bend in the track hid him from view.

The rest of my journey remains a blank...

Monday, March 15, 1965, 10 p.m.

Wendy strains her eyes beneath the overhead light to scan each word for spelling mistakes and what her teachers called "excess baggage." But no. Each painful word matters, and before closing the diary and boiling a kettle for her hot-water bottle, she glances up at the back of a photo frame on the stonework mantelpiece.

Her French ID card. That JUIVE word still too big. Too grotesquely red.

"Don't turn it round."

Doing so might bring the same bad luck endured by Benjamin and Sarah Horowitz, clinging to a slender thread of hope during their last summer, and then...

Why she's never used a shower since...

And what if they'd known their flower-filled house in the Rue de L'Abbé and his adjoining shop were seized before that year was out, is now a garage?

Tears blur her vision as she fills the blue hot-water bottle. Her one companion, who lies alongside her in her single bed. An old friend grown more thin-skinned. Whose stopper has twice worked loose. But can she get rid of it? No, because it's all she's got since...

Enough.

And in that deep Welsh darkness, she feels its heat through her pajamas and is back again in that steaming hot camp, seemingly in the middle of nowhere. Waiting and waiting...

Tuesday, March 16, 1965, 8 a.m.

She silences the second buzz of her alarm clock, slips her legs out of bed—another item she still can't part with—and finds her worn slippers. Having washed, then dressed in jeans and a hand-knitted jumper, she switches on the convector heater. Its hum reminds her of where she spent the third stage of her journey.

Like many living around the mountain, she used a wood-burner until a chimney fire left her unwilling to trust such a solid-looking stove ever again.

Just as she's finished her shopping list for a trip to the grocer's up in Bwlch, her doorbell rings. The letterbox is forced open. John Thomas, the postman, is earlier than usual, with a sealed-up package bearing six almost-blacked-out stamps and an AIR MAIL sticker. It could have come from anywhere in the world.

She draws that door's four bolts aside.

"Sorry, bit big for your box," he explains, withdrawing the mystery object none too carefully and handing it over. He then looks her up and down, his red van's engine still running. "You don't seem your usual self, if you don't mind me saying so, Mrs. Williams. Are you alright? Been nearly a year now, but..."

Mrs....

A shock whenever she hears it, even though she's worn a ring on her wedding finger for the past twenty years to stop tongues wagging in such a tight-knit community. It represents a fictional Londoner who'd died there.

"I'm fine, *diolch*." She manages a small smile and begins to close the door.

With a wave, the postman's gone. A reliable, hard-working widower in his mid-fifties. Surely not interested in her...

She rebolts the door—a habit since gypsies, come up from the valleys, camped in her plot for three days, refusing to move. Her nearest neighbor Eifion Hughes, complained to the Council and saw them off. A man who'd never left his farm since the day he'd been born, but someone reassuring to have nearby.

Wendy stares at the package, not recognizing the blue ballpoint handwriting or its dark, smudged postmark, before suddenly thinking "bomb."

My God...

"Rubbish!"

She then feels its mysterious layers of parcel tape from corner to corner, eyes the scissors on what has become a desk. Finally taking a chance...

***

Help...

After the bone-numbing shock of finding something so puzzling, she can barely drive her old Ford the three miles to the grocer's but must, because she's not only run out of coffee, bread, and things to eat, but also aspirin, dispensed from that store's back office. Pills she can't live without. Her "little Saviors..."

Back home in Allt-y-Fedw and still unsteady, she swallows two of them, her hands still shaking, then makes space on her desk for what had been so thoroughly wrapped.

No...

A Nikon F camera she'd immediately recognized, but with no message, just memories of a time when the future had seemed to brighten.

All lies, she knows that now.

Wednesday, September 8, 1942

A series of welcome but crowded lifts in carts, trucks, and other vehicles brought me and my fellow escapees to Bayonne. The busy, rain-soaked streets leading to the harbor were almost flooded. The bay was filled with every kind of boat from yachts to naval vessels, while queues of the damp and bedraggled tried to board whatever lay closest. Handing over what was probably all the money they had. When my turn came, I was almost pushed down into the choppy water below the quayside by older, stronger people, Papa's fifty francs tight in my fist.

"*No es suficiente,*" sneered a rough-looking Spaniard stinking of fish. A filthy hand, lined with greasy scales, outstretched.

"*Todo que tengo,*" I explained in poor Spanish, and he was about to shove me aside when a middle-aged woman in a fur coat slapped several notes onto his palm. Two hundred francs...

"Can't you see she's only young?" Her Spanish far better than mine.

"Thank you," I whispered, grasping her wet arm. "I'll never forget this. Where's this boat going?"

"England." She opened her bag. "Do you have a Nansen passport like this? As a stateless person, you'll need one."

***

Later, still anxious about what she'd said, I'd hoped to thank her again, but during that stormy crossing aboard *La Estrella Blanca*, I'd heard the awful news that a few older passengers had slid overboard from that huge trawler's slippery deck and never been seen again. Even now, I wonder what became of her. Nameless, but a saint.

During that chaotic journey, I heard many different languages. Those who'd been trapped while visiting relatives in occupied countries, or those on the run from the Free Zone's zealous police.

After five endless days and nights mostly spent outdoors, clinging to whatever we could, and no questions asked about where I'd come from, finally the white cliffs of Dover appeared, with seagulls swooping and wheeling overhead, almost as if in welcome. Some travelers began to sing, louder and louder as those cliffs drew nearer, but not me, with no idea where to go once we'd landed.

Unlike Europe's luckier Kindertransport, or salvaged youth, I'd no other family to go to. Instead, I was starving and thirsty, longing to feel clean again, constantly worrying about where my parents might be. Were they still alive? If so, how might I possibly send them a message?

Not until I'd walked with squelching shoes to Dover's railway station did I have the miraculous luck to meet Esther Cohen, who'd fled the hospital in Tarbes where she'd been training as a nurse. A tall, self-possessed twenty-one-year-old who, unlike myself and Anna Berg, didn't look remotely Jewish, and whose parents and two older brothers, from the Marais district in Paris, were already interned in Drancy. She offered to accompany me to North London, where her widowed maternal grandmother owned a large house where I might be able to stay.

I couldn't stop expressing my gratitude, and promised to one day repay her somehow, but she just smiled and combed my awful hair into some sort of order before we caught the last train north to Victoria Station.

Tuesday, March 16, 1965, 10:15 a.m.

With a fresh cup of the last of her coffee to hand, and the old radio on—as it is most of the day, in case of any breaking news—Wendy's trembling fingers open the camera and ease out a roll of Kodak film from its tight sanctuary. All the while, her mind races back and fore.

She knows whose it is. Forgets about compromising other possible fingerprints.

Whether the film's used or not, she can't tell, and glances at her watch. Not hers either, but just then it doesn't matter. What does matter is that she go to Davies & Jones, the chemists in Abergavenny, as soon as possible. Only after Christmas did this enterprising pair begin a same-day developing service, proving almost too popular. More reason to get there pronto....

***

Having cheekily parked in the Black Bull's car park, she stands in the chemists' slow-moving queue. Twenty minutes later, the ringless Roderick Jones, who reminds her of Prince Charles but with red hair, returns from the darkroom, rubber-gloved hands still damp.

"Your film's only partly used," he announces. "Five color prints. All of Carys." He eyes her with some concern. "Are you sure you want to see them?"

He remembers her.

But Wendy is puzzled, grips the edge of the counter. Suddenly, those enlarged, happy, grinning faces on some family's seaside holiday pinned to the wall behind it seem almost grotesque. Her hastily swallowed coffee lurks in the back of her throat.

"But not on her own," he adds, raising a portion of the counter so she can follow him into the darkroom, all too aware of those people behind her, staring hard. Ears pricked.

"Are you ready?"

He's shut the door behind them and switches on a powerful overhead light. She still feels unsteady, but must focus, because there may just be some clues in these five photographs which she and the police, in both Abergavenny and Cardiff, might still need. All are dated Thursday, July 9, 1964. One day away from the biggest milestone in Carys's life.

Her mother even finds herself praying as the first wet print dangles dripping from his pincers.

Monday, September 13, 1942

Despite having too many other passengers all around us, Esther slept most of the way to London, while I couldn't help crying as our train bore us north from the coast, through unseen countryside and small Kentish towns which I later looked up on maps of the area. Curious about this new kingdom whose capital city had spread so far south of the Thames.

I wondered if her grandmother's house in St. John's Wood might be vulnerable in an enemy attack, but no mention so far, and no early newspapers at Victoria Station, either. After too many questions, ID cards scrutinized, and Esther's impassioned begging, we were allowed through. We assured the busy gatekeeper that within two days we'd each have a brown Class B National ID card and, at last, a Nansen passport.

Since then, I've never traveled anywhere without my papers.

***

After forty long minutes in a black cab, where neither of us gave the curious driver our names or told him where we'd been, he stopped outside Number 2, Grosvenor Walk, a curving cul-de-sac lit by one flickering street lamp. Once again, Esther kindly paid my fare.

"Posh place, this," observed our driver. "Alright for some." His tone had changed. " 'Specially the chosen ones."

A sudden chill seemed to surround us, and, even before we'd begun to walk toward Number 6, he'd sped away, leaving dust hanging in the sharp morning air.

"Forget it," said Esther. "Bigots are everywhere." She put her purse away, then checked again that he'd gone. "Why I didn't want him seeing where we were going."

Number 6.

I stared over its trimmed boundary hedge at a large front window, behind which stood a gray-haired woman I guessed was in her late seventies. Grief in her eyes.

"Just wait there. There'll be no problem, believe me. I'm her only grandchild..." Here she paused, as if to wipe dust from her eyes, but she'd begun to cry too. "Why can't I just blot everything out? The thought of never seeing my parents or Jonathan or Sam again is unbearable."

"Maybe in death," I said inwardly, secretly believing it.

Soon that same window's curtains were swiftly closed, and a hall light came on. The front door inched open because I was a stranger and, with the looming threat of Hitler attacking the capital, strangers weren't to be trusted.

***

That fine home smelled of polish and cleanliness. An ordered world, away from the reeking fishing boat which had saved my life. With tearful introductions over, and photographs of her missing family members spontaneously shared, Dora Rosenbaum, using a black cane which tap-tapped on the hallway's tiles, led me through to a small room which might previously have been a larder. Its pale green walls were lined with empty wooden shelves, and in a far corner stood a square basin, maybe once used for washing fruit and vegetables.

"Esther will bring down the folding bed from her room," said my generous host in a noticeable German accent. A small, striking, gray-haired woman who, her granddaughter said, had once been a singer. "And I'll find a heater from somewhere. Autumn nights can be cold here." As before, she looked me up and down, settling disconcertingly for a moment on my stomach. "You need to eat, Myriam. You're just skin and bone."

"I will. But..."

"No buts. Yes, we've had rationing for two years, but our butcher and fishmonger help out, saying even though we're Jewish, we're all God's people..." Her voice wavered, and those sad brown eyes again began to glisten. "Kind words, but our daughter and son-in-law, with their two boys, are still trapped in that Vélodrome hellhole in Paris...No matter I was born in Bonn and my late husband in Munich. Solid Germans, with my own father fighting for them in the First World War. But did anyone listen to our fears?"

The old woman glanced at the open doorway.

"Esther tried persuading her parents and brothers to leave Le Marais, as she herself did, but they knew best."

Just like Papa...

She wiped away those fresh tears with the corner of a black shawl draped around her slender, stooped shoulders. "You and Esther are the lucky ones, so be very careful what you say and to whom." She then eyed my hair. "From tomorrow, you'll both be blonde, your eyebrows lightened. Also, a name change, as we too are planning..."

"Good idea. Myriam and I must get our new ID cards and passports organized."

Esther, still in her gray nurse's coat, then delivered a folded lightweight bed and clean spare bedding.

"I've put a towel and your own soap in the bathroom," she said, her voice fading with her footsteps.

"Thank you," I called after her, then turned to her grandmother.

"I'll explain more about me later, Mrs. Rosenbaum, but..."

"Dora to you." She gave a small smile.

"If you hear any news of an Anna Berg or a Daniel Klein, please do tell me. I last saw them in *La Maison Verte*, a supposed 'safe house' near Axat, in the eastern Pyrénées. Like me, they'd previously been at Rivesaltes..."

"The *Sahara du Midi*? How dreadful. I've heard even more poor souls have been taken there. Children and babies, too, mainly from Toulouse. But why do you ask?" I hesitated, but once I'd finished my story, I knew that here was another rare friend in a world of vipers.

Tuesday, March 16, 1965, 11:20 a.m.

"Do you recognize this other woman?" asks Roderick Jones.

"Yes." The word almost blocks Wendy's throat.

Even though that hair is pale gold and straight, ending on her shoulders, the pretty face is almost the same. "Anna Berg."

"This'll help the police trace her. She's quite distinctive."

"I want to kill her."

He pauses before pinning the photo to a wire strung between one wall and another, adjacent to several almost-dried larger prints of dogs. She stares at her daughter's beautiful, beaming face. Her summer tan glowing, even in the shadow of Cardiff Castle. Anna Berg's arm around her waist, as if best friends, but for God's sake, how? And who'd taken the photo? A passerby? Someone from her university? Or whoever had sent the package? Unless...

The shop's bell is busy.

"You go," Wendy says. "I know what to do."

With that, he passes her his damp gloves and pincers. Closes the door behind him.

Alone with these grim reminders of what came next, Wendy peers at the next print, showing Carys outside the city's library, giving Anna Berg a hug.

Damn...

***

Moments later, with the photos carefully rewrapped in the original packaging, inside a clear plastic bag, she returns to the darkroom to focus on the third image, taken in front of Cardiff University's imposing entrance. Here, Carys's Senior Lecturer, the bearded Geraint George, stands proudly between her and Anna Berg, whose white summer dress has been blown upwards by the breeze, just like Marilyn Monroe's in *Some Like it Hot*, to reveal her toned thighs. Legs which later on had enabled her to escape.

Psychopath...

The last two prints are similar, with even wider smiles, if that were possible. A clear blue sky is their common denominator, yet to Wendy's breaking heart, it's about to fall in.

2 p.m.

It takes her ten minutes to walk to the police station, still so preoccupied by those prints and wanting desperately to turn the clock back that she almost collides with a teenage cyclist tearing along the pavement.

Once inside the quieter reception area, Wendy explains why she's there. How her problem is urgent. Within two minutes, she's in Detective Sergeant Damian Richards's office where, after studying her newly dry photos, the stocky, mustachioed officer arranges for the forensics team at another site to examine them and the camera.

"We'll get back to you with any results." He gets up and indicates the door. "As for how and when this Anna Berg entered the UK, we'll check Immigration and airports' records again, so nothing's missed. Although, if she'd been living here for some time, then..."

Wendy shakes her head.

"She turned up for one thing only." She looks him in the eye. "And I'm next."

***

Back home in Allt-y-Fedw, she must calm down. There've been too many shocks for one day, but she still manages to close the front gate's padlock and make sure all the bolts on her front door are drawn before sitting down at her makeshift desk and opening her diary.

Thursday, May 6, 1943

During those almost eight months living in Grosvenor Walk with Esther and her wonderful grandmother, I'd searched various haunting archives on Jewish deportations from France's Free Zone, but found neither Daniel Klein nor Anna Berg, his clinging admirer. However, several times, my parents' passport photographs had appeared with others from Rivesaltes and equally familiar faces from *La Maison Verte*. It was painful enough seeing them all, and *Maman* smiling, in her best suit, with *Papa*, more serious, his gaze fixed on me from behind his spectacles. Worse, if possible, after their cattle-truck number for Auschwitz came, "Myriam Naomi Horowitz, their seventeen-year-old daughter, survived."

For what?

My answer was ready and waiting.

***

Baby Carys came into our lives a week early, after my shift at the Montpellier Hotel down the road. I'd chosen that name as Wales was already beckoning. A far better place to grow up in. Safer for both of us in a wicked world. Why my own name, like Dora's and Esther's, had already been changed.

Although I'd grown big, struggling more and more to get my jobs done, there'd been no sign that Carys was on her way. Luckily, Peggy, the hotel's owner who'd served in the WRVS, was at hand, and, on that sunny May morning in her private sitting room, the newcomer made her entrance.

She soon opened her inquiring, dark blue eyes—later to became brown, like mine and her father's—then let out such a long, loud yell that we missed the doodlebug's dreaded twelve-second silence before its strange, intermittent noise and the deafening blast which followed.

That solidly built hotel shuddered, and several ornaments fell to the floor while soot tumbled down the chimney into the empty fireplace, but it is the aftermath which still freezes my hand to this day.

Not until midday, with us and guests evacuated and the frantic Fire Service trying to contain nearby fires, did I realize that Number 6, Grosvenor Walk was a heap of rubble, with no survivors. Everything gone. Those who'd welcomed me and my unborn baby as if we were family. Margot Bailey (Esther), on a rare day off from her nursing job, and Deirdre Knight (Dora), who'd learned only a week ago what had really happened to their loved ones crammed onto two separate convoys from Drancy.

I must stop now. It's too painful to even think the house might have been targeted deliberately...

Tuesday, March 16, 1965, 6 p.m.

Already the afternoon has faded, bringing a breeze-blown rain smearing her cottage's windowpanes and causing the single telegraph wire to swing back and fore. The wire's also connected to the small Horeb Chapel half a mile away, where Carys's unmarked, undecorated grave lies behind the building, away from the wrong eyes. Normally, since the interment in her degree regalia, mortarboard and all, she'd have fresh flowers every week, with roses each May. The least Wendy could have done, but never now.

The phone's ring interrupts her thought that Carys could have invited the fiend over, from wherever she was, for her graduation ceremony.

"Mrs. Williams?"

"Yes. Who's that?" Sharper than intended.

"Dr. Lloyd Roberts, head of the forensic team. I've been checking everything DS Richards brought to my lab. Very interesting indeed."

"Thank you. But in what way?"

A crow alights on the windowsill to preen its blue-black feathers.

"The camera's packaging, for a start. Triple thickness, applied in a way suggesting panic. Fingerprints unclear, but the stamps' remnants of Roosevelt's face confirm it came from New York."

She blinks. That same crow flies away.

"Any particular district? "

"From other marks, my colleague thinks Manhattan."

Wendy gulps as the rain strengthens, beating against the window's glass and dropping down the one unused chimney.

"Daniel Klein, the film actor, lives there," came out too quickly. Then came a brief backstory.

Silence.

"We'll check that, too, and the handwriting giving your address."

"You've been very prompt. Thank you."

"We need to be. Incidentally, Mrs. Williams, to me, that writing suggests a male. Sociable but privately secretive."

That would tie up...

"No saliva trace yet."

Having thanked him again, Wendy ends the call and, giving the mountain a final glance, draws her curtains and picks up her "immortal" pen, wondering why Klein might have taken the trouble to post that camera. How would he have known its significance?

Unless...?

Friday, July 10, 1964, 1:40 p.m.

Both Deirdre and Margot of 6, Grosvenor Walk had been as generous in death as in life, and thanks to both their legacies from that valuable site's sale, Carys and I left our rented flat in Tooting for Allt-y-Fedw with money over.

So there I was, on another warm, cloudless day with her in Cardiff. Though looking forward to the afternoon's degree ceremony, she seemed nervous. Constantly looking over her shoulder.

"What's the matter?" I asked, as we left the Park Hotel after a nice lunch.

"Nothing, Mam. Just nerves."

I should have pursued it, but with her, it was usually best to wait, so we walked to the university, where she'd almost an hour to get ready.

***

I hardly recognized her when she emerged from the changing rooms. Luminous was the only way to describe her. That smile, the same as my late mother's. Daniel Klein, too, especially her eyes and hair color. Now forty-one and well-known for his crime thriller roles. Knowing his career-threatening wartime secret, I'd kept track. Checking on his love life, showing no Anna Berg or anyone else. I'd told Carys nothing about him. Her birth certificate gave "Unknown." Fine by me. But what secrets might she have been keeping?

"When this is all over, I'm going to be blonde, just like you," she beamed. Then came a hug before making our way toward the main Hall, where already a small orchestra was tuning up, and a steady stream of proud parents and others began to occupy the seats. She gave a brief wave, then made her way to where her group were gathering,

***

Forty long minutes later, it was her turn to step forward and climb the short flight of steps to the huge stage filled with dignitaries, ready to receive her degree. First Class Honors in French History. To better understand it.

Keep writing, I tell myself. You must...

The gunshot savaged the air and my radiant girl's head, before she crumpled in a spreading pool of blood. After that came pandemonium and, once I'd fought my way to the front to reach her, I caught a glimpse of a woman with shoulder-length, almost white hair, wearing a black trouser suit, pushing her way out the nearest exit before it could be barricaded.

Enough...

Friday, March 19, 1965, 9 a.m.

Winter has returned with a vengeance to Llangynidr, bringing hail from an almost purple sky. Not a good omen. Even Eifion Hughes has corralled his sheep and lambs into his big barn; their din woke her too soon. The shared telephone and electricity cables are rocking back and fore, and twice there's already been a brief power cut. On days like this, she worries about Carys's grave flooding, but right now there are things to do.

First, to discover if Daniel Klein knew where she lived, even if it might cost a week's housekeeping to find out. Secondly, why send her Carys's camera? How had he got hold of it?

She must call Detective Sergeant Richards.

Half an hour later, she learns that a Post Office cashier new to the job in Manhattan's Broadway, near Klein's luxury apartment, recalled being thrilled to serve such a celebrity. How he'd a film shoot to get to, and no time to wrap his parcel tidily.

Wendy makes another call, only able to guess how Daniel Klein might have had Carys's camera.

***

"You beat me to it," begins the Detective Sergeant. "Caught out by a burst drain..."

"Bad here, too."

"Are you ready, Mrs. Williams?"

Her already anxious heart misses a beat.

"There *is* an Anna Berg living in Roath. Nice part, that. Not cheap. Began renting a detached house there in May 1963. Ex-directory. No info yet on any job. We'll liaise a search with Cardiff tomorrow."

"Roath? Good God."

But God isn't good, and all Wendy can see is Carys dead on that stage.

"No one else with that name in Wales, and none of her age in New York. Seems she'd known your daughter for at least six months. Socialized regularly, apparently."

I bet they did...

Hailstones punish her windows. A brief blackness.

"Are you alright?" he asks.

Silence, save for the bad weather.

"I will be once she's caught. What's her exact address?"

"We do know, but you have to stay safe, Mrs. Williams."

Safe?

Sick joke. Then she relates Berg's earlier obsession with Klein. How Berg's been hell-bent on punishing her for...

"What?"

Two minutes later, he knows.

11 a.m.

With no let-up in the storm, Wendy switches on her radio for the national news. After a grim meteorological report, particularly for Wales, and a fatal traffic pile-up in Staffordshire, comes a name which makes her grip the table's edge. Turn up the volume as far as it will go.

"New York actor Daniel Klein has been reported missing for four days by his concierge in the Broadway apartment block where he's lived for ten years. His car's still in its underground car park, while his studio boss confirms he was due to begin filming a new thriller last Monday and has never missed a shoot."

Her first thought is that perhaps someone else from the past caught up with him. Revenge for his betrayal at *La Maison Verte*, maybe?

Hang on...

"That same concierge also recalls seeing a woman of around his age, with straight, pale-blonde hair, outside the apartment block's main doors on Sunday evening. He had to leave his desk to use the lavatory. When he returned, she'd gone."

Rather than bother DS Richards again, Wendy rings Eifion Hughes, just indoors after checking his barn. Breathless, he's probably too local to know.

"New York to London by air? Eight hours, I'd say. And five behind us. Why?"

Having finished her news, he promises to be along once the lambs have been checked.

Her phone. DS Richards.

"Just got this," he says. "Heathrow flight records show both Daniel Klein and Anna Berg's plane landed at three this morning."

12:10 p.m.

Eifion Hughes's thick, gray-streaked hair lies wet against his head. His anorak dripping on her step. A rifle in his right hand. The one he uses for rabbits.

"Best come with me, *bach*. But be prepared."

"Why?"

"You'll see."

Shrouded in her waterproof coat and hood, Wendy takes his hand, walking into the onslaught, past his silent farm, toward the chapel's modest graveyard. Despite the wind and rain, determined crows are hovering.

"I'll go first." He keeps her back. "It's not good."

***

Carys?

Only her modest headstone, bearing an angel's image, is intact. Wendy's frozen gaze rests on the hollowed-out, empty grave, the rotted remnants of her daughter's oak casket.

No words, just that cool, dark hut in Rivesaltes, smothering everything save that hot breath. Those urgent thrusts into her unwilling body...

Where she came from...

And there, from the corner of a weeping eye, she sees him again. Even more handsome than on the screen. Tanned, crew-cut, but not alone. Both drenched, motionless. The woman, mud-stained, filthy, clings to a large, equally dirty bag of some kind.

Now...

With Eifion briefly distracted, Wendy snatches the rifle from his grasp. She's used it already, under his guidance, when she first moved to Allt-y-Fedw. Just in case. Now she's running toward the couple, poised to fire.

"Give it here, *cariad!*" Eifion yells after her, but she's suddenly deaf. Daniel Klein already holds a pistol at Anna Berg's throat. Her hand still grips the kind of bag used for builders' rubbish. It's full.

My baby?

Klein inches closer to his target. His accent also familiar. Wendy can hear her heart.

"You never stopped mentioning me and Myriam. You're obsessed. Could have gone to another 'safe house,' but oh no. Then stalking me all the way to Manhattan with your blackmail threat, when all along, *this* was your diabolical mission. To dig up and destroy what's left of our daughter, with Myriam next. Why I tailed you, but my hire car broke down, so you got here first. Sicko."

"That's *my* Glock," she snarls. Her white-blonde hair hanging like so many pieces of string. Brown eyes leaking mascara, full of hate. "Hand it over, or I'll tell the media about your rape at Rivesaltes, and that other dirty trick at *La Maison Verte*. I heard you with that police officer, giving him the list, being paid. All those poor Zyklon B kids." She laughs. "No more stellar career for you, *con*."

"Dream on, sex-starved maggot. My remorse grows every day. I want to come clean and I will. I also wanted Myriam but couldn't find her..."

Goddess...

Wendy sways a little. Steadies the rifle.

"You knew she'd survived *La Maison Verte*."

"You too, unfortunately."

He presses the barrel harder against Berg's skin.

"Our daughter." His voice falters. "Give her back. Now!"

"That's rich. Why pay me to live in a posh part of Cardiff, get pally, then shoot her? So your rotten past stays buried. Her mother was next." She stares at Wendy. "Yes, you tramp. *He* made me dig her up."

"That's slander. If only I'd known..."

"Yes, dumb mistake leaving my camera in your apartment."

"Carys's camera," Wendy corrects her.

"Who cares?"

Klein breaks in.

"I sent it immediately, so Myriam would know. Her address was in your notebook. As well as deranged, Berg, you're careless."

"How did you know where I lived?" Wendy stares at the smiling enemy. Raises the rifle.

"Carys. Easy..."

Suppressing her anguish, Wendy steps forward.

"You'd do anything to have Daniel Klein. I saw it. Pathetic. And how odd that Carys didn't speak of you at all."

"Plenty about you, though, 'specially after what I told her... And hey, look, I'm still free..."

For a split second, Wendy shuts her eyes.

"Hand it over!" orders Klein again. "She's mine, too, remember? And I swear to whatever god there is, I never paid you anything. I want our daughter to have a decent resting place. Some small atonement for what I did in France. So, take this, sicko."

He pulled back the trigger.

No ammo.

He pales. Flings the pistol down. Pulls the bag from her grasp and walks toward Wendy, who's spotted Anna Berg beginning to run away. Her legs still long and nimble...

She takes aim.

"No!" shrieks Eifion.

But he's not given birth.

Wendy fires not once but twice, sending fragments of that threaded head and the rest into the wild Welsh weather, while the crows hover expectantly and the wealthy man from Barcarès, who could lose everything, flings his wet, desperate arms around her.

"Please forgive me. I could have done so much more..."

"Me too. Even the world is not enough."

The Man from Crocodilopolis

Keith Moray

Hanufer grimaced at the sight of the male body, naked except for a simple short-sleeved tunic. It had been dragged out of Lake Mareotis that morning and laid upon a trestle table in the old boathouse so that he, Alexandria's new overseer of police, could see the corpse and decide whether any further action was needed.

"He looks Greek," he mused, pulling the tunic down to inspect the skin. "Certainly not Egyptian. About forty years old. A slave, judging by this brand on his shoulder."

Sabu, his tall, broad-shouldered, shaven-headed sergeant, looked down on the body from the other side of the table. "Whoever slit his throat was not taking any chances that he would survive, my lord."

Hanufer raised one of the corpse's hands. "He has been in the water for some hours, yet not too long, as his eyes have not been eaten by the fish. His skin is wrinkled, and the flesh is rock-hard and stiff, so it is not clear whether he had labored much. Yet, by the look of him, I think he was a high-class slave, a house servant used to some ease."

He pursed his lips as he bent closer to look at the throat wound. "The deep cut extended from just under his right ear across his throat to slice through his windpipe, and then it tails off before reaching his left ear. He must have bled considerably, but it has washed away in the water."

He brushed aside some strands of hair that had fallen across his eyes from his wig. "Roll him toward you, Sabu, so that I can see his back."

Clasping the corpse's shoulder and hip, Sabu pulled him over so that Hanufer could scrutinize him from behind.

"Do you think he might have been carrying something of value belonging to his owner, sir? The body was found in the lake southwest of the city. It is not far from the Necropolis, or indeed near the Serapeum. He may have had money for votive offerings and been set upon by a cutthroat and dumped in the lake."

"It is possible, but he could have been thrown into the canal just about anywhere and drifted down to the lake," Hanufer replied as he moved the tunic to examine the body.

"No marks on his back," he said. "So he was not ill-used. That is in keeping with him being a high-class slave." He ran his fingers up the spine to the base of the skull, where he felt under the lank, soaked hair.

He straightened. "It is true, as you said, Sabu, whoever slit the throat did not intend that he should live. Yet I do not think that the cutthroat was what killed him."

Sabu's eyes shot wide open in surprise. Unlike his boss, Sabu's head was shaven, and he wore no wig as befitted his rank according to the Egyptian fashion. "You don't think this killed him, my lord? Then what did?"

"Roll him right over onto his front and I will show you."

Sabu did as he was told.

"This may have killed him!" Hanufer replied, beckoning his sergeant to lean closer as he cleared the hair away to reveal a small wound at the base of the skull.

He reached into his chiton, for, ever since he arrived in Alexandria, both of them had adopted the Greek style of dress, and drew out his sandalwood writing case. Opening it, he took out a reed pen and placed it over the puncture wound. Gingerly, he pressed against the tissues, swollen after being in the water, yet still he was able to slip it upwards into the wound at an acute angle as deep as four finger widths. "You see. The weapon entered the large hole at the base of the skull, where the spine joins it. His brain would have been punctured."

Hanufer withdrew the reed pen and handed it to Sabu to clean. "A narrow instrument like this, or something equally thin and sharp, could have been used."

Sabu wiped the gore from the pen on the dead slave's tunic, then rolled the body back to its prostrate position.

"So why was his throat cut, my lord?"

"To make it look like murder, Sabu."

"But it was murder already."

"To make it look like a very different type of murder."

"But why bother? Whoever did it could just have dumped him in the water. He was just a slave, after all."

Hanufer gave his sergeant a stern look. "Murder is murder, be that of slave or freeman."

His left thumb went to the ring upon his right first finger and stroked the image of the goddess Maat, with her ostrich-plumed headdress. In unison, his right thumb stroked his other ring, upon his left first finger, which bore the image of the crocodile-headed god Sobek, carved from a tooth dropped by one of the sacred creatures kept in the great temple of Crocodilopolis. He often touched them when faced with a crime that flummoxed him. It was his way of secretly asking the gods for help.

"Our first day in office after his majesty King Ptolemy Philadelphus appointed me, and already we have a puzzling crime to solve."

"You will solve it, sir. The pharaoh has faith in you."

Hanufer harrumphed. "Perhaps he does," he replied cautiously, "yet you must get used to referring to him as the king when you are in Alexandria, Sabu. He is both king and pharaoh of Egypt, but remember that Alexandria is essentially a Greek city, and the Greeks consider him their king."

Sabu bowed. "I will burn it into my brain, sir. But what must we do first?"

"Quite simply, our first task is to find out who this slave was and who owned him."

***

A mere two weeks beforehand, Hanufer had been the captain of the Medjay police in Crocodilopolis, the ancient city on the west bank of the Nile, southwest of the great Memphis. His work had mainly been to protect property, investigate tomb-robbing, pursue petty criminals, and solve the odd murder. Indeed, a particularly unpleasant murder of a local businessman and his family had caused mayhem and the outbreak of local feuds, with reprisals and counter-reprisals that threatened to spread out of control. The Greek nomarch in charge of the district had been so impressed with Hanufer's solving of the case, and his handling of the threatened riot, that he had sent a letter to King Ptolemy Philadelphus himself, who had already made it known among his nobles and officials that he planned to appoint an Egyptian to the office of overseer of the police in Alexandria. His intention was to unite the two countries by permitting high-ranking Egyptians to hold important offices. So it was that Hanufer and his most trusted Sergeant Sabu found themselves in the wondrous city founded by the conquering Alexander, who was anointed as Zeus-Ammon. After him, his general Ptolemy Lagides became King Ptolemy I Soter, Pharaoh of Egypt, followed by his son, Ptolemy Philadelphus, the present king and pharaoh.

On the second day of the Dionysia, the great festival held in honor of the god Dionysus, when plays were performed, poems read, music played, and festivities were held all over the city, Hanufer was sent for by the king.

The great and good of Alexandria were assembled along either side of the great atrium of the palace, along the corridors, and ultimately on either side of the great hall. Though they were all keen to see, they knew that they must stay at least two paces behind the rows of armed guards whose purpose, everyone knew, was to protect the king from assassination.

Among all these Greek nobles, Hanufer, the lone Egyptian official, walked the length of the hall, conscious of all the murmurings about him. Finally, he prostrated himself at the foot of the dais, where King Ptolemy Philadelphus and Queen Arsinoe the Second sat enthroned.

The king and all the Greek nobles were bearded and had their hair groomed in the Greek style, making the clean-shaven Hanufer stand out all the more in his neatly styled black, shoulder-length wig.

"So, you are the crime-solver and police captain from Crocodilopolis?" the king asked, after gesturing for Hanufer to rise.

"I am that humble person from Crocodilopolis, your majesty. It is my honor to serve you and her majesty, the queen."

"And what think you of Alexandria?"

"I am in awe of it, your majesty. Everyone in Egypt knows of the great lighthouse that you have built, and of the magnificent library, that I hope to visit often. My sergeant and I walked all over the city, familiarizing ourselves with its landmarks, the different quarters, and the problems that may be encountered within the city. I was particularly impressed by the temples to your gods, your majesty. Especially the huge Serapeum. You and your father, and the Great Alexander before him, have created wonders within wonders. The world will marvel at them for centuries."

Ptolemy Philadelphus, whom Hanufer estimated to be of the same age as himself, not yet three decades old, laughed with a hint of self-deprecation. "Yes, we are pleased with the library. You may already have heard that our intention is to have a copy of every book or papyrus ever written. Every ship that arrives in our harbors is obliged to hand over any books they may be carrying. These are copied in the eastern quarter by one of the many copying businesses. That copy is given to the library and then the original is handed back."

"That must be a monumental task, your majesty."

The king's eyes twinkled with amusement. "You must know that we Greeks also have many scribes, just as do you Egyptians."

It was more clear to Hanufer than ever that the king considered himself to be a Greek king, even though he was also the pharaoh of Egypt.

"But you are right," Ptolemy Philadelphus went on, "we in Alexandria are fortunate to have the great god Serapis to look after us. Yet the city that you came from is famed for its crocodiles and the god Sobek, is it not?"

Hanufer affirmed the king's question, knowing full well that the king knew this for a fact. He was also very aware that the king was very shrewd and was determined that his dynasty of Greek rulers should succeed in unifying the whole of Egypt. He knew that he meant to do this not only by putting Egyptians like himself in certain key positions, but also by having the Egyptian gods Osiris and Apis amalgamated with the Greek gods Hades and Dionysus and the goddess Demeter into the new cult of Serapis.

"Sobek is one of our oldest and most revered gods, your majesty. Like everyone else from Crocodilopolis, I venerate the great protector Sobek, yet I also worship the goddess Maat. And now that I am in Alexandria, I will make offerings to the god Serapis as well."

He was wary of saying anything that could be construed as an offence to either the king or queen. He was aware of the rumors that Arsinoe had poisoned her first husband, the Macedonian King Lysimarchus's first son, before fleeing to Egypt where she married her half-brother Ptolemy Keraunos, before leaving him and marrying her other brother, Ptolemy Philadelphus. Incest and duplicity were as common among the Greeks as among the Egyptians, it seemed to Hanufer.

"Yes, we also appreciate the goddess Maat here in Alexandria. The goddess of truth and justice is to be venerated everywhere in Egypt. My nomarch in Crocodilopolis informed me of your allegiance and your skills in mob control as well as crime solving, which is why I was eager to have you as overseer of my new police force."

Hanufer bowed low. "I am grateful and honored, your majesty."

Ptolemy Philadelphus laid a hand on his queen's shoulder. "Queen Arsinoe's great friends were murdered in Crocodilopolis. It was you who brought the murderers to justice. For this we have decided to rename the city in her honor. From now on, it will be the city of Arsinoe. You, Hanufer of Crocodilopolis, may take some share in that honor. Come closer, and I shall put the pectoral of office around your neck. Tomorrow, as my overseer of police, you shall have the honor of keeping Alexandria safe and free from crime."

Hanufer bowed low, and, when he looked up again to move forward to receive his pectoral of office from the king, he saw that Queen Arsinoe was smiling at him. But he was not sure whether it was a smile of pleasure or of queenly benevolence, or yet simply one of amusement at him, an Egyptian, being given such an unenviable task.

***

After the ceremony, the theatrical plays and celebrations continued. Allowed to go as they pleased, Hanufer and Sabu watched dramas and comedies, listened to choruses, and mingled with the people of Alexandria as they walked along with the processions of musicians, singers, and dancers.

Sabu, at Hanufer's discretion, sampled the local wines from the *askophoroi*, the girls carrying leather wine-skins, who were only too keen to let him partake of their goods. So too did he enjoy the loaves of bread from the *obeliaphoroi*.

As the throng started to make its way along the Heptastadion toward the temple of Isis Pharia, before reaching the great Pharos lighthouse itself, Hanufer and Sabu broke away and made for his new office on the other side of the Temple of Zeus. Once inside, he was greeted by a clerk who informed him that he had an important visitor, the nobleman Eutropius. Hanufer knew the name of the most prominent merchant and ship-owner in Alexandria from his research over the past few days. He had determined to find out who were the powerful people in the city. It came as no surprise to him that he was already being sought out, for he was well aware that was the way that powerful people operated.

"Ah, the noble Hanufer of Crocodilopolis." A large man of about forty, with thick curled hair and an affable grin, greeted him in his office. "I am Eutropius," he said, obviously expecting the overseer of police to recognize his name. "I welcome you to Alexandria and have come to invite you to my home for a symposium this evening. I have some famous guests that you will enjoy meeting, I am sure."

Hanufer bowed his head. "I thank you, Eutropius, and will be grateful to attend. I indeed feel honored to receive an invitation in person."

"Ah yes," the ship-owner replied, his friendly smile instantly replaced by a melancholic downturn of his thick lips. "I would have sent my slave, Karpos, to invite you, only I sent him on an errand two days ago and I fear he may have had some accident. I sent others to search for him yesterday, but to no avail."

"Could he have just absconded?" Hanufer asked. "Did he have someone, a lover that he had gone off with?"

Eutropius shook his head emphatically. "He was like one of the family. I was thinking of giving him his freedom at the end of the Dionysia. He knew that."

"Describe him, if you will," Hanufer said.

He listened impassively as the large businessman quickly detailed his slave's main features, including his brand.

"I must crave your attention for a while then, Master Eutropius. If you will come with me, I think I may have your slave. Prepare yourself, though. I fear that he has been murdered."

***

Eutropius had been sick upon seeing the body of his slave, and Hanufer had no doubt that it was not just the gruesomeness of the sight, but a genuine affection that he had for his servant. He had known many masters to curse at the loss of their property when a slave had died, yet Eutropius had cried tears that were of grief, not avarice.

"Could…could this have been because he carried money?"

Hanufer shrugged. "I do not yet know Alexandria, but if it is like Crocodilopolis, then yes, it is likely. People who have little will steal and take lives if they see an opportunity. Where was he going?"

"He was on a business errand for me in the eastern quarter."

Once the ship-owner had gone, Sabu grinned at his master, as if to say that he had told him so.

"Don't say a word, Sabu," Hanufer said, raising his hand. One puzzle had been solved, but there remained another. He did not feel that he should say more to Eutropius at this stage. He would get to know him better at the symposium first.

***

It was a balmy evening when Hanufer and Sabu arrived at Eutropius's villa near the Lochias Promontory, which stood directly across the harbor from the great lighthouse of Alexandria. The royal palace itself stood upon the promontory and was illuminated by hundreds of torches within and by the shining beacon atop the four-hundred-cubit tall lighthouse tower that had been planned during the king's father's reign and which Ptolemy Philadelphus had so recently completed.

A young slave admitted them and led the way through a large atrium decorated with murals of Greek gods which seemed so lifelike, it was as if they danced around a central fountain. It was very different to the Egyptian style, evidenced by Sabu's expression of wonder. At the end of a corridor an older slave, clearly the house servant in charge, suggested that Sabu might like to eat with the house slaves while Hanufer met the master and mistress.

In a beautifully furnished room, Eutropius greeted the Egyptian official as if he was an old friend and introduced him to his wife, the Lady Selene.

Dressed in a pale blue flowing peplos which did nothing to disguise a curvaceous body, she was one of the most beautiful women Hanufer had seen. A good ten years younger than her husband, her makeup was applied with sophistication and subtlety. Her eyes were blue as lapis lazuli and seemed to sparkle, despite the absence of the kohl which almost all Egyptian women of status wore.

"My lady, I am so sorry..." he began, yet hesitated when, to her side, he saw Eutropius's anxious look and slight shake of the head.

The ship-owner interjected. "No need to apologize, Hanufer. It is still early days. Our slave will turn up in due course, I am sure. I suspect that his liking for beer has overcome him and he will skulk back soon."

Lady Selene grasped his arm. "He is precious to us, husband. Do you really think—"

"That he has gone drinking? Yes, of course. He has done it before, but do not fear—Hanufer, our overseer of police, will find him." He smiled indulgently at his wife. "And do not worry, Selene, I will not be too hard on him."

Reassured, Lady Selene favored Hanufer with a smile that revealed pretty, even white teeth. "I have heard that Crocodilopolis is a fabulous city," she remarked. Then, with a shiver: "Except I do not like the idea of all those crocodiles."

Hanufer laughed. "The whole Nile is home to the creature, my lady, just as it is to the hippopotamus and the ibis. Our gods, Sobek, Taweret, and Thoth, protect us."

Selene laughed. "Yet I heard that my cousin Queen Arsinoe is to be honored by having Crocodilopolis named after her."

"Your cousin, my lady?" Hanufer repeated in surprise. "Well, it is my city that is being graced by having its name changed to Arsinoe."

Eutropius clapped a hand on Hanufer's shoulder. "I see that you are schooled in the art of diplomacy, Hanufer. A useful skill when dealing with Greeks. Selene is indeed distantly related to our new queen"—he winked conspiratorially—"which I live in hope will help my meager business interests."

Selene gave him a disapproving look, which only made him laugh the more.

"My wife is going to dine with some of her lady friends while we men have our symposium," Eutropius went on. "Now come, you will enjoy this, and it will give you, the overseer of police, an opportunity to study our Greek ways! The other guests have already arrived."

"Behave yourself, my husband. I have had the *andron* prepared for you, so you will all be comfortable. Make sure that the wine is kept well-watered this evening."

Eutropius chuckled and, with his arm about Hanufer's shoulder, they took their leave of the Lady Selene and walked through a series of corridors in the great villa, followed at a discreet distance by the chief servant, whose name, Hanufer learned, was Erasmos.

"I thank you for maintaining my subterfuge," Eutropius whispered as they walked. "I know how much Karpos meant to my wife, so I will choose the right time to tell her that he was so brutally killed. You may also have gathered that I have not told Erasmos and the other slaves. You know how they can jostle for position in a household."

Eutropius allowed his voice to rise above a whisper. "I am just a simple merchant, Master Hanufer. I have a fleet of ships and I trade around the Levant. Precious metals, grains, silks, spices, ebony, and ivory; you name it and I will find it for you and trade whatever commodity you want. People like me are useful to Ptolemy Philadelphus. I also know that it is because I am rich that I get surrounded by those who see me as a source of money for their enterprises and plans." He grinned and squeezed Hanufer's shoulder. "You will see that tonight, for all three of my other scholarly guests have need of me and my wealth. Arrogant, useless wasters are they, yet it amuses me to see them buzz about me like wasps around a honey pot."

They stopped in front of a pair of huge, heavy doors. The large businessman turned and signalled to his slave.

"Erasmos, in Karpos's absence, was appointed my *symposiarch*," he explained to Hanufer. "That means he has prepared the wine and the little delicacies we shall enjoy tonight. We always water down our wine in Greece, as a matter of good taste."

Then to Erasmos: "Have the wine pitchers been drawn from the *krater*?"

Erasmos bowed. "They have, my lord. My mistress instructed me herself. Three pitchers by every couch and the *krater* has been filled again, should you require replenishments."

Eutropius nodded. "This is an important symposium, Erasmos. I want our overseer of police to see how Alexandrian society works in miniature. I want you to lock these doors after us. We shall have much to talk about through the night, so do not unlock them until I signal for you to come in to light the oil lamps before I give them my surprise. Then, after that, bolt the door again until the morning cock crows." His lips curled and he gave a soft, short, self-satisfied chuckle.

"Come, crime-solver from Crocodilopolis, it is time to meet your fellow guests. You may judge how they all react when I reveal to them my little surprise."

He placed a hand on Hanufer's shoulder. "And perhaps you will show your skill this evening in solving crime!"

***

The *andron* where the symposium was to be held was a large windowless room with small air vents just below the high ceiling. The walls were painted with scenes of the Olympian Gods, and all around were large urns with ostrich feathers and potted palm trees and bougainvillea and vines burgeoning with grapes on tall trellises. Five couches were set in a circle around a huge glazed jar, which Hanufer supposed was the *krater* that Eutropius had referred to. Pitchers of wine with drinking bowls were placed in readiness on low tables amid plates of fruit and trays holding delicacies of all sorts. At the far end was a doorway covered with a curtain, which Eutropius informed him was a cubicle where they could relieve themselves throughout the evening.

"My friends," Eutropius announced to the three men standing chatting by the *krater*. "Allow me to introduce you to our new overseer of police. This is Hanufer, the crime-solver from Crocodilopolis."

All three came to meet him with smiles and salutations.

"This is Heraclitus, the famed physician of Alexandria," said Eutropius, introducing a benevolent-looking man with receding hair and a full, well-groomed dark beard streaked with gray.

"Not famed, but a physician in practice," replied the doctor, with a modest bow.

"I am Philemon, the playwright," announced an athletic-looking man in his early thirties. His dark hair was extremely curly, and his thick beard was well-groomed.

Hanufer bowed. "I enjoyed your play during the Dionysia today."

The playwright smiled and withdrew to allow the third man, a wiry fellow with luxuriant blond locks and a short, neatly trimmed beard, to approach.

"The poet Themistius," Eutropius introduced. "Soon to be famous throughout the land."

The young man waved a hand dismissively. "With your help only, my lord, for which I thank you."

Eutropius raised his hands magnanimously and gestured to the couches. "Noble guests, please seat yourselves and allow me to fill up your wine bowls myself."

And so the symposium began.

One by one the guests, including Hanufer, introduced themselves. Eutropius interjected frequently, adding little witty anecdotes about each person, which all dutifully smiled or laughed at, making it clear to Hanufer that Eutropius's remarks to him about them all being dependent or beholden in some way to him was true.

They drank a few toasts to King Ptolemy Philadelphus and Queen Arsinoe and praised the gods before they chatted about the overall atmosphere of the Dionysia and how the great library and the lighthouse were making Alexandria the greatest of all cities outside Greece. Hanufer contributed and gave his opinion as a visitor fresh from Crocodilopolis.

Eutropius was keen for them all to drink in unison, which bothered Hanufer, for he was more used to palm wine than the rich wines from Greece, no matter how diluted they were. Already he was feeling their effect.

Philemon was the first to take command of the conversation by talking about drama and its importance in understanding the nature of man. Playwrights such as himself, although he hinted strongly that there were none as able as he, covered the whole panoply of human emotions by staging works of tragedy, comedy, and satire.

"We are the ones who truly understand the workings of the mind. In my plays, I put words into others' mouths and stir the minds and hearts of both men and women."

The wiry poet Themistius was quick to disagree. "You are only partly correct, good Philemon. Your words do not fully tell your stories, for your actors use masks to tell the audience the emotions they should feel. Perhaps your words are over-clever for people that have to be shown comic masks to tell them when to laugh, or downturned, miserable facades to indicate when they should cry."

Eutropius took a hefty swig of wine and then guffawed. "So what would you say about poetry, Themistius?"

The poet stared at him over the rim of his wine bowl and then raised his arm extravagantly toward the ceiling. "Why, it is the highest of man's endeavors, Eutropius. Poetry is nothing less than the language of the gods. We poets are the mouthpieces of Olympus."

Heraclitus snorted with derision. "You are both suffering from a delusion of grandeur. Most people care not a fig for poems or plays. They want to eat, drink, and enjoy their leisure. They want slaves to look after them and they want physicians like myself to keep them in good health, despite their excessive eating, drinking, and debauchery. No, my friends, medicine is the true philosophy. We doctors understand not only the body, but also the mind and the soul." He raised his bowl in a toast to Eutropius. "My thanks to our host for promising to build my new gymnasium and hospital."

The poet and the playwright stared at him, then, after looking at each other, both laughed and raised their bowls.

"To Eutropius, for publishing my poetry collection," said Themistius.

"And again, for paying for a chorus to perform my trilogy of plays and publishing the texts," said Philemon.

Eutropius nodded at them each in turn and, raising his own bowl, drained it entirely. Then he belched loudly and subtly winked at Hanufer.

Standing and crossing to the door, he banged his fist on it. "I have a surprise for you all," he said with a sly smile. "You will see once Erasmos comes to light the lamps."

The door was unbolted by Erasmos and pushed open. The slave came in with a lit oil lamp and tapers, which he used to go around the room lighting the other lamps. When he was finished, he went to stand by the open door, where Eutropius was standing, waiting.

Eutropius grinned at his guests. "And now your surprise." He clapped his hands, and immediately a beautiful, scantily dressed young woman danced in with a huge basket of grapes in her arms.

"I give you Helena, the fairest praise singer in Alexandria," Eutropius announced as the girl danced, sang, and performed cartwheels around the great room, all the while tossing single grapes at each of the guests in turn, or lobbing them with great skill to land in the wine pitchers.

Eutropius guffawed. "She is the most expensive courtesan from the finest brothel in the city. And I should know—because I own it!"

Hanufer watched Erasmos leave, pulling the door closed after him. Turning to the room, he noted the expressions of the three other guests as she moved in and out between their couches, gyrating as she sang. Round and round the *krater* in the center of the room she moved sensuously, as if it were a living person that she meant to seduce.

Although the wine was affecting his vision, he fancied that he saw a mixture of lascivious and admiring looks from all of the men as they watched the girl. A glance at Eutropius told him that he too was paying keen attention to the reactions of his guests.

Breaking away from the *krater*, she tossed her remaining grapes at each of them. Themistius tried to catch his in his mouth, but it bounced off his chin and was deftly caught by Philemon, who shot out his left hand and plucked it from the air.

"Ha! It looks like an extra favor for me," he laughed, winking suggestively.

After some minutes Eutropius clapped his hands, called Helena to him, and folded his arms about her, almost as if she were a possession. Then he laughed.

"Envy me, my friends. I know you do, but she is all mine. My very own slave, ripe like a peach and now ready to do my bidding."

Hanufer noted the look of near-panic in the girl's eyes as he smacked her rear with one hand and thumped on the door again with the other. Instantly, Erasmos opened the door, and the girl danced out. "Until later, my sweet," the ship-owner called as the house slave closed and bolted the door after her.

At Eutropius's urging, they refilled their wine pitchers from the *krater*, ate delicacies, drank, and talked about his subject, the making of money and the art of being a merchant and ship-owner.

"Money and wealth makes the empire work," he said. "All of you need men such as I, yet sometimes we are taken for granted. Indeed, you three Greeks depend upon me, just as you toasted me earlier. Well, business is not always as good as it could be, so I have a surprise for you. I shall not be paying for two of your projects." He stared at them as he slowly drank his wine.

"Come on, drink up. The night is still young and the *krater* is still more than half full. In the morning, I might tell you who the lucky one is."

Hanufer blinked at him, aware that his vision was becoming blurred. He suddenly felt incredibly sleepy. He set his wine bowl on the small table mere moments before he felt himself falling backward onto the couch, and he slid into a black pool of unconsciousness before his head hit the cushions.

***

The room was full of noises as the man from Crocodilopolis started to wake. Forcing his eyes to open and his limbs to move, he pushed himself upright. The oil lamps cast a flickering light about the room, and he rubbed his cheeks vigorously as he allowed his eyes to accustom to the light. As his vision cleared, he was greeted by a shocking spectacle.

Themistius was lying half on his couch and vomiting into his pitcher of wine. Philemon seemed to be asleep, but was making snorting noises and breathing with some difficulty. Hanufer noted that his lips were flecked with frothy spittle.

"Thank Zeus you've come round, Hanufer. Help me," came Heraclitus's voice from the far side of the room.

Eutropius was lying on the tiles, his eyes open and staring upward at the ceiling. The physician was kneeling over him, shoving one of the large ostrich feathers down his throat.

"Poisoned!" Heraclitus exclaimed. "We've all been poisoned. I must make him vomit or…"

Hanufer pushed himself to his feet and staggered across to assist the physician, who was shoving the feather up and down the large businessman's throat as if attempting to unblock a pipe.

"Enough, Heraclitus," he said, grasping his wrist. "You may be the doctor, but I can tell when a man is dead." He pulled the ostrich feather from the throat of the dead ship-owner and held it to his nose. He felt nauseated, for it reeked of poison.

From somewhere outside he heard a cock crow and, just as Eutropius had ordered, the bolts on the door were shot and the door was pushed open. Erasmus the slave entered and took in the grim scene.

"Call for my sergeant," Hanufer commanded. "Your master has been murdered, and we have his killer to take into custody."

Heraclitus stared at him in horror. "But…but you cannot seriously mean me. I was trying to save his life."

Philemon and Themistius had both roused and stumbled over to gaze in horror at the ship-owner's body.

Hanufer held up the ostrich feather. "You were forcing poison down his throat with this," he said. "Heraclitus, you are under arrest."

***

News of the murder of Eutropius the wealthy ship-owner spread round the city like wildfire. The king himself was outraged by it and sent a papyrus to Hanufer commending him for the arrest of Heraclitus, the murderer of the husband of Queen Arsinoe's relative, Lady Selene. The queen herself was going straightaway to visit her cousin.

Sabu looked across the desk at his master as he studied again the papyrus from his king and pharaoh.

"Surely there is no doubt of the physician's guilt, my lord?" he asked. "The king's doctor is an expert on poisons, and he confirmed the poison in the dead man's stomach was the same as on the ostrich feathers and in the wine that you had all been drinking."

Hanufer was non-committal. "I was obliged to arrest Heraclitus, but we still have to investigate this crime fully. The question is, why would any of the three guests have wanted him dead?"

"My lord, you said that he surprised them by saying he would not sponsor them," Sabu said.

Hanufer nodded. "All three were depending on his money. Heraclitus with his gymnasium and hospital, Philemon with his play and its publication. Similarly, Themistius and his poetry publication. It could have been any of them."

"But the physician would know about poisons, and he would have access to such poison."

Hanufer stroked his chin. "But that was not the only surprise he gave them, Sabu. The praise singer, Helena, was a courtesan from a brothel owned by Eutropius. I need to know more about her, so you must go to this brothel and find out about her."

"Find out what, my lord?"

"What connection she has to any of the guests. All three look at her with desire in their eyes. Find out, Sabu."

Sabu bowed. "And what will you do, my lord?"

Hanufer rose from his desk. "I need to clear my head after all that wine and whatever was in it, so I am going to finish my sightseeing tour of the city. I'm going to begin with a visit to the great library of Alexandria."

***

The following morning, Hanufer received a further papyrus from King Ptolemy, expressing his wish to know what progress was being made.

Hanufer carefully composed a reply, which he gave to Sabu to deliver. Essentially, he said that he was holding a final investigation in the *andron* of Eutropius's villa that afternoon, which he expected would confirm the murderer's guilt.

Lady Selene, Themistius, and Philemon sat on couches in the *andron*, while Erasmos the house slave and Helena, the courtesan and praise singer, stood by the closed door, which Sabu was guarding. Heraclitus the physician sat on another couch, his wrists manacled.

Hanufer stood in the center of the room beside the large *krater*, which had been emptied of wine.

"Why is that whore here?" Lady Selene demanded angrily, scowling at Helena.

"Because she entertained us on the night of your husband's murder," Hanufer replied. "Her presence is very important."

"But why indeed are we here at all?" Themistius asked. "Surely you have the murderer. That man whom we thought was a friend."

Heraclitus looked dazed, confused at what had become of his life. Yet he looked at the poet with incredulity. "I was friend both to Philemon and to you, Themistius, and I was Eutropius's own physician. Yes, and yours, too, Lady Selene. I cannot understand that anyone would think that I could be guilty of murder."

"We all saw you, wicked man," said Philemon.

Hanufer held up his hand. "What exactly did we see, Philemon?"

The playwright pointed at the physician. "I was not well, but as I came round from the poison or drug, or whatever was in the wine, we saw him pushing an ostrich feather down poor Eutropius's throat."

"I was trying to get him to vomit," Heraclitus protested.

"How do you think the wine was poisoned?" Hanufer asked.

Heraclitus shook his head. "I think it was her doing," he said, pointing his manacled wrists at Helena. "Either she either dropped the poison in the wine when she danced around the *krater*, or the grapes she tossed at us or threw into our pitchers were poisoned and drugged."

The praise singer looked terrified. "I...I...did not—"

Lady Selene suddenly shot off her couch and dashed across the room, her hands clawing toward Helena. "You whore! You stole my husband from my bed, and you poisoned him."

Themistius immediately leapt up and intercepted her, easily holding her arms to prevent further attack. "Leave her! She is innocent."

"Settle yourself, Lady Selene," Hanufer said, soothingly. "Sit and listen, for Helena is indeed innocent."

Eutropius's wife stared at him in amazement and allowed Themistius to sit her down.

"You reacted quickly to protect her, master poet," Hanufer went on. "Which you would, because you and Helena are lovers. Don't deny it, for Sergeant Sabu found out about your meetings at the brothel."

Themistius returned his scrutinizing gaze. "I do not deny it. I wanted to buy her freedom from Eutropius, the mean-spirited old lecher. But we did not try to kill him." He stood and held out his arms to Helena, who rushed across the room and fell into them, as if he would protect her from all of the horrors around her.

"And Heraclitus is telling the truth," Hanufer announced. "He did what any physician would do when he regained consciousness and saw his host lying on the floor in such circumstances. He tried to revive and save him."

"You speak the truth," Heraclitus said, emphatically.

"The wine was drugged, but not poisoned. And it was not done by Helena, neither directly nor by throwing grapes into it," said Hanufer.

"Then how?" asked Philemon, his brow furrowing in puzzlement.

"The wine pitchers were all mildly drugged, for we were meant to drink and fall unconscious. Eutropius was drugged just the same as us, but it was when he fell unconscious that the poison was administered to him. It was indeed upon the ostrich feathers, but it was not Heraclitus who shoved the poison down his throat while we others slept. It was the murderer, who then added poison to all the pitchers. Then, when Heraclitus roused, for he would have been given the pitcher with the least drug, he saw Eutropius and grabbed one of the ostrich feathers to try to make him vomit. But it was too late."

Themistius looked aghast. "You mean it was one of us?"

Hanufer nodded. "That is correct. That is how you did it, is it not, Philemon?"

The playwright shot to his feet. "How dare you. I—"

"You are a murderer and you made the mistake of using the same murder method that you used in one of your earliest plays. Today I visited the great library and met the head librarian, Zenodotus, who, out of the thousands of books, scrolls, and papyri, took me straight to the plays of Philemon, which resided in a case along with the works of Sophocles, Aeschylus, and Euripides. Your tragic play was one of your first and has not been performed for over ten years, but in it you used the exact same murder method."

He nodded at Themistius. "I also perused your early poetry collection, in my search for clues. I found nothing but love poems, all about a praise singer."

"It is nonsense. An outrage!" declared Philemon. "Why would I murder my friend and patron?"

"Ah yes, he was patron to you all, but his revelation that he was not going to fund two of the guests at the symposium gave you even more opportunity to cover the murder that you had already planned to commit during the symposium. You wanted Heraclitus to be accused, so the ostrich feathers were the ideal way of both poisoning Eutropius and incriminating Heraclitus. If suspicion fell on Themistius as well, so be it, you thought."

"But I was asleep," Philemon protested. "You all saw that."

"No, your wine had no drug at all. You were acting. And of course, the wine that the rest of us drank was drugged by your accomplice in the first place—Lady Selene. Zenodotus also showed me a book describing almost seven hundred poisons available to a skilled poisoner. She also prepared the poison on the ostrich feathers."

Although he did not say it, he suspected that if Queen Arsinoe was skilled in poisoning, there was a good chance that her kinswoman would also be an adept.

Eutropius's wife shook her head vigorously. "It is not true."

"It was your second murder," Hanufer went on, addressing her directly. "The first was that of your slave, Karpos. Your husband thought that he had been slain by having his throat cut. I showed him the body on the afternoon before the symposium. I believe that he suspected it was because Karpos had seen something on his way to pay one of the copying businesses in the eastern quarter. King Ptolemy Philadelphus himself told me that is where books are copied. Eutropius probably also knew that Karpos had been murdered by one of the guests he had invited to the symposium because of what he had seen. I believe that was why he invited me."

He strolled round the room, circling the couch upon which Lady Selene sat, and suddenly reached for her hair, which was braided and wound around her head in imitation of the goddess Aphrodite. He plucked an ivory hairpin from it, causing her braids to tumble down.

"Here!" he said, tossing the hairpin to Philemon, who deftly caught it.

"Ah, you see, your lover is left-handed, which fits with the way he slit poor Karpos's throat. Only a left-handed man would have inflicted that type of throat wound. He did it from behind when Karpos was already dead. Of course, Philemon only slit his throat to conceal the fact that it was you, Lady Selene, who had killed him with this hairpin, or one very similar, when he had turned his back on you. You feared he would tell your husband, so you had to kill him. You pulled it from your hair and shoved it into his skull and punctured his brain."

Lady Selene stared at Philemon. "My love, what shall—"

"What shall you do?" Hanufer repeated. "Why, you will both stand trial, either before a judge that King Ptolemy appoints, or perhaps even before himself, since Lady Selene is related to Queen Arsinoe."

Suddenly, Philemon reached into his chiton and pulled out a dagger. He vaulted over the couch and slashed at Sabu's throat.

That was his mistake. Sabu ducked, caught the wrist holding the dagger in both hands, and snapped the bones. Then he spun the playwright round and punched him in the face, breaking his nose and hurling him into the wall. He struck his head and slid down in an unconscious heap.

The others gaped in astonishment before hectoring Hanufer with questions.

Helena sobbed and was comforted by Themistius, while the slave Erasmos helped Heraclitus to his feet.

"It will be a good test of Greek justice," Hanufer said, as Selene fainted at the sight of her fallen lover and collapsed backward on the couch. "When they regain consciousness, they should pray to their gods. Had they taken the trouble to look at the image of the goddess Maat, they would have seen that she wears an ostrich feather in her headdress. It is the feather of truth."

The man from Crocodilopolis kissed the image of the goddess on his ring and bowed. "The feather of truth revealed their evil hearts."

A Pinch of Pure Cunning

Jane Finnis

It was a perfect day for travelers, which made it a perfect day for innkeepers. I'm an innkeeper, and I love it when the summer sunshine brings half the empire out onto the roads. On this cloudless July morning, a steady stream of traffic came trotting along our particular road, stopping at the Oak Tree for a change of horses, a beaker of wine, and a bite to eat.

By noon the paved forecourt was packed with carriages, carts, horses, and mules of every shape and size. The barroom was overflowing, and some customers were choosing to drink outside in the sun. I wandered among them, having a word here and there and making sure nobody was dying of thirst. If Caesar himself dropped in for a jug of wine today, I thought, we'd have trouble making room for him. I daresay we'd manage somehow. But then again, being Caesar, he'd presumably expect all his drinks on the house. So maybe it's just as well he's in Rome and we're far away in Britannia, on the very northern edge of his empire.

I was saved from further disloyal thoughts by the arrival of a familiar blue-painted carriage, bringing a friend I hadn't seen for a while. She called out, "Good morning, Aurelia!" as she stepped down, and I hurried over to greet her.

"Clarilla, what a lovely surprise! It's really good to see you." I smiled and gave her a big hug, but I couldn't add, "You're looking well," because in all honesty she wasn't.

She was smartly dressed as always, in matching russet tunic and sandals; her silver jewelry was striking without being flashy, and her hair was fashionably styled so the touches of gray hardly showed. But she was tense and very pale and had dark circles under her eyes.

She returned my hug, but with only the briefest of smiles. "It's good to be here, Aurelia. I do hope you don't mind my calling unannounced."

"Of course not. You know you're welcome any time. How are you? And how's your brother?"

"He's very well, thank you. Busy as ever, but he enjoys that." He would, I knew. He was our chief town councilor, an important man in the area and an old friend. Clarilla, quite recently widowed, had come to keep house for him. "I'm fine too, in health anyway. But I'm worried, and in need of advice. I know you're bound to be busy, which is why I've come to you rather than inviting you to our villa. I'm hoping you might spare a little time for a chat?"

I laughed. "No problem. You've given me an excellent excuse to escape the lunchtime rush. The staff can cope perfectly well without me for now, and there have to be some advantages to being the boss. You'll stay for something to eat, won't you?"

"I'd love to, if you're sure it's no trouble. Is there somewhere quiet where we can talk? It's a bit, well, personal."

I was intrigued. Clarilla was usually so self-possessed. She's older than I, and I'd always thought of her as more worldly-wise than I am, yet here she was asking me for personal advice. "We'll sit in the garden." I began to lead the way. "We can be absolutely private there. I'll tell one of the maids to bring out some food and wine."

Our family garden is secluded and calm, well away from the customers, with fragrant flowers and an ornamental pond. We sat down on a comfortable couch and one of the barmaids brought cool white wine, fresh bread, goat's cheese, and smoked sausage, with one of our own lettuces.

"What a lovely spot," Clarilla exclaimed. "So peaceful. I wish our villa..." she trailed off unhappily. We ate and drank in silence for a while; at least my friend hadn't lost her appetite. Finally, she said, "You don't know what a relief it is to be away from home just now. The atmosphere there isn't comfortable. In fact, it's pretty poisonous."

"I'm sorry to hear that. You and your brother haven't fallen out, I hope?"

"Yes. Well, almost. I'm afraid we're barely speaking."

"Gods, what's happened? I thought you were happy keeping house for him. You've been with him—how long is it—six months now? And you seem to have settled in really well."

"I have. At least I thought I had." She sipped her wine. "But I've got a problem with the servants."

I hadn't expected that. I mean, everyone has problems with servants sometimes, but I'd have bet money Clarilla was equal to any of them.

She guessed my thoughts. "Yes, I know we all have servant troubles. The thing is..." She hesitated.

"Servants!" I said. "Can't live with them, can't live without them. Go on."

"One of ours is stealing, and I don't know what to do. Which makes me feel foolish, as you can imagine. After all the years I ran my own household until my husband died, I really should be able to manage."

"What's being stolen?"

"Personal things—*my* personal things. It started with small items: a bronze cloak pin, an ivory comb, nothing of any real value. I kept thinking I'd just mislaid them, and they'd turn up eventually. But they didn't, and I couldn't help starting to wonder...it's a horrible feeling."

"It must be. Nobody likes to think there's a thief in the house."

"Exactly. It makes the whole atmosphere sour and suspicious. Then expensive pieces of jewelry began disappearing, a silver ring, a pair of brooches. Again, I kept telling myself I was just absent-minded, it was nothing to worry about. But yesterday I couldn't find a gold ring with an emerald set in it, one that my late husband gave me. It's not just expensive, it's of great sentimental value too. I've looked everywhere, and it's simply vanished. I've realized I must stop shilly-shallying and do something. But what?"

I refilled our wine mugs. "At the risk of stating the obvious, first find the thief. You said one of the servants. Have you any idea who? Your brother's always had a large household, I know, and you must have brought quite a few of your own slaves with you when you came to live with him. Do you think it's one of them, or one of your brother's people?"

"Finding the thief isn't the problem. I think I know who she is."

"You *know?*"

"Well, let's say I'm almost certain."

"Have you questioned her?"

"I've questioned all the indoor servants. They all swear they're innocent, of course. Including this particular woman. But I've been watching her, noticing how she behaves toward me, and there's no doubt in my mind. It's one of my brother's senior slaves, a Gaulish woman called Orla. Very intelligent, very capable, and rather sly. I haven't actually caught her in the act, but I've checked up quite carefully, and she could have been responsible, she's clever enough. She always has some plausible explanation for where she was at any given time. Yet I'm convinced she's lying her head off."

"Do you know why she's doing it? For money?"

"I believe it's a personal grudge against me. She's made it as plain as she dares that she resents my coming to look after my brother. She has no choice but to do what I tell her, but she's unhappy, even jealous, and she's finding ways to get her own back."

"Then, if you know who the thief is, I don't quite see the problem. After all, she's a slave, you said, so you can do whatever you like. Punish her, or if she's causing you so much worry, sell her. In fact, that'd be my advice: get rid of her altogether."

"But it's not so simple. For a start, she's my brother's slave, not mine. And she's been with him a long time, twenty years or more, ever since his wife died. He came to rely on her a great deal to help run the house. She's one of the few who can read and write and manage figures, and he left her to do most of the household accounts, which I'm doing now. He trusts her completely, and he's grown fond of her. When I told him about my suspicions...oh, it was awful."

I began to see where she was driving. "He was upset to find she's betrayed his trust?"

"More than upset. He flatly refused to believe me."

I was shocked. "He believes a slave rather than his own sister? Surely not!"

She nodded sadly. "Perhaps, if I persisted, I could make him accept that she could possibly be guilty, but it would mean an unpleasant confrontation, perhaps a permanent rift. That's the last thing I want. I must find a way of proving Orla's guilt so completely that he can't doubt it. Ideally, I'd like to get a voluntary confession out of her somehow."

"A voluntary confession?" The phrase roused a half-buried memory from my childhood. We children were living with our grandmother then, and I dimly recalled that she'd faced a similar difficulty: how to make a slave admit to some misdemeanor. But I couldn't remember the details.

"Aurelia? What are you thinking?"

"Sorry, I was miles away—that is, years back in time, when I lived in Italia."

"Ah yes, your original home was in Pompeii, wasn't it?"

"For a while. The family moved around quite a bit actually, and our grandmother brought us up, after Father was widowed. And I vaguely remember she had a similar problem to yours, with one of her servants stealing...gods, it's frustrating, I wish I could recall the details. She was a wily old bird, our grandmother. She used to say, 'If the truth is hard to find, remember a pinch of pure cunning is worth a box of brute force.' "

"A pinch of pure cunning," Clarilla repeated. "I like the sound of that. What did she do?"

"She set some kind of trap, I think. But it was all so long ago."

One of the maids appeared just then, bringing a fresh jug of wine and a plate of honey cakes. She picked up the empty jug and turned to go, then paused. "Mistress, you haven't seen Dido anywhere, have you? She hasn't been in at all this morning, not even for her breakfast. We're hoping nothing bad's happened to her."

I said, "She was fine just after sunrise. I saw her near the stables, eating a baby blackbird. I told her she should be breakfasting on mice, but she ignored me. She'll be sleeping it off in one of the haylofts."

"Naughty thing! But I'm glad she's safe."

Clarilla raised an eyebrow. "Dido? A new maid with unusual dietary tastes?"

I laughed. "No, but she's on the staff in a way. She's a clever little black cat the kitchen girls have adopted." And suddenly memories came flooding back to me. "Of course! Clarilla, it was a cat that helped Grandmother get a confession from her maid."

"A cat? Seriously?"

"Yes. And we could use Dido to do the same for you. I'm sure it would work. Let's see...have you a couple of reliable servants you can trust absolutely?"

"Yes, my personal maids. They're twins, they've been with me since they were children. They'll do anything for me."

I smiled. "Then, with a pinch of pure cunning, we'll make your thief confess."

By the time I'd finished explaining, Clarilla was smiling too.

***

I arrived at Clarilla's bright and early next morning, and the twin maids were waiting for me at the bottom of the long drive. They were young and pretty and eager to help. They took me and Dido, who was safely in a covered wicker basket, to a wooden garden shed, then one went off to fetch Clarilla while the other showed me around inside. It was dim and mysterious-looking, barely illuminated by a tiny oil lamp on a wall bracket; indeed, it took my eyes a while to adjust to the gloom, which was excellent. It had been cleared of garden clutter, and one corner was curtained off with some dark fabric to make me a hiding place from which I could see without being seen. I couldn't have asked for better.

Clarilla bustled in, brisk and cheerful, yesterday's uncertainty quite gone. "Good morning, Aurelia. Will this shed do?"

"Good morning, Clarilla. Yes, it's perfect, thank you. Are the servants ready?"

She nodded. "All the female staff are waiting in the kitchen. They'll come and line up outside here when I send for them." She glanced at the basket on the table. "And how is Dido today?"

"In fine form. See for yourself."

I took the cover off the basket, which was really a wicker cage with a hinged lid and a carrying handle. Dido got up and stretched, yawned, looked around, then sat down and began to wash her paws. She'd had a large breakfast of pigeon, and now, well-fed and sleepy, she was content to wait and watch, the pupils of her yellow eyes large in the semi-darkness.

I reached in through the widely-spaced wicker bars. "She can't escape, but anyone can slide a hand through and touch her." I stroked her gently, and she stopped washing and began to purr. Clarilla followed my example, and so did the twins. Dido twitched her ears and purred more loudly.

"She's rather sweet," Clarilla said. "Very well, let's get on with it." She glanced at one of the twins. "Go and fetch the rest of them. And my brother too, of course." The girl nodded and hurried out.

I was surprised. "Your brother is coming to watch?"

"Oh yes. He still refuses to believe Orla is a thief, but after I'd visited you yesterday, I raised the subject again. When I told him you had shown me a way to find out for sure, he agreed to let us try. I haven't told him what we're up to, I'm not telling anyone except the twins."

"Quite right. We'll keep it to ourselves. An air of mystery is what we need."

"Yes. But...Aurelia, you're sure this will work, aren't you?"

"Positive. If you and your girls play your parts, Dido will do the rest."

"Right. I'll send for them all now, and they'll come in one by one, as we agreed."

Soon we could hear chatter and shuffling feet outside our door, and Clarilla left the shed. I gave Dido a final caress, then moved into my hiding place behind the curtain.

Clarilla's speech to the assembled servants was masterly. She said they probably all knew that someone in the household had been stealing from her, and she was determined to discover who it was. She had sought help from a wise woman (this made me smile) who had brought along a very cunning cat which could detect thieves and liars simply by their touch.

"You will each of you take a small test," she went on. "Go into the shed there and stroke the cat gently, and with your hand on her back, say these words: 'No thief am I, and if I lie, may all the world hear you cry.' The cat will cry out when the thief touches her. Be sure to speak the words loudly." She repeated them. "I'll be outside listening. Now, any questions?"

There were gasps and murmurs from the servants, and a voice asked, "How does it know, Mistress?"

"By touch, Orla, as I said. The simple touch of a hand tells her who is honest and who isn't."

"But how?"

"By her own native cunning, of course. She comes from a family of cats that were reared by priestesses in a sacred grove. When she's anointed with holy oil, as she is this morning, she acquires divine powers. The woman she belongs to says she never fails."

The woman she belonged to was delighted by such inventive nonsense but didn't fail to notice the questioner's name: Orla, the suspected thief.

Clarilla started ordering them all into line. "You twins first, then the rest of you, in order of how long you've been in service with me or my brother. Orla, you've been here longest, I believe?"

And so it began.

The twins entered in quick succession. Each stroked Dido and recited the rhyme loudly enough for those outside to hear. The cat sat still and purred.

I listened closely as each twin left the shed. The first said, "Ugh, that cat's got something greasy in its fur. I suppose it's the holy oil they've put on it."

The second said, "By the gods, I've got that holy oil on my fingers too."

"Go and wash your hands then," Clarilla said, "and get back to your work."

"Well done, girls," I breathed. "Now for the real test."

Orla came in. Even in the gloom, I could see she was tense. She approached Dido's cage and whispered softly, "You may be cunning, pussy cat, but so am I." She kept her hands firmly by her sides as she spoke Clarilla's rhyme aloud, paused for a few heartbeats, and went back outside, exclaiming, "Gods, that sticky stuff's all over my fingers. But the cat's proved I'm no thief, anyway, hasn't it, Mistress? Shall I get on with my work?"

"Yes, you may go, Orla. Now, whose turn is it?"

The rest of the slaves, more than thirty of them, went through quickly, each touching the cat and declaiming the rhyme. Dido lay down and continued to purr, bearing the ordeal with more patience than I did. But at last it was over.

When I finally emerged, blinking in the sunlight, only Clarilla and her brother were waiting.

"My dear Aurelia," the chief councilor greeted me, shaking my hand. "Welcome to our humble abode. We very much appreciate your efforts to come to Clarilla's aid. These thefts have been most distressing for her."

I smiled at him. I knew from past experience that beneath his pompous manner there was genuine warmth and friendship. "You know I'm always glad to help you and your sister."

"That's very gratifying. I'm only sorry your test doesn't appear to have worked."

"But it's worked beautifully. We know the thief for certain now, and Clarilla was completely right in her suspicion."

She gave me a beaming smile. "Good. So it's Orla, as I thought."

"I don't understand." Her brother's expression of bafflement was almost comic. "The cat did not cry out. Not for any of them, and certainly not for Orla. How can you conclude she is guilty?"

"Orla didn't touch Dido," I explained. "She believed that would give her away, so she spoke the words, but didn't put her hand on the cat at all. I was watching carefully."

"But she must have done. She said she felt the stickiness on the fur, from the sacred oil."

"There's nothing on the fur," Clarilla said. "Orla mentioned the oil because the twins both did. But they were play-acting, as I'd ordered them to. Orla followed their example, believing it proved she had stroked the cat's back, whereas it proved just the opposite. You noticed none of the other girls commented about the fur being sticky?"

We brought out the cat-basket and he stroked Dido himself, confirming that she had no oil on her coat. But even now he couldn't shed his doubts completely. "Orla a thief? I still find it incredible. All right, I realize we can't let matters rest as they are. Send for her now, please. I shall question her myself."

But there was no need to send. Orla was hurrying toward the shed, and, when she saw her master there, she broke into a run. She dropped to her knees in front of him and burst into tears.

"Forgive me, my lord," she sobbed. "I am guilty. I've stolen the mistress's jewels. I've done you both wrong."

"You admit it?" He was horrified. "Even though the cat didn't cry out?"

She nodded. "I didn't touch it, I just pretended. Now the other girls tell me it had no oil on its fur. Even the twins, they say so. If only I'd stroked the pesky animal myself, I'd have known. But I didn't dare, because then it would know I was lying."

His stern look told us he had no more doubts. "I'm very disappointed in you, Orla. How could you do such a wicked thing? After all the years you've been with me. And why? Have you sold the jewelry?"

She was shocked. "Oh no, my lord! I threw the things in the river as offerings to the river god. I prayed he would make Mistress Clarilla go away."

"But why?" he repeated.

She began to cry again. "I just want things to go back to how they were before she came. I was happy then. You needed me. Now you don't." She hung her head.

"Clarilla is here to stay," he answered. "You'll be the one going away."

"No!" she shrieked. "Don't sell me, Master, please don't! I swear I won't do it anymore!"

He looked at her for a few heartbeats, making up his mind. At last he said, "I shan't sell you, Orla. You've served me well until now. I shall send you to one of my other estates, somewhere you can make a new start. You have many good qualities, you can still be useful to me. But if I ever hear you've misbehaved in any way..."

"I won't, my lord. I'm sorry. I'm so sorry. Thank you." She rose and slowly walked away, wiping her eyes.

He sighed as he watched her go. "I can still hardly believe it. I must confess I could have wished for a different outcome. But we wanted the truth, and now we have it."

"You've done the right thing, brother," Clarilla said. "I couldn't have stayed here happily while she was under the same roof."

"I know. I'm sorry you had to put up with something so upsetting." He turned to me and smiled. "Aurelia, we're most grateful. But tell me, could your cat really have detected that Orla was lying, merely by touch?"

"Of course." I reached between the bars to stroke her. "You're a very cunning cat, aren't you, Dido?"

She stood up and gazed at me. I could swear she was thinking, "It takes one to know one." Then, purring loudly, she nodded her head in a graceful bow.

Flesh of a Fancy Woman

Paul Magrs

"You always was a scrubber, Lily Mahon," my Patrick laughed at me, and I swear down I could have gutted him then and there. I had nothing to lose, did I? I'd been drawn in to his hideous pit of bloody awful horror and it was everything I could do to keep control of myself. I just glowered at him and kept on scrubbing, didn't I? Whatever else was I going to do?

He'd brought us into disaster, like everyone said he would. Deep down, I'd always believed in him and so I always defended him. I wouldn't let no one say a word against my Patrick. He was perfect in my eyes, even when he wasn't.

And I would always do anything for him.

So that was why.

So, there I was: scrubbing out the master bedroom of a bungalow in Bournemouth. Floor to ceiling. Skirting boards. All the fixtures and fittings and the bedding and the furniture and all that. He'd got it everywhere, the dirty little bastard.

Oh, I'd have loved a weekend in Bournemouth. A little bungalow like this. A couple of days away, somewhere I could catch my breath and stretch my limbs and feel like he cared, just for a bit.

But it wasn't me he brought here, was it?

Just his bleeding floozies.

Red and brown and scabby and reeking like something out of hell. That's what that bungalow in Bournemouth was like. You see, by the time I got there, things had been rotting for a little while. Rotting down like compost does, and it stank to high heaven behind that door. I was horrified enough at what Patrick had done, but somehow...making a muck of that lovely seaside cottage, making it stink like that. Well, that seemed just awful to me. Obviously, not the worst thing he was guilty of. But it was like added insult to injury, you see. That's what it was. That stink! I've got it in my nose right now, when I think of it.

The stink of his fancy woman. Lying there in Bournemouth. Like she hadn't a care in the world. Well, she hadn't, had she? Not anymore.

The details are gruesome, dear. Do you want to hear it all? I bet you've heard everything, haven't you? You've heard it all before. Here, let me fetch us another drink, old mother. More gin. They water it down to nothing here. It's hardly gonna get us pissed, is it? But I need to wet my whistle if I'm gonna tell you more.

Here, watch my bag, old woman. Keep an eye on that Gladstone bag, me old duck, will you? Don't open it, though! Don't touch that clasp! Not if you don't want a shock like what I got. I felt such a fool. Standing in the lost luggage office at Waterloo Station. Well, I almost screamed. I had my neighbor with me, Mrs. Turton, and she nearly screamed as well, and she ain't no softie. She's had as hard a life as I've had, nearly. But I wouldn't go prying in that bag if I were you, dear. You won't say no to another gin, will you? Hang on, I'll be back.

And then you'll read my fortune, won't you? When you've had another tot. You'll tell me what the stars hold. I'm hoping it's something good. I could do with an upturn in my fortunes. The past week's been bleeding awful.

***

It began with his good jacket. I know I shouldn't go poking my nose in, but I do. I've lived seventeen years as his wife and I know when he's up to no good. Though he said he'd been away at the races, there was more to it, I knew. And Mrs. Turton from next door was round for a cup of tea and she said there weren't nothing wrong with it. Just going through his pockets in case there was money in there. I brushed his jacket and felt through the pockets with impunity. And that's when I found the ticket.

"Oooh, treasure," said Mrs. Turton. She spooned the gloopy sugar from the bottom of her teacup and sucked it with relish.

The ticket was for the cloakroom at Waterloo Station.

"What's he left in safekeeping there, that he couldn't bring home?" I wondered. My curiosity was piqued, and my neighbor was egging me on.

"Let's go and find out," she kept saying, crunching her way through all the biscuits. "You've got your suspicions about him. He's probably nicking stuff. He might be nicking stuff from you!"

"Huh, I've got nothing," I laughed. "He took anything what I had years ago and flogged it off."

Mrs. Turton (she's a bored old soul) works on me and winds me up all evening. And the fact that Patrick doesn't come home until one in the morning, reeking, and not telling me anything, makes things even worse.

The next morning me and Mrs. Turton catch the omnibus up to Waterloo Station. "Good girl," the old ratbag commends me. "Best to grasp the nettle. Best to find out what's really going on."

When we get there, it's all a-bustle and a-swarm and a great big echoing marble hall and I wonder: how did I end up sneaking around the edges of my husband's life? I'm investigating him. I don't trust him an inch, do I? Then I'm queueing at the desk and the young man there is examining the ticket and looking up to study Mrs. Turton and my good self. We both look respectable, don't we? We don't look like no kind of disreputable trollops. I'm a decent wife, concerned about things. Mrs. Turton smells of brandy a bit, but she's bad with her nerves.

The young man makes a meal of being officious and in charge. He goes over to the little lockers and the board displaying all the tiny keys. Then he finds the right door and unlocks it. He pulls a face. There's a smell. No, more than a smell. A right stench.

It's a Gladstone bag. It was once Patrick's dad's. It was something he was always proud of. Polished smooth with use. Old, soft leather. Like butter, it felt that soft. His dad was supposed to have been a doctor, but I doubt it. Safecracker, probably. Housebreaker. That would be more likely.

The young man plonks it down on the desk and his face is all curdled and grim. The bag really hums, and Mrs. Turton cries out, "Good heavens!" She gasps and wafts her hands.

"Take it away," the young man says. "We've been thinking we could smell something funny in here."

It's an infernal stench. A smell out of hell. I'm ashamed to pick the bag up and take it out of there. I'm ashamed that people on the omnibus going home are going to think it's something to do with me.

"Open it up!" Mrs. Turton keeps urging all the way home to Peckham Rye. "Have a look inside!"

But I won't. Not till I get home. I'm not opening this thing in public. It'd be like setting off a bomb. Let's wait till we're back in my parlor, with all the windows open and away from prying eyes...

***

And then comes the bit when Mrs. Turton turned against me. Honest, she hasn't spoken to me ever since that moment. We were in my parlor and she turned on her heel and walked right out of there.

"I want nothing more to do with it," she said in this thundery voice. She put down the glass I'd poured her. Drained it first, of course. "I've had my trouble, Lily. I've had an awful lot of bother in my life and I don't want no more. You, ducks, are on your own."

Then Mrs. Turton was gone. My front door slammed.

And I was alone with that Gladstone bag.

And its contents.

The silk lining was ruined. It was black with blood. And there were rags inside and you could see what they were covered with.

Clarts. Muck. Gobbets of flesh.

I was reminded of chopping up scrag-end and the worst cuts of meat for a stew. Even with the stench rising up to meet us, when I opened that bag I was thinking of food. But that's obvious, I suppose, because the only time I ever saw meat like that it was supposed to be food.

Not this. Not this.

Not the remains of a fancy woman.

Because I figured it out. Soon enough. I was only seconds behind canny Mrs. Turton in the figuring-it-out stakes.

This was human remains. Just a lot of bloody rags and some gobbets. When I dug around gingerly in those filthy recesses, I saw some other bits, too. Ah yes. That was human all right.

I snapped the bag shut and I went to be sick. The gin fumes were making it worse. When I came back, the gin fumes made it better again. I poured a glass or two, turned up the wicks of the lamps and sat waiting for Patrick to come home.

The Gladstone bag still sat on the dining table. Fastened shut, but that fetid, almost shitty smell still seeped out and tainted our living room.

And it set Patrick's red nose twitching when he came in, late that night.

"Christ, is that the drains?" he snarled at me, bursting through the door.

"No," I said. I must have given him a deadly look because he stepped back, one look at my face. I'd been drinking all evening, I admit it. And my look must have given him pause for thought.

Then he saw the bag on the table and realized what the source of that reek was.

"Ah, fuck," he said. "What's that doing here? How did you..." His face darkened with anger. "What have you been doing, Lily Mahon? You been spying on me?" And he raises those pan shovel hands against me, like he had done so many times in the past.

Now I guess I got real reason to fear them, haven't I? They don't just administer slaps and stinging blows. They deal death blows, don't they? My insides thrill with horror and...yes, excitement, too. 'Cos now I know. My hubby. My beloved of seventeen years. Now I know what you can do. "You been chopping women up," I tell him, and that halts him in his tracks. "Who was she? Whose bits were in that bag of your old dad's?"

***

Do you know what he told me, old mother? Here, have the rest of mine. Steady your nerves. Yeah, this is scary stuff, I know. You need a gulp just to take it all in. But don't get too pissed. I still want my fortune-telling. Don't go insensible now. I want you to hear the rest of this.

He said, "Ah, that's just dog meat, dearie. Don't you worry about that. It's a little racket I been involved with. Just a harmless little deal. Dog meat. I been bringing it from the knackers at the races, you see? Bringing it back to town. It's ruined Dad's old bag, but the stitching were going anyway. I didn't know what else to put it in. And then it stunk so badly afterward...I didn't know where to put it. So when I went through Waterloo, I thought, I'll leave it in a locker and get it cleaned later. But that's all it was, my love. Just dog meat. Plain old dog meat."

"Patrick," I told him, and the air was going smeary and swimmy with the lateness of the hour and the wicks burning down. "You take me for a fucking fool, don't you? I've had seventeen years with the wool pulled over my eyes while you've done everything and anything you wanted."

"Dog meat, my dear! It's dog meat! It's horseflesh that's been in there! That's all!" He gave a loud, boisterous laugh, like the bastard didn't have a care in the world.

Funny, it was the laugh that made me more scared than anything. I thought: you can even convince yourself that you've done nothing wrong.

"Patrick," I said. "We ain't got no fucking dogs. Why'd we need horsemeat for 'em?"

Then he laughed long and hard at his foolish, gullible, ignorant wife. "I was selling it, wasn't I? I sold it to them who *has* got dogs. And a tidy few quid I made, as well. It ruined the bag, but I made a few quid. That's life."

"Patrick," I said to him. I was keeping tight grip on my sanity and what I had seen in that bag. I knew I had. I knew he couldn't tell me fucking otherwise. "Patrick, there's an ear in that bag. And it ain't no horse's."

***

I made him tell me everything.

That's how I came to be in Bournemouth.

He told me he couldn't do it by himself. He'd got in too deep. He couldn't get the place clean at all. There was still evidence everywhere.

He only had the place on lease till the Tuesday.

"And you've always been a scrubber, ain't you, love?" he asked, with this snide little giggle. I thought *Ooh, you're chancing it*. By then I was up to my elbows in the scabby grime and gore.

But what could I do? I could never refuse him anything.

I made him sit down in that glorious front room of that bungalow and tell me the whole sordid tale. There was a picture window. A picture window looking at the beach. Oh, my heart wept for the sight of that. Why did he never think of me? When he was bringing fancy women here? Why did he never think: Lily'd like the view from here. I should bring her sometime.

Well, now he has. And now we sit here, knee to knee, and he confesses:

"I can deal with it when they come on too strong. Usually, I can. But this one. She was like a fucking steamroller, Lily. She wouldn't take no. She was all, let's run away to the continent together. Fucking Europe. I never heard the last about Switzerland and Paris and Madrid from her. She had all kinds of poncey friends abroad and she said she could run away any time and live with them, and she wanted me to come too.

"Well, I played along for a while. I was enticed a bit, and my head was turned. But I was always coming home to you, Lily. You know that, don't you? And when that one talked about divorce and setting me free and getting all the papers and a proper solicitor, it fair turned my stomach. I thought: she's building up her part. She tried to get me to get myself a passport, just like she had. Badgered me to fill out the forms. Well, there were unforeseen difficulties there. She didn't know that moving around and names and stuff, they're all a bit difficult for me, with my past and everything.

"I know you understand that, Lily. You understand everything about me.

"And then came this bank holiday weekend and she turns up at Waterloo and she's beaming and extra lah-di-dah. She's pleased with herself and I can't work out why. By then it was on the wane for me. I promise that, Lily. She was looking old to me, and boring. And all the talk that used to thrill me with its sophistication—about opera and pictures and fancy restaurants and that— was getting on my wick, to be honest. I thought: you're no better than me and my Lily. You've just read a few more library books and been to a few more galleries and you married money with your first bloke and that don't make you any better than the scrubber you are. Beg pardon, Lily, no offence.

"So then she started on how she was up the duff. Yeah, I know. It was a cruel blow. Here, don't cry, Lily. Please don't cry. I couldn't stand that, on top of everything. I've caused enough upset. But I thought...yeah, don't that just put the tin hat on it. She goes and gets herself pregnant. She knew, she absolutely knew that she was rubbing it in. I'd told her you was barren. I told her there was no hope. And there she was. Easy as anything. Showing off, really. Stood where you are now. Soon as we arrived on the Friday night. 'I'm expecting our child, Patrick!' Like I was gonna be glad. Like I was gonna jump up and change everything round. Like I was gonna start dancing to her tune. Yeah, she thought she'd won."

***

Ah, you'll need a tot more gin for this bit, I think, old mother. You don't mind me calling you that? You see, I lost my own over ten years ago. Patrick said it was for the best. And it was so peaceful, her just slipping away in her sleep like that. But when there's bother, I do miss her advice and her comforting.

This was the hardest bit. Getting rid of what was left.

A lot of Emily Kaye he smuggled away in his Gladstone bag. Piecemeal. Gradually. On the train back and forth to Waterloo.

How he kept from screaming and going out of his mind, I don't know. He can be quite steadfast, methodical. He can be a good little worker when he tries.

He'd get a carriage by himself. He'd pull the little curtains on the corridor. Then he'd work quickly. Up went the window. Whoosh went the wind. Shriek went the engine and the whistle. He unclasped his father's leather bag and he'd bring out a piece of Mrs. Kaye at a time.

And then he'd chuck her.

Off she'd fly! Bit by bit!

Bye-bye Blackbird!

A long, elegant forearm tossed into a hedge.

Her thigh (which one?) flung into the depths of a forest.

A field full of meadowsweet and larkspur got a smooth, pale shoulder.

A bagful of guts was dropped in a canal.

I can't imagine what he went through, steeling himself to do these awful acts.

But he wasn't caught. He was brazen. And no one even noticed the disposal of Mrs. Kaye.

Here, don't choke. Don't gag.

And don't go. Please don't go yet. I'm sorry. I know... I understand that this is hard stuff. Even on a strong stomach like yours, old mother. But I'd like you to stay to the end. Hear the last of it. Then I'd like you to tell me my future.

I want to know, you see, whether it was all worth it.

He isn't a monster, you know. The most tender bit, the most heartbreaking bit, that's coming up now. You see, the unborn child—he wasn't such a brute that he threw that from the window of the train, along with the rest of her. Now, the little child he kept for a day or two. Like a little fairy child, delicate in its squashy bag of stuff. He kept it for me to see, which was thoughtful, I suppose. It looked like a little pixie or a gnome, all curled round. We both looked at it and imagined that it was ours.

Then, in a special little ceremony, we took it out into the bluebell woods near that cottage by the sea and we buried it a few feet down under the flowers. It was really quite moving.

When we was back indoors, we took stock of how much was left. Mostly it was dirt. That, I could deal with.

But it was the question of the head, you see.

Not something I'd thought of, but of course, he couldn't go chucking that out of the train. What if someone had recognized her? When he explained, I thought, *Oh yes, it's obvious, isn't it?*

He'd put her in the grate and tried to set a match to her, to burn her face off, kind of thing. But that hadn't worked out for some reason. It turned his stomach.

"You must help me," he said, in his most helpless voice.

"I'll put her in the river," I promised him. "She'll sink. She'll go all the way down to the bottom. Especially if we stuff her full of beach pebbles and rocks. We can't throw her in the sea because the tide will bring her back. But if I take her into town in that bag...I'll go down to the river and drop her in. Some quiet dock. Some nasty little corner where the water's black and oily and bobbing with all kinds of jetsam and the like. No one will notice one more bit of trash."

"Oh, please, oh please," he begged me. "Just get her out of my sight. Those eyes keep following me. I can't stand her face. Once she's gone, that last little bit, when you've done that, we'll be able to start again, Lily, don't you see? All the mess will be gone, and we'll be free to live our lives with no interference. Now, go on. There's a train back to London at half past six."

And so there was.

And here I am. Drinking gin in the closest parlor I could find to the river. We're right on the front here. It's all clabber and clarts outside this door. Just a few steps away and it's the scummy heart's blood of the city, flowing past us in the twilight. That's where I'm gonna drop her, and then she'll be gone for good. We've stuffed her good and proper to make sure she won't float. That would be awful, wouldn't it? To set her free and step back and watch and then she didn't sink? I dunno know what I'd do then.

Do you want to see her? Do you want to look at her face? Maybe you could say a little prayer or something? You've got a nice face. A kind expression. It might be nice if the last face that looked at her was a kindly one. Someone who meant her no harm. Here, I'll undo the clasps. Sit this way, facing away from the room. Don't let anyone else see. You can come with me, in a minute, if you want, and watch me drop her in the river. It might be quite emotional.

Of course, I'll stand you another drink first.

Also, if you'd do that thing? Would you read my fortune? I'd love to know. I need to find out. I'm staking everything on this. My life...our lives...Patrick and mine...they're gonna get better, aren't they? Now that we've got rid of his fancy piece. We're gonna be happy in the time we have left? Tell me it's true, won't you, old mother?

The Hill of Hell

Bernie Crosthwaite

Assisi, Italy, 1298

The light in the basilica was fading. I could barely see as I added the finishing
touches to the halo around the head of San Francesco. I was almost trembling
with fatigue. It had taken a whole day's work—my *giornata*—to paint the
saint's noble face, surrounded by its golden disc.

I took a step back on my platform, the wooden boards and the scaffolding
that supported them creaking with the sudden movement. The yellow paint
glowed in the gathering dusk. San Francesco's eyes expressed kindness, his
cheeks were rounded, his lips soft. I had created a real human being, not one
of those flat symbolic creatures I had been taught to paint. It wasn't perfect—
nothing was, after all—but the plaster was hardening now and would take no
more pigment. Tomorrow I would mix paint with egg yolk and touch up the
fresco, applying the tempera onto the dry wall.

I put down my brush, sighed, and stretched. The work was hard, the
hours long. This was my first big commission: twenty-eight frescoes, each one
a vivid scene from the life of Umbria's favorite saint. Of course, the job was
too big for me alone. I employed several apprentices who painted the images
according to my designs. We had been working on the project for nearly two
years already and still it wasn't finished.

It was almost dark. There was only a feeble gleam from a rushlight down
below. I groped for the ladder.

It wasn't there.

I had sent my assistants away early: Michele with his painful twisted
back, young Niccolo eager to meet his girl, and Luca, a hard worker but a
poor artist. As the days became shorter and the nights colder, I had taken
to sleeping in the basilica rather than trudging back to my lodgings along
the dark streets of Assisi. I would go to sleep as soon as I'd eaten my meager
supper, and, in the morning, rise early and get started. As usual, after I'd
finished my *giornata*, I was tired and hungry, desperate for rest. But it seemed
I had an intruder to deal with first.

I knelt down and peered into the vast space below. Soon the basilica
would be a wonder, rich with decoration, but right now it resembled a

building site. I could see the pails of water, the mixing tubs, the humped outlines of sacks of lime and sand. One of them moved.

"Who are you? What do you want?" I called out.

A stifled groan, barely human.

"What's the matter? Are you hurt?"

There was nothing for it. I gripped the upright pole of the scaffolding and clambered down. I had only taken two paces when someone reared up and ran at me, screaming. I felt a heavy blow on my shoulder and crashed to the ground.

A figure loomed over me. The dim light showed a pale face, a wispy beard, and the glittering eyes of a madman. He brandished a wooden stave, ready to strike again. I caught the glint of a knife tucked in his belt.

"Are you going to kill me?" I asked, straining to keep my voice level.

"If I have to!"

I sat up slowly. The man stepped back. I could see he was afraid too. The weapon in his hand wavered.

"You don't have to." I struggled to my feet. I massaged my sore shoulder, thanking God that he had missed my head.

"Who are you?" the man asked, his voice shaking. "You don't look like a friar."

"I'm not. My name is Giotto di Bondone."

I held out my hand. He stared at it as if he had never seen a hand offered in friendship before. "What's your name?"

"Lorenzo. Lorenzo Torelli. I took your ladder...I was scared when I heard noises up there." He cast his eyes down. "I hit you because I wasn't sure if you were a...ghost."

"Why are you here, Lorenzo?"

"I was born here, in Assisi. I left because... I spent many years...away."

That made me wonder if he had been incarcerated in an asylum.

"I had to come back..." He gazed around the church. "My grandfather was hanged here."

"You mean...in the basilica?"

"No, before the church was built." His eyes flared. "They called this place the Hill of Hell, where thieves and murderers were put to death—a merciful sword for the rich, the slow, agonizing rope for the poor." He threw the stick onto the floor with venom. The sound of wood on marble echoed around the lofty building like a roll of thunder. "My grandfather was the last man to be hanged right here, seventy years ago. But he was innocent! I've lived with the stigma all my life. It's made me..." He clutched the sides of his head.

Perhaps he wasn't insane, just crazed with shame and grief.

"It's made you sad," I said. "And angry too, I think."

He stepped closer to me. I could smell sour wine on his breath.

"What are you, Giotto di Bondone?"

I pointed at the half-painted walls. "I'm an artist. Let me show you."

I lit a candle from the rushlight and, with Lorenzo beside me, walked along one side of the nave and then the other. I showed him the completed frescoes and described the pictures that would fill the empty spaces. When we'd finished, his eyes had lost their mad glint and were filled with wonder.

"It's as if San Francesco is still alive; he looks so human."

I couldn't help a swell of pride. "That's exactly what I'm trying to do. You know, when I was a student, I painted a fly on a picture, and my master—Cimabue—he tried to flick it off. I'd painted it so lifelike he thought it was real!"

There was no trace of amusement on Lorenzo's face. Instead he stared at me intensely. "You understand people, don't you? You can see into their hearts."

"I'm not sure I can do that."

"You listened to me and understood straightaway. You believed me."

It was nearly sunset. My belly was empty and my eyes sore with fatigue, but I recognized that the need in this man was so strong it radiated from him like a smoldering fire.

"Come," I said. I led him to the work table, littered with dishes of dried pigment and egg yolk, broken brushes, the punched sketches of my designs and sooty lumps of charcoal. I pushed the mess aside, grabbed two pewter cups, and poured out the dregs left in the flagon of wine. "I'd like to hear your grandfather's story. Tell me."

We sat down on low stools. Haltingly at first, then with growing fluency, Lorenzo told me how his grandfather (Salvatore Torelli) had been accused of lying in wait in an alleyway one evening for a man he believed had cheated him in a card game and stabbing him to death. But his wife Isabetta insisted that her husband had been with her all night. He was there when she went to sleep and there when she woke up in the morning. Her evidence was discounted, and Salvatore was executed for the crime. Isabetta had watched her husband swinging on a rope on the Hill of Hell. "They have killed an innocent man!" she had cried bitterly, over and over again. She suffered such mental anguish that she became mute a few days later and never spoke another word for the rest of her life.

"Poor Isabetta," I murmured. "She was clearly a very loyal wife." But I was thinking about my own Ciuta, how she would fight to defend me, whatever I had done. If it meant saving my life, I had no doubt she would twist the facts to help me, and then believe they were true.

"I know what you're thinking," said Lorenzo. "But my *nonna* was a devout religious woman. She would never have lied."

"If you're right about that, then Salvatore was wrongfully put to death, and the real murderer walked free."

He stood up, knocking his stool over. "My mother was only a baby when her father died. Isabetta and her child were shunned, ostracized. They lived in poverty and shame all their lives, and when I was born, so did I. They are both dead now. This is my last chance to clear the name of Torelli." He grabbed my arm. "You must help me. Seventy years...I came back to Assisi to mark the day. Of course, almost as soon as I arrived, I was recognized. Nobody would give me shelter, except a farmer outside the city walls. He lets me sleep in his barn with the animals. No one listens to me. They think I'm a lunatic. But you..."

"Me?"

"I'm sure someone here knows the truth about my grandfather. You're an artist, a respected man. If you find out what really happened, everyone will believe you, Giotto di Bondone."

"But it was too long ago, my friend. Who will remember? And I don't even come from Assisi. Florence is my home. People round here wouldn't take kindly to me poking into their affairs. Anyway, where would I start?"

Lorenzo reached into the leather pouch that hung at his waist. "With this." He pulled out a piece of rope.

I recoiled. "I hope that's not the rope that choked Salvatore to death?"

"Look closely."

He handed it to me. The rope wasn't old. It was clean and white, with three knots tied at intervals toward the end of its length. I frowned as I examined it. There was something familiar about it...

"It's a belt, like the ones worn by Franciscan friars," said Lorenzo.

"Of course. I've seen these many times."

"You know the community here?"

"It was the head of the order, Padre Giovanni, who commissioned me to paint these frescoes. I see him regularly to report on progress, and sometimes I have supper with the friars."

"Last night a small package was left at the place where I stay. It contained this belt, along with a note..."

Lorenzo pulled a piece of paper from his pouch and handed it to me.

I've atoned for my crime. Leave me in peace.

The strip of good quality rag paper had been torn from a larger page. On the back I could see the lower half of a line of writing, carefully scribed in fine black ink. I guessed it had been ripped from a book, a prayer book or hymnal perhaps. I read the scrawled message several times.

"Interesting."

"You will help me?"

I thought for a while, then nodded. "But first..." I took a ducat from my pouch and slapped it on the table.

"I don't want to take your money. I should be paying you...but I have nothing."

"It's not charity," I said. "It's a fee." I reached for my sketchbook and picked up a piece of red chalk. "You have an interesting face. I want to draw you."

***

The horizon was a blaze of red, the sky a deep blue, almost as luminous as the precious pigment lapis lazuli. The artist's bag that went everywhere with me was slung over my shoulder. It contained my sketchbook, drawing materials, a mixing board, and, tonight, the rope belt and the note that Lorenzo had given me for safekeeping.

I breathed in the sharp cold air, then took a steep flight of steps down to the adjoining building, the Sacro Convento. I hesitated for a moment in front of the door, then rapped on the wood. It was opened by the maid Agnella, who ushered me in out of the cold. Her pronounced limp meant the arthritis in her knee was worse than the last time I came.

"Just in time for supper," she said, smiling. "Come in, come in, the soup is ready."

I made my way to the refectory. Peering in, I saw about twenty friars, dressed in brown woolen habits, sitting on each side of a long table. Their ages ranged from young men barely out of boyhood to the very old, who nevertheless looked alert, a testament to their healthy and spiritual way of life. Could there possibly be a murderer among them? It seemed so unlikely I nearly turned away, but the smell of warm broth made my stomach rumble.

As I entered, they turned their heads in unison. At the head of the table, Padre Giovanni stood up and spread his arms wide. "Master Bondone! Welcome. Have you been working all this time? It's late. You must be ravenous! Please...sit down and eat."

Fra Antonio and Fra Bernardo shuffled sideways on their bench to make room for me.

"Thank you." I slipped my bag from my shoulder and placed it on the bench beside me.

Agnella appeared with a steaming bowl and placed it in front of me. The soup was thin and watery, but pieces of onion and zucchini floated in it, and it warmed my hungry belly.

"How is the work going?" asked Fra Antonio on my left. He was barely out of boyhood, though the tonsure on his head, leaving his crown bald, made him look much older.

"It's going well, thank you." I let a moment pass. "I learned something strange today. Apparently, this spot used to be known as the Hill of Hell." I spoke lightly, as if it were a fact of no great importance.

Around the table, chatter stopped, spoons paused in mid-air.

"Sadly, that is true," said Padre Giovanni. "But the name was changed when our beautiful basilica was built. Nowadays it's known as the Hill of Paradise."

Fra Bernardo gripped my arm with a bony hand. "They say the ghosts of the executed still haunt the place..." He turned his large square face to me and held my gaze for a tense moment.

Across the table, Fra Matteo tapped his spoon against his dish. "Don't talk nonsense, brother. There are many sad stories, but there are no ghosts. Can't you see you're frightening our guest?"

The friar let go of my arm and burst out laughing. "Just joking."

"Thank you, Fra Matteo," I murmured.

He nodded. His face was gaunt in the candlelight. He was one of the older brothers, and though he looked a little like a skeleton covered in skin, his mind was still sharp. The friar sitting next to him, Fra Filippo, leaned across, his double chin wobbling.

"Who told you about the Hill of Hell?"

"Just...someone I overheard in the piazza."

Fra Filippo frowned. "This is a holy place now," he said. "You're here to celebrate the goodness of our founder San Francesco, not rake up memories of evildoing."

"Of course," I said. I turned to Fra Antonio. I knew he came from Florence. I told him about the building of the new Duomo, that I'd heard the façade was to be patterned with slabs of green, pink, and white marble. He told me how he used to play on the banks of the Arno with his friends and catch writhing fish with his bare hands. He smiled at the memory, looking like an innocent young boy.

Agnella cleared the soup bowls. Platters of bread and pecorino were handed round. I saw Fra Filippo cut a larger piece of cheese than the others. His flabby face and soft belly suggested he wasn't as frugal in his tastes as a Franciscan friar should be. Fra Matteo waved the cheese away, took a small piece of bread and nibbled it slowly. Fra Antonio took his share then passed the dishes to me.

"Please, take plenty. No, that's not enough; take more. You do not have to observe the Rule like the rest of us. Meager food, nothing but water to drink, rising from our beds in the middle of the night to pray..." He sounded wistful for a less austere way of life, and I wondered if his vocation had been the right choice.

A cup of wine was placed at my elbow by Agnella.

"No, no, water is fine."

But Padre Giovanni waved away my protest. "You are our guest, Giotto. Drink, drink!"

As I raised the cup to the padre in thanks, a sharp pain made me wince.

Fra Domenico stretched his arm across the table. "Are you all right?" he asked me.

I rubbed the shoulder where Lorenzo had landed his wooden stave. "I...fell off my ladder. It's a bit bruised, that's all."

Fra Domenico stood up. He was very tall and lean, with a mane of white hair, his shoulders bowed from years of stooping. "Come with me."

I knew he was skilled in medical matters and the making of herbal remedies. He led me to a small room along a gloomy corridor. I took off my jerkin and shirt and let the friar rub ointment into my sore shoulder. I caught the scent of rosemary oil. It made me giddy with longing for Ciuta's cooking, and for the warm embrace of my children, far away in Florence.

Fra Domenico stirred fresh green herbs into a flask of water.

"Drink this. It will help with the pain."

The taste was bitter and made me think of swamps, but I drank it down. "Feeling better?"

I nodded as I dressed myself. "Thank you, much better."

When we returned to the refectory, the low murmurs stopped, and everyone looked at me then swung their heads toward Fra Antonio, whose cheeks flushed red with embarrassment. He was fiddling with something on the bench beside him. When I sat down, he handed me my bag.

"Sorry, Master...I...I reached for more bread and it fell on the floor. Things fell out...but I've put everything back."

"Please don't worry about it, brother."

He smiled gratefully. "You are a fine artist, Master Bondone. We are very lucky to have you here."

"Thank you."

I finished my simple supper. The food and drink were making me sleepy. It was time to leave. I had learned nothing here. These were good men with open hearts and clear consciences. None of them was perfect, but who was? I began to think Lorenzo had been lying to me, or really was insane. I stood up, a little unsteadily.

"Where are you going?" asked Fra Filippo.

"I need an early start tomorrow. There is so much to do..."

Padre Giovanni wagged a finger at me. "I've heard that you've taken to sleeping in the church, Master Bondone."

"I hope you don't mind."

"Not for the moment...the state the place is in. But not tonight. It's late. We have a spare cell for you; you can sleep here. You won't have to share the dormitory with the brothers, and we won't rouse you at midnight for Matins." A rumble of amusement passed around the room. "You can rest in peace and rise with us for prayers at dawn."

"That's a very kind offer..." An appealing one, too. I was so tired I could barely keep my eyes open. "Yes...I would like to..."

Padre Giovanni clicked his fingers. "Agnella, take fresh bedding to one of the empty cells. Sleep well, Giotto."

***

When I woke up, the sun was streaming through the small high window of the tiny cell. Something was digging into my back. I rolled onto my side and pulled it out. It was my artist's bag. I must have fallen asleep still clutching it, and from its flattened, creased appearance I had lain on it most of the night. Yet the discomfort hadn't roused me. And why hadn't I woken to the sound of bells at dawn, to the brothers chanting their prayers in the chapel? I raised my head, but it felt heavy, my limbs sluggish. I could barely move. My shoulder was throbbing painfully, but that was only natural. The rest of my symptoms, I began to realize, were not.

I had been drugged.

The wine. Who gave me the wine? I couldn't remember. Who could have tampered with it before it reached my lips? Almost anyone in the room, especially after I went with Fra Domenico to his apothecary. And more importantly, why? Whoever did this, it had to be something to do with Lorenzo, his innocent grandfather, and the Hill of Hell.

There was a scuttling noise. I forced my head to lift. Caught in the beam of sunlight was a dark shape the length of my hand: eight legs, two pincers, a segmented tail that ended in a vicious point.

Scorpion.

I knew that most scorpions were harmless. But some scorpions could kill with their venomous sting. Was the presence of this one an accident? Simply bad luck? Had it crawled in through the window? Or had someone placed it in my room during the night, knowing that the drug I'd been administered meant I wouldn't wake up? And in the morning, when I rose unsteadily from my bed and stepped onto the floor...

I shuffled to the end of the bed. The creature darted in the same direction, as if shadowing me. I could see my shoes, kicked off carelessly last night, near the door. I swung myself off the bed and grabbed one of them just as the scorpion raised its tail in an angry curve, ready to strike. I bent down and slapped the shoe on top of it. The shoe moved. I reached into my bag for my mixing board, shoved it under the shoe, then, holding both with shaking hands, stretched up to the window and parted shoe and board in a jerky movement, flinging the creature out into the open air.

I leaned against the wall, my knees weak. Whoever had drugged me and put a scorpion in my room meant to warn me, harm me, even kill me. I had doubted Lorenzo's story, and sometimes his sanity. But I had no doubt now.

I have atoned for my crime. Leave me in peace.

The real murderer was here.

***

I crept down the stairs and out of the building without breakfast, or even a sip of water. I hurried along the streets, through the arch of the eastern gate, and into the farmland beyond.

Only a few minutes along a rutted stony path, I saw the farmhouse and the dilapidated hut beside it. A man was working a nearby field. He straightened up as I approached, watching me with suspicion. He held a sharp curved sickle in his hand that reminded me of the scorpion's tail. Although the sun was bright, I shivered.

"Good morning," I called. He said nothing. "I'm looking for Lorenzo."

"Gone."

"For good?"

The farmer jerked his head toward the barn. "His cloak is still there. He'll be back."

"Right. Someone left a package for him a couple of days ago. Did you see the man who left it?"

"No."

"Ah." I stared at the stony ground. "Thank you anyway."

"The dogs barked."

"I'm sorry?"

"It was at night. The dogs barked. So I came out." He tested the sickle's weight in his hands, suggesting he had been armed that night too.

"But you didn't see him?"

"It was a woman."

"A...woman?"

"She saw me, left in a hurry. She had a limp."

I was speechless for a moment. A woman with a limp... Agnella? Had one of the friars used her as a messenger?

"Please...don't let me keep you from your work."

"There is always work." He plunged the sickle into the dry ground. "My wife has made honey cakes. Breakfast seems a long time ago."

I smiled ruefully. "And I haven't had any yet."

"Then come with me. You look as if you need a square meal."

***

I crept round the back of the convent. The kitchen door was open. Agnella was stirring a large iron pot hung over the fire. She looked startled when she saw me.

"I need to speak to you."

"Master Bondone...are you hungry? Can I get you something to eat?"

"No, my stomach is full of honey cakes. They were delicious." I paused. "Made by the wife of the farmer who lives just beyond the eastern gate."

Her mouth gaped open.

"You delivered a package to the vagrant who shelters in the barn, didn't you?"

She backed away from me.

"There was a note too. Did you read it?"

"Read? Me?"

Of course. The woman was illiterate. Few women had an education—my Ciuta was an exception.

I stepped closer. "Who asked you to deliver the package, Agnella? I know it was someone here at the Sacro Convento."

She crossed her strong arms in front of her, a defiant look on her face. "He's a bad man."

"Who? Tell me his name."

"I mean that lunatic. That friend of yours!"

"I only met Lorenzo yesterday."

"You're partners in this! You drew a picture of him!"

"How do you know—"

"We all saw it, while you were being treated by Fra Domenico. Your bag fell to the floor and things fell out. Fra Antonio should have left it alone, but no, he had to take a look in your sketchbook, marveling at the pictures. 'Look at this,' he said, and showed us the latest one. Somebody recognized Lorenzo the Lunatic, who left Assisi years ago and should never have come back!"

No wonder the young friar was embarrassed, scrambling to put my things away when I returned to the refectory. Somebody in the room had seen the link between me, Lorenzo, the Hill of Hell, and the death of Salvatore. They had drugged my wine and set a scorpion trap. And that person was a murderer.

"Who sent you to Lorenzo with that package?"

She shook her head firmly. Her loyalty to the order was too strong. I had never bullied or beaten a woman to get what I wanted, and I wasn't going to start now.

I had to think of another way.

***

Michele, Luca, and young Niccolo were already at work on their platforms when I entered the basilica.

"Good afternoon, Master," said Niccolo cheekily. It was barely halfway through the morning. "Too much wine last night?"

"Or was he missing the arms of the lovely Ciuta and looking for... comfort?" asked Luca.

"Careful, Luca. You made a mess of San Francesco's robe yesterday. Mix some tempera and fix it *a secco*. Now." He disliked working on dry plaster, lacking the skill for fine detail.

Michele was mixing lime and sand with water in a large tub. He straightened up, rubbing his aching back. "Is something wrong, Master?"

"No, nothing."

He shrugged but had the sense to leave me alone.

For the rest of the day I gave half of my concentration to painting a tall tower in the background of my panel, the other half to the Hill of Hell. My drawing of Lorenzo, the knotted belt, the note torn from a prayer book... someone had come to my cell to retrieve and destroy them. But I was sleeping on top of my bag. So, the scorpion. Even if its sting hadn't killed me, I would have run terrified from the room and they would have taken their chance to steal the items that could incriminate them.

As the day wore on and my hand grew stiff and sore from holding the brush for so many hours, I tried and failed to think of ways to catch my prey. Then, as I applied the last few touches of paint, it struck me that I didn't need to be a hunter. All I had to do was be patient and, like a spider, wait for my prey to come to me.

As each artist finished his *giornata*, he tidied up and silently left the church. I was barely aware of their departure. When I climbed down from my platform, I was glad of the absolute silence and solitude. I had things to do. I hurried to the work table. I took a block of red ochre and placed it in a mortar and ground it with a heavy pestle into fine powder. But instead of adding water to create pigment for painting, I tipped the fine dust into a bowl.

I glanced around the church. The vaulted ceiling was supported by pillars placed at intervals along the nave. The base of each pillar was a block of heavy stone which provided a narrow ledge. I took my bag and put it on the ledge opposite the panel I was painting, about halfway along the nave. I stepped back. It looked as if I had casually left it there.

Then I took the dish of ground-up red ochre and scattered it carefully in front of the base of the pillar. Finally, I extinguished all the rushlights except the one nearest to my chosen pillar. It emitted a feeble glow, just enough to illuminate the area around it. In the gloom I inched my way across the nave and fumbled for my ladder. I climbed onto my platform and lay down on my stomach. My eyes adjusted, helped by moonlight coming through the high windows.

All I had to do was adopt the infinite patience of a spider.

***

I must have dozed off. The noise of the door creaking open startled me. A hooded figure carrying a dark lantern entered the church. The figure paused, then cautiously walked along the center of the nave. I peeped over the edge of the platform, frustrated that the cowl was pulled so far forward I couldn't see the face.

The work table blocked the way. The figure paused, raking through the muddled contents of the table, and, not finding what was wanted, shoved the whole mess onto the floor with a vicious sweeping gesture. A glance to the right, to where the rushlight, smoking and guttering, was about to burn down. The figure turned and made a straight line toward the bag resting on the base of the pillar.

I rose onto hands and knees and made my way to the corner of the platform. I swung my leg out, found a foothold, and grasping the wooden pole, began to climb down as quietly as I could.

I wasn't quick enough. By the time I reached the ground, the figure was heading for the door.

"Stop!" I shouted.

My prey broke into a shuffling run. The door was banged shut in my face just as I reached it. I wrenched it open and flew out. The marble pavement glowed white under the moon.

Something tripped me up. I fell onto the ground, my cheek smashing against the cold stone.

Winded and dazed, I felt my arms being wrenched and tied together behind my back. Then my feet. I was rolled like a log to the edge of the flight of steps.

With every scrap of energy I had left, I thrust my bound legs into the body of the person who was trying to kill me. I heard the expulsion of breath, the wince of pain. The rolling stopped, and at that moment I heard a cry in the distance.

"Master Bondone? Giotto! What's going on?"

Lorenzo.

The hooded figure didn't wait. It scuttled away toward the Sacro Convento. I heard Lorenzo running toward me.

"What happened to you? Who did this? I saw someone... Should I follow?"

"Just cut these ropes with your knife, will you? Don't worry. They won't get away."

***

I hammered on the door of the convent. It was long past supper time, but I hoped the friars would still be awake, studying the psalms, getting ready for evening prayers and bed. I rapped my knuckles on the solid wood until they were sore.

At last Agnella opened the door a crack.

"Let us in," I said.

She glanced over my shoulder and saw the looming presence of Lorenzo. She stepped back silently, and we entered the hall. A large handbell stood on the table by the door. I lifted it and clanged it loudly. It echoed through the building. Gradually, one by one, the friars emerged, looks of consternation on their faces. I heard mutters of *fire* and *plague* and *war* as they struggled to understand the commotion. One of them, of course, knew exactly why I was here.

Padre Giovanni came forward. He was frowning, his usual good humor gone. "Master Bondone...and Lorenzo the..." He stopped himself saying *lunatic*, but I could see from his expression that he believed it. He turned back to me. "Explain yourself."

"I'm here to report a theft, and to retrieve my property."

"Then go to the authorities, to Perugia, to the Pope. Do not come barging in here at night, disturbing our lives of prayer and contemplation."

"The thief is here, Padre."

A mutter of disbelief rippled around the hall.

"And not only is that person a thief, but a murderer too."

Now the mutters became cries of outrage.

"I can prove it. Please line up and turn your backs to me," I instructed.

Padre Giovanni reluctantly nodded his assent.

"Lorenzo, check their footwear."

One by one, the friars lifted their sandaled feet to be inspected. None of them showed the evidence I was expecting.

"You too, Padre."

He looked angry to be ordered about but complied. Nothing.

"Are any of the brothers missing?" I asked.

They burst into chatter, pointing, counting. Fra Antonio stepped forward. "Yes, Fra—"

"I'm here," came a stern voice from the depths of the hallway.

The group parted as Fra Matteo walked toward us. He looked older than before, his features sharp as blades where the bones lay just under the skin, which was a sickly yellow. He looked tired, too. The exertion of tying me up and rolling me along the ground had exhausted him. Or was it guilt that added years to him?

"Show me the soles of your feet," I said.

Fra Matteo frowned, unwilling. But the eyes of the community were fixed on him. He lifted one foot toward me, then the other. The rope soles of both were deeply ingrained with red dust. I explained what I had done.

Lorenzo rushed forward to lash out at the man who had caused him and his family so much grief for seventy years. I stepped between them, my palms against Lorenzo's chest to hold him back.

"You killed a man and let my grandfather take the blame!" he cried.

Fra Matteo smiled grimly. "How little you understand. Yes, I killed a man, and yes, I let someone else take the blame. But it wasn't your grandfather who was hanged to death on the Hill of Hell."

Lorenzo's knees buckled. I had to hold him up.

"What do you mean?" I asked.

"My name is Salvatore Torelli." He reached out a skeletal hand. "I am your grandfather."

There was a moment of profound silence before the room erupted with noise. Lorenzo sagged against me. "I don't understand what's happening," he whispered.

"I think I do." I set Lorenzo down on a chair and turned to face Fra Matteo.

"Your wife Isabetta, she covered for you, didn't she? She knew you had been out that night. Perhaps you came home with blood on your shirt?"

The friar bowed his head but didn't deny it.

"She broke her faith in order to lie and it destroyed her. And not just that. When she saw a man choking to death on the Hill of Hell, she cried out, 'They have killed an innocent man!' And this time she was telling the truth. It wasn't you, the real murderer, but some poor petty criminal hanged by mistake. I'm right, aren't I?"

"He was thrown in jail for stealing bread, if I remember rightly. We were locked up for weeks together in that stinking cell. We were both filthy, our hair matted, our beards unkempt. The guards were paid next to nothing. They were often drunk. Was it my fault that on the day of my execution they came to our cell and dragged out the wrong man?" He looked around at the brothers for sympathy but met only stony stares. "When I had served my sentence, they let me out. I left Assisi, started a new life, but..."

"Guilt?" I prompted.

"It took a few years, but yes, remorse began to eat into me. I had let an innocent man die. I came back to Assisi, joined the Franciscan Order, and tried to atone for my sin. Ever since, I have tried to live a good and blameless life."

"Until Lorenzo came back. You tried to warn him off, the poor simple lunatic you thought he was, but it had the opposite effect. He told me his story, and then he had an ally. You saw me as a serious threat and tried to get rid of me." I told the assembly about my drugged wine, the scorpion in my room, the attempt to roll me down the steps. They listened in stunned silence. "Not such a blameless life after all."

"Lorenzo, I'm sorry," said the friar, without looking at his grandson. Then, without warning, he collapsed.

Fra Domenico, tall and stooped, stepped forward and gave instructions. The younger brothers carried Fra Matteo to the infirmary. The rest melted away until only Padre Giovanni was left. He shook his head sadly. "Poor Fra Matteo."

"He killed someone and let an innocent man take the blame!"

"He's a sick man, Giotto. He will die soon. Who are we to judge? Let God decide."

He ushered Lorenzo and me to the door. We heard it close firmly behind us.

***

A week or so later, when I was working late in the basilica, Padre Giovanni bustled in, staring up at me with an expression on his face both worried and elated. I climbed down the ladder.

"Master Bondone, there is good news, and there is bad news."

"What's the bad news?" I hadn't heard from Lorenzo and feared that it concerned him.

"Fra Matteo is dead, God rest his soul."

"I see." I couldn't keep the coolness from my voice. "Did he talk to his grandson before he died?"

"No. Lorenzo came several times but was refused. Yesterday, he told me was leaving Assisi and that he would never return."

"That's sad. And even worse, Fra Matteo has escaped justice."

"He did apologize," said the padre gently.

It was true, but my heart was sore for poor Lorenzo and for the unfortunate man who had died instead of Salvatore Torelli. Nothing could change the tragedy of their lives now.

"But the good news is..." Padre Giovanni waved a letter at me. "Rumors about your fine work here in Assisi have reached the ears of Pope Boniface, and he wants to commission you to decorate the Lateran Church in Rome!"

"That's wonderful, but..." I looked around helplessly at the empty panels. "There is still so much to do here."

"True, but your designs can be followed. The work will be completed by other artists. Just one thing..."

"What?"

"The Pope would like to see an example of your skill first."

"And your word isn't good enough?" I felt a rising tide of anger. "No? Then tell him to come here and take a look for himself."

The padre spread his hands. "He's a very busy man..."

"Alright then."

I went to the worktable, furiously ground a block of red ochre to powder and mixed it with water. I found a fresh sheet of paper, selected a long thin brush. Then, without a moment's hesitation, I painted a perfect circle.

"There you are. There's an example of my skill. Send that to the Pope."

When Padre Giovanni had gone, I set about clearing up. I sighed deeply. Had I been too hasty, too rude? It wasn't the padre's fault. But my heart had been churned up, saddened beyond bearing about Lorenzo and the grandfather he had lost, found, and lost again.

I opened my sketchbook at the drawing I had made of Lorenzo. I examined the pale face, staring eyes, and wispy beard. The very first image in the story of San Francesco, a panel I hadn't been able to paint yet because of the construction of the rood screen, concerned a simple man, perhaps touched by madness, who nevertheless recognized goodness when he saw it. He laid his cloak in front of the saint, a sign of his reverence.

Lorenzo would be my model for that man. It would give him a kind of immortality. It wasn't much, but it was all I could do.

I sighed. Life was unpredictable, complex, and often out of our control. The sublime was impossible to achieve in this world.

Apart from one thing, of course.

My perfect red circle.

Murder and the Cucumbers

Amy Myers

"You're the new chef then?" Inquisitive eyes studied him.

"Temporary chef," Auguste Didier replied firmly.

In fact, he would only bestow his presence on Little Mincing for one more day. Two days at the manor house were sufficient to spend in this quaint village. He had long considered that English customs were quaint to say the least, but the highlight of today's proceedings was unforgivable. If he had understood correctly, the Battle of the Cucumbers would be using this precious vegetable for its weapons. In this modern age of 1895, cucumbers should be stuffed and gently fried in butter or puréed into cream sauces with parsley; they were an honorable inheritance from ancient Roman times, they were *not* an instrument of war. Surely he must have misunderstood? This village's actions needed to be regarded with caution, as did those of its neighbor and rival, Mincing Magna.

"Look into my crystal ball, Mister," urged this striking lady with dark hair, dark eyes, and a somewhat menacing expression. Mistress Griselda, as she styled herself, was tugging him by the arm into her tent in order to tell his fortune—or rather misfortune, as this Cucumber Day promised to bring.

Auguste surrendered and obediently clasped the crystal ball between his hands.

"Ah, now, young gentleman," she whispered, peering into its depths, "it's a long and happy life I see." Then to his alarm she stopped abruptly, her face white with shock. "There's darkness," she whispered. "Take care, Mister Chef." She peered in again. "I see a rose, I see someone you know, a policeman, and I see trouble ahead."

Auguste paled. If this mysterious rose was coupled with the someone he knew, could that be Chief Inspector Egbert Rose of Scotland Yard?

"Beware," she hissed, still huddled over the magical crystal ball.

Auguste pulled himself together. This was nonsense. The villagers of the two rival parishes of Little Mincing and Mincing Magna were at present engaged in another strange custom, the annual Beating of the Bounds, which would be followed by the Battle of the Cucumbers. Unappealing though these were, they hardly seemed to foretell the arrival of a Scotland Yard inspector.

Named with typical English humor, Little Mincing was twice the size of Mincing Magna, but even so Beating the Bounds sounded relatively harmless. Sir John Abbot-Smith, squire of Little Mincing and his temporary employer, had explained that he and the squire of Mincing Magna would each lead a march around the entire boundary of his village, thus apparently establishing their rights to the land. For part of this procedure, they would be meeting on their shared boundary, the exact details of where this was still had to be agreed. If they were not—and they never were, so Sir John's brother Mr. Charles had said, laughing—the dispute would be settled at the Battle of the Cucumbers.

Auguste could already hear the two approaching armies in the distance, judging by the low rumbling and periodic outbursts of shouting.

"They're coming!" cried Mistress Griselda.

Auguste seized his chance for escape, but she was close behind him as he reached safety outside the tent. The battle was to take place in the field bordering the narrow River Dollop, and indeed this field looked rather like a medieval battlefield with a cluster of stalls and tents. A makeshift stage had been erected near the river for the great fight to come.

Auguste could already see the first group of villagers arriving, perhaps fifty or sixty, of all ages and led by a stalwart gentleman of mature years carrying a banner proclaiming, inexplicably, "Victory! Stickleback is ours."

"That's Percival Thorn-Hawking, squire of Mincing Magna," Mistress Griselda told him gloomily. "Curses on him. We just call him Squire Percy."

The cheers that accompanied him were now being drowned out by the yells of fury coming from the second group, stumbling behind the first and led by Sir John. Sir John was a kindly gentleman and one whom Auguste much respected. By the look on his face, though, kindliness was not on the manor menu at the moment, nor did his brother Mr. Charles look any happier.

This did not bode well for the victory dinner Sir John had hired Auguste to present this evening. The Battle of the Cucumbers would now decide the issue of Stickleback, Mistress Griselda informed him. What Stickleback was remained a mystery to Auguste.

While the villagers continued to swarm over the battlefield in protest, the contestants in the battle to come went grimly on their way to don their tabards and pick up their weapons. Auguste longed to leave in order to avoid the hideous slaughter of cucumbers that would undoubtedly follow, but, in respect for Sir John, he had to stay. He became an instant victim for the indignant villagers of Little Mincing, who, like Mr. Coleridge's Ancient Mariner, were only too eager to tell him their tale of woe.

"Stickleback's lost," roared an elderly man, half sobbing, half spitting in fury as he grasped at Auguste's lapels. "What's to happen? We're doomed and so's Little Mincing."

With some difficulty, Auguste deduced that Stickleback must be the name of another river or pond, but how either could be *lost* remained unclear. He did his best to sympathize, however, as he carefully disentangled his jacket. "My sympathy, monsieur, but the battle may yet be won."

"The crystal ball never lies, Mr. Didier," Mistress Griselda instantly snapped. "Farmer Brockway's right. There's trouble brewing if Stickleback's gone. That pond's the lifeblood of Little Mincing, and Squire Percy gave orders to throw a load of stones our side to stop our lads from rushing into the pond and river to claim them. Then those big-booted jossers from Mincing Magna rushed into Stickleback and then along the River Dollop and claimed them."

"But where legally should the boundary lie?" Auguste enquired, even more puzzled.

"Who's to say but the Good Lord above who gave it to us?" growled the farmer, beard bristling. "Where's the water coming from for my fields if Sir John loses the Cucumber Battle too? There'll be no stopping Squire Percy then."

"And then what's Griselda and me to do?" Tom Sharp (Mistress Griselda's husband and the village constable, she had explained) arrived with a younger man, both trembling with fury. Tom Sharp looked as though he was usually a mild man, but today his calm had deserted him.

"Whoever wins the Cucumber Battle," he moaned, "Squire Percy will still be turning us out of our cottage. Wants to sell all the cottages in the village and most of the land on the estate. No more renting, he says, knowing we don't have the money to buy. No cucumbers going to stop that, are they, Sam?" He turned to his companion.

"Right, Tom,"

Sam Carter had a grievance. "Gave me the order of the boot, did Squire Percy. Said I was no gardener, the cucumbers were too small. No strength in them, he said. That means no job, no roof over our heads. And the wife with a babe on the way."

Tom Sharp, Sam Carter, and Farmer Jacob Brockway, as Mistress Griselda introduced them, weren't the only villagers with a grievance. It was all too clear to Auguste that the trouble Mistress Griselda had foretold was arriving all too quickly. The jubilant Mincing Magna villagers were enjoying the fruits of what Auguste hoped would be a premature victory with mugs of beer, while their Little Mincing counterparts were licking their wounds with a chant that was far from friendly:

> "Squire Percy
> Shows no mercy
> Bring on the hearse
> To the devil goes old Squire Perce."

Auguste shivered. This was no jolly country festival; there was definite menace in their sinister chorus. Whatever the outcome of the Battle of the Cucumbers, there was indeed going to be trouble.

Initially he had been enthusiastic when Sir John had asked him to center this evening's banquet at the manor on the cucumber. Auguste had long thought that the cucumber was too often ignored, despite the magical possibilities it presented for mankind. In early times it was classified as being under the influence of the moon. It was a mysterious herb that could both cool and cure as well as delight the palate, and he had been full of enthusiasm at Sir John's proposal. Sir John had omitted to mention to him, however, that cucumbers were also to be used as a weapon of war prior to the banquet, although not, Auguste hoped, the same cucumbers.

Sir John, an erudite man, had explained that, centuries ago, the lord of both Little Mincing Manor and that of Mincing Magna, having imbibed too much of the local wine, had foolishly handed over the lordship of the latter to his rival in a game of chess, which he had lost. The only condition he had made was that, should his rival have no son to inherit Mincing Magna, it would revert to the lordship of Little Mincing. For centuries the squires of Mincing Magna had duly produced the required heir, but so far neither Percival Thorn-Hawking or indeed Sir John Abbot-Smith had a son. The Battle of the Cucumbers had first been celebrated annually to remind the Thorn-Hawking family of its delicate position, which had by now been enshrined in law. However, as the years passed, the battle had come to have more pressing motivations, such as the fight for Stickleback Pond, which together with the River Dollop was central to the economic vitality of Little Mincing.

"Do the two squires fight it out between them?" Auguste asked Mistress Griselda.

"No. Each of them has two knights fighting with him," she replied. "My Tom and Sam Carter are fighting with old Squire Percy, and Sir John's brother Charles is with him—"

"And I'm fighting for Sir John too," Farmer Brockway snarled. "What's going to happen to my farm without Stickleback?"

"Best fight well, Jacob," Griselda said darkly.

"If Squire Percy wins the battle, does he keep both the pond and river?" Auguste asked, appalled.

"Not for long, if Tom and Jacob Brockway can help it, or Sam Carter. Sam's going to have a word with Mr. Charles, hoping to get a job at the manor now Squire Percy's given him the boot, but he won't stand much chance. Who wants vegetable gardeners if there ain't no water?"

Auguste looked inside the tent where the contestants were gathering and saw Sam inside, already talking to Mr. Charles. They were the only two of the six contestants not wearing their chain mail hoods over their heads as yet, although all six had donned tabards. Auguste blinked. Tabards and chain mail? This was getting stranger by the minute. They were taking this Cucumber Battle very seriously. Auguste had never tried swinging a cucumber at anybody and so could only guess at the cucumber's sturdiness as a weapon, but to him the only point in its favor seemed to be that it was unlikely to cause any major harm (except to the cucumbers).

The level of noise outside the tent had died down now, but the villagers seemed to be divided into two groups; their children were playing together regardless of their parents' loyalties. Inside the tent, though, the noise level was rising, and Auguste waited in trepidation to find out what would happen next.

"They're ready!" Mistress Griselda's doom-laden voice announced as she peered inside.

The six men trooped out in silence, clutching their cucumbers, all now with their chain mail hoods in place, which had the effect of obscuring their identities. A wise precaution, Auguste considered, as tenants might be lashing out at their own squires. Four of the belligerent forces wore blue tabards, the other two red. The latter, Auguste presumed, were Sir John and the unloved Squire Percy, although it was hard to tell who was who as they were of much the same build. As a result, they looked like Mr. Lewis Carroll's Tweedledum and Tweedledee, each clutching his cucumber, ready for battle, while the crowd murmured insults. Auguste could hear that chant again:

"Bring on the hearse
To the devil goes old Squire Perce."

The six men were accompanied by a much jollier-looking man, without a tabard, who carried a box of cucumbers. The reserve weapons? Auguste wondered.

"That's Jack Trudy, the miller," Mistress Griselda explained. "He's

"Lift your cucumbers," he shouted. *"Fight!"*

Auguste could hardly bear to watch, but, as Mistress Griselda had pushed him right to the front of the crowd, he had no choice. These cucumbers, he thought wistfully, would have made a superb cucumber ketchup with wine, anchovy and spices, Mrs. Rundell's great recipe of ninety years ago. Mix in a little cream and *voilà*, the perfect accompaniment to fish, or veal, or poultry. Both good by themselves, but add one to the other and there is perfection.

The battle began slowly between the two red-tabarded men, Squire Percy and Sir John, and as they clapped their cucumbers together, the other four contestants awaited their opportunity.

"Who wins?" Auguste asked, in a valiant effort to ignore the fact that the cucumbers were suffering.

Mistress Griselda didn't seem to know the answer. "The first one to knock a cucumber out of the other's hand has the advantage," she offered rather obviously.

Tweedledum and Tweedledee had been twisting round each other at close quarters so quickly that it was now even harder to sort out who was who, but Auguste winced as the first cucumber was knocked flying. That was immaterial though, because as its owner turned to seize another, a blue-tabarded man decided to join the battle.

"Avaunt," he yelled, as he struck out with his cucumber, and immediately the other three followed suit. As far as Auguste could tell, they were all attacking at close quarters one of the red-tabarded men, who was cowering under the assault. Fighting technique varied, he observed. One of the contestants was using a two-handed approach with his cucumber, perhaps for stability; another favored a left-handed attack, and some a right-handed. Technique didn't seem to matter as all six men were now in a communal scrum on the floor, grappling, as far as he could see, with whomever was nearest. There was no way of telling whether each was fighting for his own village or just bent on bashing someone up with a cucumber. The real Tweedledum and Tweedledee would have fought more elegantly, Auguste decided, watching the heaving mass of bodies, all too aware that among them were the soon-to-be-homeless village constable and Sam Carter, and the disgruntled Farmer Brockway. The course of the battle in general was unclear to him, but it was all too clear that the English were even more strange than he had realized.

"Cucumbers are being knocked out of their hands, but they still go on fighting," he pointed out to Mistress Griselda, completely at sea.

Her eyes were fixed on the battle, but she did offer some more guidance. "If they lose a cucumber, they're allowed to get another, up to a total of three. The side that has no cucumbers left loses."

"But how can they tell who to hit?" He received no answer to this.

"Lay down your cucumbers," roared Jack the miller.

So the battle was over. But who had won? It made no sense, Auguste thought, as he watched five men painfully scrambling to their feet.

Five? One, he saw with apprehension, was not moving, despite a kick from one of the contestants. He wore a red tabard and lay face-down.

What was this? Auguste's stomach lurched. The man must be hurt. A terrible fear seized him as he ran to the man's side, with Mistress Griselda close behind him.

"Trouble's here," she cried.

Bring on the hearse. Auguste shuddered as a crowd began to gather around them. No one moved, just stared down at the motionless man. He nerved himself to kneel at the man's side and feel for a pulse, but there was none. Gathering his courage, he turned the man over and horror struck with full force.

"It's Sir John," he whispered unbelievingly.

A screech from Mistress Griselda. "That's the wrong man!"

***

The wrong man? Auguste clutched at the words, still trying to grapple with them some time later as he watched the Sevenoaks police cordoning off the stage and the area around it. *Sacre bleu*, what was he doing here? He should be far away, not here in the Kentish countryside that looked so fair and yet produced such horrors. There was little doubt that Sir John had been murdered. The probable weapon—a sharpened tent peg that had been used as a stiletto—had fallen to one side and blood had covered his chest. Auguste had seen violent death before, so where did his duty lie now? At Little Mincing Manor, where Sir John had so looked forward to his victory banquet, or here where he might help?

Even as that unwelcome thought crossed his mind, Mistress Griselda came hurrying up to him, clearly very agitated. "They're going to lock up my Tom, Mr. Didier. Him being one of the suspects and a policeman too. They think he killed Sir John. As if he would. They're sending for some inspector at Scotland Yard."

Relief flooded over Auguste. "Perhaps that is my friend Chief Inspector Egbert Rose. He will find out the truth. You saw a rose in your crystal ball."

She paled. "So I did. I knew trouble was coming, but I didn't know it was for my Tom. And it's not even Squire Percy dead," she wailed, "but dear old Sir John."

Auguste wavered. Should he leave this to Egbert Rose to pursue? No, when people were in shock, they did not always guard their tongues. "Squire Percy was the *right* man to be murdered?" he asked cautiously.

"Yes," she replied vehemently. "And a thousand of us in Mincing Magna would say so, and in Little Mincing too. There's scores of us suffering under him like Jacob Brockway is here with the loss of Stickleback. And where are Tom and I to go now Squire Percy's still lording it? And Sam Carter too."

Auguste sensed he must grasp this nettle quickly. If the wrong man had been killed from the murderer's point of view, then Egbert would need to know about this. As there had only been two men in red tabards, mistaken identity was indeed a possibility, even a likelihood, given what he had learned about Squire Percy, whereas Sir John was widely popular. But regardless of the murderer's target, the gristle in the mincer—given that it must have been a preplanned murder because of the use of the tent peg—was, why had the murderer chosen such a time and place to carry out his terrible deed? With so many onlookers and so much chance of his stabbing the wrong man, it seemed a strange place to choose.

"There's Tom coming now." Mistress Griselda was crying with relief, pointing to where Sam Carter and Farmer Brockway were emerging from one of the tents. She rushed up to them and Auguste followed.

"They let you go then?" she asked her husband.

"No. We've been told to wait in the dressing tent till this Scotland Yard bloke arrives. There's a copper there to make sure we do."

Auguste seized the moment. "What happened when you were fighting on the stage floor?" he began. "Was there any sign that Sir John had been stabbed before he fell, in the seconds during which Sir John and Squire Percy were fighting alone?"

Tom Sharp and his wife looked at each other, perhaps longing to say yes, he thought, but hesitating in case the others disagreed, or perhaps deciding the dressing tent was preferable to interrogation here.

Sam broke the short silence. "I reckon it was when Sir John turned to get another cucumber and Squire Percy saw his chance. Quick stab sent him reeling and we all fell on each other. After all, it was only a bit of fun," he added hastily.

Tom and Jacob Brockway instantly agreed. "But he could have been stabbed when we was all on the floor," Tom added conscientiously.

"Jacob here said we should all have a go at Squire Percy," Sam said, until
he saw the others' expressions. "As I said, just a bit of fun," he added quickly.

Farmer Brockway didn't deny it though. "Mistress Griselda says
you know this Scotland Yard bloke, so what's all this about?" he asked
Auguste suspiciously.

"I do know him, and he's a very good detective," he replied firmly.

"How's he going to find out what's been going on? He don't know us. You
going to tell him?"

"He'll talk to everybody," Auguste replied.

"We could any of us slipped in that tent peg good and proper, but there's
no proving who did," Sam said belligerently.

"Weren't none of us," Jacob Brockway growled. He seemed anxious to
leave them, Auguste noticed.

"Someone did it," he pointed out.

Now he could see the reason that Farmer Brockway was already setting
off for the dressing tent. Mr. Charles, accompanied by Squire Percy himself,
Auguste deduced, was approaching them. Tom and Sam now saw them, and
they too made a quick departure. Squire Percy, whether the "right" target or
not, was not to be trifled with.

Squire Percy, although the same build as Sir John, bore no resemblance to
him otherwise. "You're the cook, eh? What are you doing, meddling here? Get
about your business."

"He can't, Mr. Thorn-Hawking," Mr. Charles said quietly. He looked ashen
and no wonder, Auguste thought. "I should explain, Monsieur Didier, that
I regret the manor banquet cannot go ahead this evening. Your fee will of
course be paid."

"My sympathy, Mr. Charles," Auguste said, ignoring his companion's
orders. "A terrible blow for you."

"Indeed," Mr. Charles replied. "A terrible and inexplicable mistake."

Auguste was startled. Mistake? Did the grieving Mr. Charles also think the
wrong man had been killed?

Perhaps Mr. Charles realized the implications of his statement. "An
accident, of course," he said hastily. "The peg must have slipped out of
place somehow."

Auguste accepted this unlikely explanation politely, but Squire Percy did
not bother with courtesy and consideration.

"Accident? Balderdash," he snorted. "Poor old Sir John, though. Good man
that. But this changes nothing, Abbot-Smith. I'm still selling up the estate
with the Dollop and Stickleback and there's nothing to stop me. I'm honoring

the agreement our ancestors made, though. The house will come to you after I'm dead, but that won't be for a long time yet. You're welcome to it. It's falling down."

Auguste made his way back to the manor kitchens. The preparations for the banquet looked as forlorn as Mr. Charles had. He surveyed them gloomily. It had been hard to think of a dessert including cucumbers, but then he had had an inspiration based on a cucumber mousse. It would be wasted now. Even worse was that the cucumber ketchup would never be united with the fish he had planned to accompany it. Together they made a superb dish.

"Admiring your handiwork, Auguste?" Egbert Rose had crept unnoticed into the kitchen and came up behind him. "They told me I'd find you here. Might have known you'd be mixed up with a case like this. You surpass yourself. Your idea about that Battle of the Cucumbers, was it?"

"No, Egbert," Auguste said sadly. "I was forced to watch it though, and look what a tragedy took place."

"You *watched* it? Then tell me about it. I've heard the story from a dozen other people, but I'd welcome your account of it."

Auguste obliged, beginning with the crystal ball and Mistress Griselda.

"Village eccentric, is she?" Egbert asked.

"The wife of Tom Sharp, the village policeman."

"Ah yes, one of the suspects. Bad do, that, being a constable. They all had a chance to get hold of a tent peg and sharpen it up, so what about their motivations for killing Sir John?"

"None at all," Auguste replied. "But, Egbert, Mistress Griselda believed that the wrong man was killed. That Sir John was murdered after being mistaken for Squire Percy."

"Possible?"

"Yes." Auguste explained why. "Tom Sharp, Sam Carter, and Farmer Brockway had every reason to wish Squire Percy permanently out of their lives."

Egbert consulted his notes. "What about Charles Abbot-Smith, the victim's brother? I gather he inherits the estate."

"He would gain nothing from Sir John's death, as he would be inheriting an impoverished village with more problems than anyone would wish to cope with. Nor would he gain from Squire Percy's death, as the estate would have reverted to Sir John, not him."

"Ruling him out, that means there are no motives for killing Sir John but three for killing Squire Percy. That's your "wrong man killed" theory. Tell me more about this scuffle on the floor."

He listened intently as Auguste went through the story again with every detail he could remember. Then he grunted. "So any of them could have stabbed him, including Squire Percy."

"But he had no reason to kill Sir John either," Auguste pointed out. "With Mr. Charles alive to inherit, the estate would go to him and Squire Percy would be no better off." He hesitated. "I do not see how anyone could have stabbed Sir John while wielding a cucumber in the middle of a cucumber fight."

Egbert Rose sighed. "Talking of that, any food left over for this evening, Auguste? I have a feeling I'll need strengthening up."

Auguste brightened up. "There is a great deal of food left over. The banquet was planned around the cucumber. Both fish and veal," he added eagerly, "together with a splendid cucumber ketchup to make the dish complete."

Egbert Rose grunted. "Fancy a meal at the pub instead? Nasty indigestible things, cucumbers."

Auguste remained silent, with difficulty.

***

When he reached the King's Head an hour later, there was no sign of Egbert Rose, but there was—to his amazement—a group of laughing, cheering men, including a beaming Constable Tom Sharp, Farmer Brockway waving a beer jug, and Sam Carter, who seemed to be performing a clog dance in huge gardening boots.

"What are you celebrating?" Auguste asked in bewilderment.

"They've arrested him, that's what, Didier," roared Farmer Brockway.

"Who?" Egbert had made no mention of this.

"Squire Percy," shouted Sam. "It was him killed Sir John."

Auguste could not make head or tail of this. "I thought you believed Squire Percy should have been the victim."

"Ah well, we may have got that wrong," Sam chortled.

"But why arrest him?" Auguste asked.

"Don't go upsetting things, Mr. Didier," Tom Sharp said anxiously. "My missus just got it wrong about the wrong man being croaked. She was upset, like, being fond of Sir John."

"Mistress Griselda must have thought," Sam chimed in eagerly, "that we might have wanted to croak Squire Percy because of him not wanting my services no longer. Now he's been put away, Mincing Magna's going to need me back."

"And I'll be keeping my cottage too," Tom Sharp chortled.

"And Little Mincing will be getting its water back," roared Farmer Brockway, tipping the last of his beer down his throat. "All gone well, ain't it?"

Except for Sir John, Auguste thought sadly. And why had Egbert said nothing to him about Squire Percy's arrest? It was true that Squire Percy had the best chance to kill Sir John, and that Auguste had seen for himself that either he or the other red-tabarded man seemed to be reeling from a blow which might have been the tent peg going in, but he had no motive.

Something was surely amiss with this recipe.

***

It was another hour before Chief Inspector Rose arrived at the King's Head, took one look at its noisy celebrating customers, and hired a private room for himself and Auguste.

"And I've ordered a nice steak and fried potatoes for both of us," he informed Auguste.

"Splendid." Auguste did his best to sound enthusiastic. "Egbert, I'm told you've arrested Squire Percy. Has he confessed?"

"Not yet."

"He won't."

"Know that for a fact, do you?"

"It is a matter of logic," Auguste declared. "Even though he was in the best position to kill Sir John, he had no reason to do so."

"Wrong. Squire Percy had very good reason. Mr. Charles told us a different story."

Auguste was taken aback. "You believe he was working with Mr. Charles to obtain both village estates together?"

Egbert Rose laughed. "I hadn't thought of that one. No, it wasn't a put-up job. Squire Percy wanted to sell off a large chunk of his land and cottages, but he needed Sir John's permission to do so and he couldn't get it."

Auguste hadn't known that, and it took him aback. "He must have assumed Mr. Charles would agree."

"No. Squire Percy knew perfectly well that he couldn't do so. Back some years ago, Sir John put that clause about seeking permission into the deeds, but whoever drew it up made a howler. He put Sir John's name only. It didn't apply to his successors, so with Sir John dead, Squire Percy could do what he darn well liked with the cottages and land. Only the manor house would revert to Little Mincing. How's that for a motive for killing Sir John? Squire Percy wanted to sell that land and make his fortune."

Auguste surveyed the meal before him, which suddenly looked even less appetizing. "So you believe this could be a case of the right man being killed, in the murderer's view?"

"It is. You may be back with the wrong man theory, Auguste, but I'm sticking with Squire Percy."

***

Auguste walked back to the manor through the field that had so recently been the scene of murder. The wrong man or the right man? He was thinking hard about that when his foot struck a discarded cucumber lying on the grass and he picked it up out of sheer pity. How ridiculous to think that way, he told himself. It was merely a battered, inedible cucumber. It wasn't evidence of a crime. No tent peg could have been hidden within it to stab Sir John, because buried within the cucumber it wouldn't have sufficient force when it struck, and the murderer would need to act quickly. Yes, this murder had been carefully planned indeed. Six men fighting. How could any one of them be singled out as the murderer?

He was about to lay the cucumber down again when he gave some more thought to it. How would the murderer have held it when he had the tent peg to maneuver too? Auguste gripped the cucumber in his right hand and looked at it: four fingers were on the right side of the cucumber with his thumb on the left. No chance of carrying the tent peg in the same hand. Remembering what he had seen in the battle, he transferred the cucumber to his left hand, and this time his fingers were on the left with the thumb to their right. Did that make any difference?

In the Battle of the Cucumbers, he had observed different methods of attack once the men were fighting on the floor, and he summoned up his memory of it. Three of the men had reason to kill Squire Percy, one of whom killed the wrong man. Did he just carry the tent peg with no cucumber, or were the six men brandishing cucumbers? No, all the men had to have cucumbers, otherwise it would surely have been noticeable that one was missing.

He began to think very hard about the wrong man theory.

***

Dawn found Auguste knocking on the door of the King's Head, to the annoyance of the innkeeper. Grumbling about Scotland Yard and its demands, he led Auguste to a disgruntled Egbert, who was consuming a boiled egg with no great pleasure, it seemed.

"Let's get this straight." He glared at Auguste after listening to his story. "You want me to line up all the suspects, including Squire Percy, give them all a glass of beer and see if there's a left-handed killer amongst them."

"Yes, Egbert."

"Because you think the killer was wielding the cucumber in his left hand."

"No, Egbert."

"What then?"

"A left-handed murderer would have been holding the cucumber in his right hand and the tent peg in the left."

"What difference does that make?"

"It means none of the five suspects would have been waving the cucumber with his left hand."

"And you saw that one of them was doing that?"

"Yes, Egbert."

"Could you oblige me by telling me who?"

"No, Egbert."

Egbert Rose sighed.

"I suggest that if you test Squire Percy with a teacup in prison, he will pick it up with his right hand," Auguste said meekly.

***

"Right-handed. The lot of them," Egbert Rose duly reported to Auguste after summoning him to Scotland Yard some days later.

"Including Squire Percy?"

"Yes. But it tells us nothing, Auguste, save that one of them murdered Sir John. If it's not Squire Percy who made no mistake about killing the right man, then I agree we'll have to find which of those three killed the wrong man."

As Auguste rose to leave the room, he was thinking desperately once more about the three suspects for the wrong man theory, who were all nevertheless rejoicing at what the "mistake" had resulted in. Wrong man, right man: two theories but in practice coming back to the same outcome. Unlike his cucumber ketchup combining with the fish or veal to make a superb dish though, the outcome of this theory had been a terrible one. He stopped short.

"*Egbert!*" he yelled racing back into Egbert's office. "*Cucumbers!*"

"What about them?" Rose growled.

"Wrong man theory, right man theory. It was the *right* one. The murderer's motivation was to make one dish, cucumber and fish."

"Pardon?"

"Stage one: kill Sir John," Auguste hurled at him. "Stage two: wait for Squire Percy to be found guilty of the murder and sentenced to death. Outcome achieved. He would inherit both Mincing Magna and Little Mincing. Only Mr. Charles had a motive for wanting the death of both his brother and Squire Percy."

Egbert Rose thought and nodded. "That's what I call a digestible case, Auguste. Despite the cucumbers."

Gracie Saves the World

Michael Bracken & Sandra Murphy

I shrieked as the tepid water turned shockingly cold. I managed to step out of the shower without tripping, but as I bent to turn off the taps, shampoo ran into my eyes and made it impossible to see. Most of the time, counting to sixty and turning the water back on would return temperatures suitable for a final rinse. Not that morning. That morning there was no water at all.

I'd found trying to dress in the damp bathroom made it impossible to drag dry clothes over wet skin. I wiped the shampoo from my eyes, wrapped myself in a towel, and escaped from the bathroom steaminess. My efficiency's one big window opens onto the fire escape, and it stays shut no matter the temperature. For privacy, I dry off and dress behind a three-part thrift shop screen I lugged up four flights of stairs.

I was glad to work as a mechanic instead of being stuck in a secretarial pool. No garter belt, stockings, or drawing a line down the backs of my legs with cocoa powder to simulate a seam because silk and nylon were needed to make parachutes for our troops in Europe and the Pacific. As a mechanic, a job I could never have gotten before the war, despite my experience maintaining and flying Uncle Jed's crop duster, bib overalls with my red, white, and blue ankle socks was acceptable attire. My grandmother used to tell me, "Stand still long enough and the entire world will pass you by," and it seemed to be passing me faster in the city than it ever had on the farm.

Because there was still shampoo in my hair, I would have to cover it with a bandanna. Luckily, there's a beauty shop at the plant, and I could stop in during my lunch hour. I wanted to look nice. My friend Celia and I were going to the USO to dance with servicemen, in hopes of cheering them up. Even though I would miss my bus if I didn't hurry, I took the time to pick out my best dress and stepped around the screen to dig out my fancy shoes, which I had stashed under the bed.

I was fastening the left shoulder strap of my overalls when I saw a pair of shoes. Men's shoes. On my bed. With a man wearing them.

My screams brought Stella, the neighbors, and the police.

Uniformed officers pounded up the fire escape, guns drawn. The first cop through the open window scanned the room, and the second unlocked the door for more who flooded the room from the hallway.

Stella, her tow-headed grandson Bobby, and other neighbors crowded the landing, trying to see what had brought the police.

I was shoved aside by one officer and pulled into the hallway by another. An unseemly pat-down proved embarrassing as well as that I was unarmed. Thank goodness for bib overalls.

I spent a good portion of time sitting on the stairs while the photographer's flash lit up my apartment every thirty seconds, recording the dead man's likeness from every conceivable angle. I had to move when they transported the body.

Stella sidled up to me. "Only answer what they ask, don't volunteer nothin'."

"No talking!" The cop on the door shot a dirty look our way.

I felt warm breath on my ear. "How often do you have men in your room?"

I whirled around to get my first look at Detective Marsden. I hadn't seen anyone so handsome off the movie screen, ever. He was tall, with black hair pomaded into place, a hint of beard stubble despite it being barely breakfast time, and hazel eyes that drew me into his penetrating gaze.

Stella jabbed me in the ribs to break the spell. I said, "I *never* have men in my room."

"Never?" he asked. "You're a pretty gal and—"

"Gracie never has nobody in her room," Stella interrupted. "She's a good girl."

"Might be more believable if you weren't covered in blood." Marsden's eyes scanned my body head to toe. "You got some on your face. Got pretty close to him, huh?"

"He was trying to speak, so I leaned in, slipped, and landed on him."

"What did he say?" Marsden looked around at his men, like my answer didn't matter.

"He coughed blood onto my face, and then he was gone." I squirmed. The aroma of drying blood in the hot and humid hallway was getting to me. "Can I change clothes and wash up now?"

"Not until I'm done. Wait here." Marsden walked off.

Thirty long, boring minutes later, after the photographer and half the uniforms had filed down the stairs, he returned.

"How'd you know the dead guy?" Marsden scribbled in his little notebook.

"I didn't."

Stella stuck her nose as far into my place as the flatfoot guarding the doorway would allow. "You sure you never seen him, Gracie?" She turned toward Marsden. "That's Mr. Rory. He has the room right over Gracie's."

"I know who he is. I recognized Second-Story Rory the moment I laid eyes on him." Marsden sighed and ordered one of the uniforms to take Stella's statement.

After Marsden and I were alone, I asked, "Second-Story Rory?"

Marsden answered my question with one of his own. "How could you not know him if he lived upstairs?"

"I heard him walking around at night, but I never saw him," I said.

"So, why'd you let him in?"

"I didn't! The door was deadbolted, with the chain on. He came in the window. Look, there's a handprint on the glass."

"Maybe it's yours."

"That print's the size of a ham!" I held up my hand. "Not mine."

His questions continued, as if I hadn't spoken, and after a bit he finally let me phone my employer.

My boss wasn't happy when I requested the day off, but he relented when I told him about the dead man in my bed. I spent that night and the next few on Stella's couch before the police let me back into my apartment. Stella helped me scrub the place and gave me the late Mrs. Krueger's mattress to replace my blood-soaked one. Friends and coworkers, Celia especially, made me repeat the story about finding Mr. Rory.

Celia rescheduled our dance plans, so that Friday I showered as soon as I returned home from work. I put on my best dress but hesitated before stepping from behind the screen, afraid there might be another dead man waiting for me. The bed was empty. I put on my dancing shoes, did my hair and makeup, and drew a thin seam up the backs of my legs. I'd just finished when I heard a knock at my door.

"Coming, Celia! You've got to check my seams to make sure they're straight."

Instead of Celia, I found Detective Marsden on the landing. He whistled softly. "You clean up pretty good, Miss O'Malley," he said. His gaze gave me goosebumps, a combination of excitement and anticipation. "Going somewhere?"

"Dancing," I said. "My friend Celia, from work, is due any minute."

"You like to dance?"

"Haven't danced since Miss Bernice's School for Young Ladies when I was thirteen," I said. "We're going to the USO. It's my first time, but she's a regular.

We would have gone last week, but, you know, Mr. Rory. It didn't seem appropriate, and you wouldn't let me get my dress and shoes."

"You don't need a fancy outfit to attract attention." He smiled. "You got mine when you had on bloody overalls."

"Did I? Hard to tell, what with you accusing me of murder and of being the sort of woman who would invite a man to her bed."

"You were in a locked room with a dead man, so I felt obligated to question your involvement."

"Convince me I'm not a suspect, and I might be able to forgive you."

"You are not a suspect." He smiled, and a dimple showed. I caught my breath. "Do you think after you practice on those poor, unfortunate soldiers, I might be able to take you dancing?"

I felt my face grow warm, so I changed the subject.

"I don't expect this was a personal call," I said. "Why are you here, Detective?"

"Call me Bill. I do have other questions for you, Miss O'Malley."

"Gracie."

"Gracie," he repeated with a smile. "I do have other questions for you, Gracie."

"Shoot," I said before realizing how inappropriate that word might be, given how the detective and I had met.

"We gave your apartment a pretty thorough going-over—"

"I noticed," I told him. "Particularly my lingerie."

"Did you find anything, anything at all, that Second-Story Rory might have left in your apartment?"

The only thing Rory ever left me was some loose plaster on my floor. I didn't know what he did in the weeks before he died, but when I heard him moving around overhead, I always found plaster dust in the northwest corner of my room. I didn't think that's what the detective wanted to know, so I shook my head.

"Nothing at all?"

I shook my head again.

Before Detective Marsden—Bill—could ask another question, Celia arrived. We heard her high heels tap up the last flight of stairs. Bill turned, and I saw Celia's eyes open wide in surprise.

Following introductions, Bill turned back to me. "I may drop in again, Miss O'Malley," he said, now that we had an audience. "I have a *lot* of questions."

"Any time, Detective," I said.

We stared into each other's eyes for a moment longer than necessary, and I hoped what I saw in his gaze was reflected in mine. He turned to go, but looked over his shoulder to say, "By the way, they're straight, those seams."

As she watched the detective descend the stairs, Celia whispered, "I would let that man interrogate me any time."

***

The USO was located a block from the train station, easily accessible for soldiers traveling to report for duty. Celia and I took the streetcar.

As we approached the front door of the USO, I hesitated. "I'm not a dancer," I said. "Maybe I can just pass out doughnuts and coffee."

"Don't be silly." Celia patted my arm. "A lot of these men can't dance a lick. The memory of a warm place, good music, and pretty girls will mean a lot when they're on the front lines. Now, put on a big smile and let's go in."

Celia was right. Some of the men danced non-stop, while others talked to the junior hostesses or leaned against the wall and watched. My plan to hand out doughnuts and fill coffee cups lasted only a few minutes. I was swept onto the dance floor by a young man from Omaha. Then came Chicago, Peoria, and Duluth. After that, I lost track. My feet were glad when the band took a fifteen-minute break.

Celia brought me a doughnut and coffee. "I saw you with all those boys," she said. "Isn't this fun? Being questioned by Detective Marsden has given you confidence. You should find a dead guy in your bed more often."

"Once was more than enough, thank you."

"Excuse me," said a dark-haired woman standing near us. "I didn't mean to eavesdrop, but did you say you found a dead man in your bed?"

Celia, having already heard the story several times, launched into a colorful version. I slipped away. A few minutes later, the trombone player belted out a long, warbling note to let us know the break was over. Omaha was about to lead me back onto the dance floor when the evening's hostess caught my attention. Celia stood beside her, staring at the floor.

"Thanks so much for having me, ma'am," I told her as soon as we were close enough to hear one another talk. "This has been more fun than I'd even hoped."

"Miss O'Malley, as you are well aware, we strive to have the highest caliber of women for our soldiers to meet during their limited free time." She held out my paperwork. She'd written "Rejected" in big red letters.

"Rejected? I was cleared weeks ago. What's the problem?" I looked at Celia, but she glanced away.

"You've been questioned by the police. In the matter of a *murder*. And the dead man was found in your...bed." Her mouth puckered so tightly, I wondered how she got the words out. "This is unacceptable. We cannot expose our soldiers to such behavior. I'll have to ask you to leave. Immediately."

"If she goes, I go." Celia grabbed my hand. "She's my friend, and she's done nothing wrong."

"No, Celia, stay," I insisted. I looked at the hostess. "I had *nothing* to do with that man's death."

I left without looking back, unsure what to do next. Once outside, I stopped to catch my breath, fairly shaking with anger.

"Excuse me, miss?" A good-looking blond airman, a lieutenant, stood about six feet away. "Are you leaving? I'd just gotten the courage to ask you to dance."

"I appreciate the offer," I said, "but I'll not be allowed back inside."

He looked at me expectantly.

"It's a long story."

"Well then, it's a good thing we can hear the music from here." He held out his arms. When I didn't step into them, he continued, "Please, miss. I bribed the band leader to play a few slow tunes. It's the only way I know to dance."

"How much was the bribe?"

"I gave him two dollars."

Two dollars? I only made thirty a week. "Then I guess we'd better dance, Lieutenant."

"Nathaniel," he said, introducing himself. "Lieutenant Nathaniel Caldwell."

Later, we sat in the diner across the street and talked about flying until the dance broke up and Celia stepped outside. When I stood to go, the lieutenant paid for our coffee and walked me across the street.

After I thanked him for our dance and conversation, he said, "I'm sure we'll meet again, Miss O'Malley."

As the lieutenant walked away, Celia looked at me with envy. "Gracie, I don't know what's come over you, but if you figure it out, teach me."

***

Celia was right. Despite being surrounded every day with posters proclaiming "Loose Lips Sink Ships" and the news a week earlier about a wealthy businessman accused of leaking secrets, my newfound confidence caused me to take chances with men that I never would have before. Several times I almost let slip what it was I actually do.

I'm a mechanic but not the kind who changes oil and tires on Jeeps. Thanks to Uncle Jed, who taught me to fly his crop duster and helped me get my pilot's license, I work on big transport planes. Reading about the Women Airforce Service Pilots during my breaks made me want to do more than repair the planes.

Marsden took me to dinner several times, at a place where the waiters all knew him. White tablecloths, wine with dinner, butter and cream sauces— didn't restaurants have rationing coupons too? There was always a dance floor. Marsden held me a bit closer than was acceptable, weakening my resolve every time we were together. Frankly, my mind cautioned me to slow down, but my body had other ideas. Since neither of us could talk about our jobs, we kept the conversation light, except when thoughts of Rory intruded.

At the apartment building's front door after our third date, he kissed me. He pulled me into his arms, and I didn't even try to resist when he planted his lips on mine. I don't have much experience with that kind of thing and hoped I did it right. From the grin on his face, I guess he was happy with it. If Stella's grandson Bobby hadn't arrived right then, it might have been more than a kiss. Marsden said, "I'll see you soon, Gracie," and left.

Bobby chattered as we went into the building, never noticing I was still weak in the knees.

Despite my woeful lack of experience with men, I enjoyed the lieutenant's attention too. Our dates weren't so fancy. We talked and ate at the diner, danced between the tables after, to the music from tabletop jukeboxes. Sometimes the waitresses joined in.

It was my first romantic dilemma, and I wasn't sure I wanted anything to change. To distract myself, I decided to find out just what Second-Story Rory had been up to before he died on my bed.

***

I expected to pick the lock on Rory's door with a hairpin and was surprised to find the door open. Inside, Stella eyed the mess the police had left behind. She saw me and said, "I don't know what they were looking for, but them coppers done a job on this place."

A small sofa was upended, the mattress tilted off the bed, and Rory's meager wardrobe was scattered on the floor. Every drawer and cabinet had been emptied. Only the carpet remained intact. The place smelled of days-old food set on the table and forgotten.

Rory's place, a duplicate of mine, was a large room that served as bedroom, living room, and kitchen all in one. Unlike other converted apartment buildings, each tenant in our building had a small private bath. I saw a shaving brush, soap, and safety razor dumped in the sink. No sign of spare blades. Cheap cologne, nail clippers, and tweezers had landed in the trash can.

"You want help?"

"Sure, could use some," Stella said. "Get rid of the food before it attracts rats."

I shuddered. The last thing I needed was rats.

Empty beer bottles, moldy bread, and a stale hunk of cheese large enough to be black-market goods told of an unmarried man with doubtful scruples. Two button-front dress shirts, two pairs of chinos, pockets turned inside out, and a pair of wingtip brogues in the small closet, half a dozen boxer shorts, undershirts, and paired black socks in the dresser.

Stella put the dead man's clothes in a box for Lonnie, a sporadically employed photographer living on the third floor. When the apartment was as clean as we could manage, she invited me downstairs for coffee.

"I really hate chicory," I said. "I so want a cup of good coffee."

"I don't know how they decide what to ration, don't make any sense." Stella set mismatched cups on the table next to her nearly empty book of ration stamps. "I want sugar and cream in mine, but I'm out of sugar and the cream's gone bad. What I wouldn't give for a good piece of chocolate cake to go with it."

I sighed at the thought. "Maybe we can pool our stamps next month and bake a cake to share."

"Let's do that," Stella said as she filled our cups and settled onto the chair opposite mine. "So tell me what's happening with that handsome copper who's sweet on you."

I suspected I was blushing when I said, "Bill—Detective Marsden—is just doing his job. He's investigating a murder and he has a lot of questions."

"Sure, sure." Stella grinned. "Does he always ask them with his mouth pressed against yours? I saw that kiss. And what was that I heard about you dancing in the street with an Air Force lieutenant?"

"I, uh, well—" I couldn't think what to say, but then in a rush blurted, "I never had a man so interested in me and now two at once! I don't know what to do."

"Enjoy it, Gracie. Just enjoy it." Stella laughed and mercifully let me change the subject.

***

That night Celia went back to the USO while I met Lieutenant Caldwell at the diner across the street.

"Gracie, I admire you. A lot of women wouldn't want to take a job," he said.

"Well, I tried knitting socks, but I think soldiers would consider them a violation of the Geneva Convention. I wish I could do more."

"You can, by paying attention to the people around you. It's hard to know who you can trust these days," he said.

"Are you trustworthy?"

"Oh, yes," he said. "I have a note from my mother saying so."

We had a good laugh. He picked another tune on the jukebox and, as we danced, he dipped me. While I was bent backward, he kissed me. As he pulled me upright, he said, "I can't bring myself to do that in front of Celia."

The waitresses, and even the cook, applauded. I was red-faced, but whether from the kiss or the dip, it was hard to say. Liking two men at once was more difficult than it looked, but I wouldn't change a thing. The lieutenant was one sweet kisser. I was still trying to catch my breath when that night's USO dance ended and Celia joined us in the diner for our trip home.

I was still thinking of the lieutenant's kiss when I opened my apartment door. So it took a moment to register that my apartment bore a strong resemblance to Rory's—before we cleaned.

Clothes were off the hangers, the linings of my shoes removed, book spines slit open, and the tin of cocoa powder I used for stocking seams poured onto the floor. I nearly cried. Cocoa was damn expensive. The only thing intact was the mattress, as if the culprit knew it had been replaced after Rory's death.

***

I called Marsden instead of the precinct.

"I was right all along. Rory did give you something, or why would somebody search your place?" he said after he eyeballed my apartment. His eyes were hard, his voice professional. "There had to be a reason for him to come down the fire escape and die in your apartment."

I had no response.

He grabbed my arms, and I knew he wasn't about to kiss me. "Stop playing games, Gracie. I know what Rory gave you. Where is it?" His grip grew painful. "I need that package. Hand it over!"

I tried to squirm away, but he held me tight, pressed his body against mine and my body back against the wall. "He didn't give me anything. How many times do I have to tell you?"

"Give it to me!" He raised his voice and began to shake me, hitting my head on the wall until I saw pinpoints of light.

"Let me go!" I tried to scream, but his hand covered my mouth before I could make a sound. I bit him. In spite of the pain, he held firm.

"You stupid cow! To think I wasted my time and money buying you dinners and listening to your inane prattle. If that package surfaces, you'd better deliver it to me, unopened, or else." He gave me a final shove and stepped back, breathing hard.

He'd been using me! I tasted blood, whether from my split lip or his bitten hand I don't know, but it made me angry and anger won out over fear. "Or else what?"

"Or else it could be bad for your health." He yanked the door open and rushed down the stairs. The doorknob left a dent in the wall.

Knees weak, I slid to the floor.

Stella found me sitting there, next to the open door.

***

"How could I have been so stupid? I thought he really liked me. He kissed me, danced close, bought me fancy dinners. What was all that for? Some stupid package that doesn't exist?"

Stella had put three spoonfuls of my rationed sugar in my coffee, to ward off shock, she said.

"Thanks for this." My face was wet with tears. "Do you think he meant any of it?"

"Sure, the copper was a good-looking swell, but look at them bruises. And don't your head hurt? What are you going to do about it?" Stella handed me a towel to wipe my face. "You can sit here and cry or do something."

"Do what? Me against a police detective?"

"Well, if it was me and I got treated like you did, there'd be only one answer." Stella nodded as she spoke.

I sat up straighter. "What's that?"

***

We began with the lieutenant. With Stella's encouragement, I called him the next morning and made a dinner date for that evening, hoping to take my mind off what a jerk Marsden had been.

In the hallway later that afternoon, I saw Bobby, Stella's fifteen-year-old grandson. He's small for his age but an eager beaver, especially if there are a few pennies involved. He was torn between wanting the war to end and hoping it wouldn't before he could enlist.

"Bobby, would you like to help me solve a problem?"

"Yes, Miss Gracie, do you need me to run to the store or move some furniture?"

"Let's take a walk." I opened the front door and scanned the sidewalk. "How about the park?"

I bought lemonades from a street vendor and sat on a bench, far enough from other people to not be overheard. "I've been dating an Army Air Force lieutenant. Of course, he can't talk much about his job, but there are things I need to know about him. Could you follow him without being seen?"

"You think he's got another bird?" Bobby slurped his lemonade. "I could find out."

"This is about the war."

"I'd be like a spy?" The kid's eyes lit up.

"Exactly," I said. "You'd have to be careful. This isn't a game. It's serious."

"Somethin' to do with the dead guy?" His face was grave.

"That's what we need to find out."

His chest puffed as he sat up, lemonade forgotten. "I got the moxie for the job. What first?"

"Here's the plan." I asked Bobby to follow the lieutenant after our date that evening and then, the next morning, to tail him to work. It would give me an idea of what the lieutenant's job and intentions really were.

My dinner with the lieutenant went well, but I was suspicious of him after the way Marsden had treated me. Unfortunately, I winced when he took my arm to dance. Before I could stop him, the lieutenant lifted my sleeve and saw the bruises Marsden had left. "What happened? Were you attacked going home? I knew I should have seen you home last night." His concern was touching.

"Nothing to worry about. Let's just have a nice time."

"There's something you're not telling me."

"What I'm not telling you is how much I want to dance," I said, deflecting his attention. "Hold me close and let's dance slow."

He did, and we did, and, after he walked me home, I saw Bobby pick up his tail.

***

Back at the apartment, the dent in the plaster from Marsden's tantrum reminded me of the dust I saw after one of Rory's late nights. I pulled a kitchen chair to the corner and climbed up to inspect the ceiling. There were hairline cracks in the plaster. The chair left me a little short, and a small squeak sent me running for the broom. If there were a rat's nest between my ceiling and Rory's floor, banging the broom around might scare the rats away.

I climbed back onto the chair and raised the broom handle just as I heard a rustling noise. Startled, I stepped back, banging the broom on the ceiling as I toppled off the chair. I landed on my behind, and plaster shards rained down on me.

I tried to catch my breath but only inhaled powdery plaster. Coughing, I looked up to see the damage. Dangling from the newly created hole was a small box. I climbed back up, used the broom handle to dislodge the box, and carried it to my kitchen table. One look inside told me I was in serious trouble.

***

Bobby came to my apartment the next morning and handed me a piece of paper with an address written on it. "Here's where the Loot lives. Following him was a gas."

"Without being seen?" The last thing I wanted was to put Stella's grandson in jeopardy.

"Man, I was like a real gumshoe. Wanna know where he went this morning?" At my nod, he went on, eyes gleaming. "He's like a Fed, only one of the troops."

"He's *what?*"

"Army Intelligence. I talked to one of the dames coming out of the office for lunch and made like I wanted to enlist, told her my buddy said this was the place to talk to somebody about being a cook instead of a grunt. She laughed and told me they're like spies in there. I don't think she was supposed to say that, on account of her friend elbowed her hard and gave her a look."

"I don't suppose she should have, but I'm glad she did." I stood. "Let me think about this. We'll talk in a couple of days. In the meantime, don't go near him or that building. Got it?"

"Copacetic. See you in two." He ran down the hallway as I put the chain on the door.

***

Rory's stash included loose gemstones, a large amount of cash, small engraved metal plates, and a box, formerly used for spare razor blades, now used to store several brown strips of photo negatives.

I took the negatives to Lonnie, the sporadically employed photographer on the third floor. He had converted his bathroom into a darkroom, where he developed film and made his own prints. I knew he would help for a small fee.

I put it out of my mind—until he knocked a couple of hours later and pushed me inside as he closed the door. Before I could protest, he said, "Christopher Columbus, are you trying to get us all killed? Here're your pics. I don't know what it means, and I don't want to. You don't know me, you never met me, got it?" He rushed into the hallway and slammed the door behind him.

A few minutes later, I understood his panic. One of the photos was of a German Nazi ID badge. The picture on it was a familiar face. The name beneath it: Wilhelm Marsden.

I ran for the bathroom and threw up.

***

Once I recovered, I checked again to make sure the door was locked and the chain was on. I ducked behind my dressing screen, like that would help, and spread everything on a small table. I found a black velvet bag I hadn't noticed before. I dumped my little dish of hairpins, tipped the bag, and out came—diamonds. Dozens of diamonds. Even to the naked eye, they were sizable and of good quality.

I stared. Etched metal plates caught my eye. White plaster dust coated several. I grabbed a photo album. By pressing the plaster-covered metal plates against the black pages, I made readable imprints of them.

It took time for my brain to process what my eyes saw. The image was familiar. Ration stamps. I got my book and held a page to the light. The paper wasn't anything special. I put everything back in the box, hid it in a space behind the clawfoot tub, and paced. Why ration stamps?

Because they were as valuable as cash.

With those blanks, a little ink, some flimsy paper, and a lot of know-how, I could print my own. Stunned, I thought, what if that was the plan? Flood the black market with counterfeit ration stamps, create demand for products needed for the troops, wipe out any surplus. It would have the same effect as a run on the banks during the Great Depression. Genius. Evil.

The diamonds and cash would finance the paper, ink, printing, and distribution. The loose gemstones were likely Rory's savings plan from his heists. Marsden needed ID when the plan went into effect, but not on him, hence the photo.

Something had prevented Marsden from getting the package through usual channels. Could be the wealthy man taken in for questioning by the FBI that I'd read about. Maybe Marsden blackmailed Rory into retrieving the package. Rory double-crossed him and kept it, feeling patriotic or, more likely, to sell it and skip town.

I knew Marsden had searched my place, just as he had searched Rory's. That meant he had to be Rory's killer, which explained why the coppers had been so quick to flood my place when I screamed. Marsden had been upstairs, had likely shot Second-Story Rory mere minutes before I found him in my bed, and he had already called for backup when he realized Rory had slipped out behind his back.

I knew better than to leave the building with what I had found. Marsden would be on me in a flash. So how could I reveal Rory's killer and save the nation?

I went to find Bobby.

***

"It was jake! Just like we planned," Bobby vibrated with excitement. "I skated down the sidewalk as the Loot came out for grub, looped around a couple of dames and crashed right into him. I fumbled like I couldn't get my feet under control, slipped the package into his pocket, slick as a whistle. When he tried to help, I whispered, 'Miss Gracie sends her regards' just like you told me. Then I skated off, fast as one of our planes."

"You *cannot* tell anybody about this, not even Stella."

"You said, a bunch of times. It's cool. I can keep a secret. I'm a spy, right?" He danced a few jitterbug moves like that was proof. "Now what do we do?"

I hated to tell him his days as a spy were over. "We wait."

Saturday morning, I heard the newsboys shouting, "Extra! Extra! Read all about it! German spy ring busted!" I threw on clothes, grabbed a dollar, and met Bobby in the hallway. We bought copies of the *St. Louis Post-Dispatch* and returned to my place to read about what had happened.

Sweet revenge, there was a front-page photo of Marsden in handcuffs, identified as one of the ringleaders. In all, two dozen conspirators were arrested.

On Sunday, a large box arrived for me. Inside was a bounty of several pounds of real coffee, five pounds of sugar, and ration stamps—real ration stamps—to use for perishables. Stella and I would make that chocolate cake after all, and we'd have enough to share with Bobby and Lonnie. There were also a small box, a letter, and a brochure. I opened the letter first.

Speaking officially, a grateful nation thanks you for your assistance in the capture of German spies on American soil. If carried out, their plan would have been devastating to the war effort. Please accept and enjoy this token of appreciation.

Speaking personally, although it was partly to find out how you were connected to Marsden, I enjoyed our time together. I hope you'll accept this gift and think of me. The rest was donated to the war effort and returning wounded.

Remember my mother, who will vouch for my trustworthiness? I've enclosed her address. I hope to see you again, Gracie O'Malley, but if the war takes us in different directions, we'll be able to find each other through Mother.

I have a feeling your life will change. I wish you happiness.

Lt. Nathaniel Caldwell

The small box contained a pair of diamond earrings. I used my eyebrow pencil to mark a dot on each ear lobe. When they looked even, I grabbed a sewing needle and a potato destined for dinner, and I pierced my ears. The earrings were stunning. I read the brochure. It looked like my future was about to change again.

The next day, I smiled and opened the door to the recruiting office, ready to join the Women Airforce Service Pilots.

Like Grandmother said, "Stand still long enough and the entire world will pass you by."

Flying, I could keep ahead of it.

The First Locked Room

Eric Brown

Gudrun led the hunters back to the clearing in the shadow of the cliff face.

He shrugged the small deer from his shoulder and dropped it before the fire, then looked around at his people. The men, women, and children stared at the carcass in dismal silence, wondering how so little meat might fill so many bellies.

He crossed the clearing to the cliff face and pulled aside the animal skin covering the entrance of the god-man's cave.

Skarn hunkered in the shadows, grinding pigment in a gourd with a chunk of stone. Gudrun stared in awe, as always, at the old man's paintings covering the walls: huge mammoth and a herd of bison galloped through grassland, and the images stirred something in his hunter's heart.

The god-man looked up, his wild eyes peering from a tangle of hair the color of ash. With a crimson-stained finger he pointed to a boulder across the cave.

"Sit," he said.

Gudrun remained standing. "The spell you cast, the one you claimed would 'charm mammoths onto our spears'..."

He told the god-man what his fellow hunters *had* brought back.

"We were as fast as the wind, as quiet as clouds, and as strong as tigers," Gudrun said. "We tracked a bull mammoth, but he escaped. Just like last time, and the time before that. Now, winter is on the way."

"I hear your words."

"But what will you do?" Gudrun demanded. He looked around at the scattered magic bones, the runes carved into assorted stones. "You can look into the future, can't you? So...what do you see?"

"The future is as clear to me as a woodland pool," Skarn declared. "Come back at sunset, Gudrun, and I will have the answer."

***

The hunters sat around the fire and ate the scrawny deer. The meager portions barely took away their hunger pangs, and the old men, women, and children had to make do with picking gristle from the discarded bones. Later the hunters chewed on dried berries and seeds collected by the children and older folk.

The hunters were still muttering their discontent at what the god-man had told Gudrun.

"Why do we listen to the old fool?" Korth said.

"He brought us here," said Lall, "and ever since then the hunting has been bad."

"And we've lost good men to wild animals."

"And more to disease."

"Why do we listen to the god-man?"

Gudrun raised a hand for silence.

"We listen to Skarn because in the past his wisdom brought us food, and rich pickings from the land. You have short memories, all of you. We moved here to get away from the Ugly People."

A collective shiver passed through the group as they remembered the attack of the Ugly People, the broken skulls of loved ones, and their screams as they were dragged off to be eaten.

"Skarn said that I should return at sunset, and he will have the answer."

His words appeased the more vocal among the hunters, but even he doubted that the god-man would have magic strong enough to bring the mammoth back.

Because, if he had such magic, why hadn't he used it already?

***

Gudrun moved to the stream and drank his fill, then emptied his bowels of a thin, foul-smelling liquid.

He turned to find that Korth had been watching him.

"You shit like you speak, Gudrun."

Korth was even uglier than the god-man. In the attack of the Ugly People he had lost one eye and half his scalp, though he had fought back with ferocity and slain his attacker. His left eye socket was a suppurating cauldron of pus, his head a blackened scab.

Soon, when Korth had recovered fully from his injuries, Gudrun knew, he would mount a challenge for the leadership.

Now Gudrun attempted to reason with the man. "And what would you do, Korth, in my position?"

Korth spat into the stream. "I would kill the god-man."

"And kill his wisdom with him?"

"What wisdom? We're starving. This land is dead, and cold—"

"You would rather we had stayed and lived in fear of the Ugly People returning?"

"The god-man cast a spell three moons ago, and again before that, magic to charm the mammoths, and what good did that do?"

"Skarn is a mortal, like you and me," Gudrun said. "Sometimes he fails, sometimes he succeeds. You have forgotten the many times he has succeeded. You have forgotten his wisdom, his healing powers. Why, it was Skarn who attended to your injuries. If not for him, you might have bled to death. Is that not so?"

Korth muttered something unintelligible.

"We need to give Skarn more time to prove his powers," Gudrun said. "I will see what he says at sunset, and when the hunt is successful, tomorrow, we will eat our fill and rejoice."

"And if we fail to kill a single beast?" Korth asked.

"You will see. We will fill our bellies and rejoice."

Korth stepped forward and thrust his ravaged face close to Gudrun's, who held his breath against the foul stench gusting from the other's mouth.

"If our next hunt brings nothing," Korth spat, "I will kill the god-man first, and then I will kill *you*."

He turned and rejoined the others around the fire, kicking aside a suckling mother and snatching a length of bone from a puling infant.

Gudrun watched him go, then climbed the rocks high above his people and stared out across the mist-shrouded northern lands.

***

When the sun hit the horizon and spread like the yolk of a broken egg, Gudrun climbed down from the rocks and crossed to the god-man's cave.

He drew aside the animal skin and ducked inside.

Skarn squatted before the embers of his fire, peering into the coals and muttering to himself. Gudrun sat down and regarded the old man.

Only the dull glow from the embers illuminated the cave, throwing an eerie light up onto the god-man's haggard face.

At last Skarn ceased his mutterings and looked up at his visitor. "I see that you have had words with Korth."

"How do you know?"

"The coals tell me."

Gudrun grunted. "And what else do they say?"

"They say that Korth is a threat."

"I don't need the coals to tell me that."

"A threat not just to yourself, but to the tribe."

Gudrun stared at the old man. "Tell me more."

"He is arrogant, and greedy. As leader, he would think only of himself, not of the welfare of everyone, young and old, man and woman. You must watch your back, Gudrun."

"During the hunt?"

"At all times." The old man hesitated. "You should act before it is too late. You should kill Korth before he moves to usurp you."

Gudrun regarded the glowing embers. "Korth fought off many Ugly People, but suffered terrible injuries. It would be wrong to challenge him when he is weak."

The god-man snorted at this. "Will you fight him when he is fit and well and stronger than you? You would be a fool if so, Gudrun. Your people need you, not Korth."

Gudrun waved the words aside. "I came here to learn how you will help the hunt, not to be told how to lead my people."

Skarn stared at the glowing coals.

"The gods have spoken," he murmured at last.

Gudrun felt his heartbeat quicken. "And?"

"They foresee a time of plenty, of successful hunts and full bellies."

For all the god-man's optimistic forecast, it did not fill Gudrun with hope as it would have done in his youth. The old man had ill interpreted the words of the gods of late.

"Successful hunts and full bellies," Gudrun repeated. "But what do the gods want in return? What must you do, Skarn?"

Skarn did not reply immediately. Still squatting, he turned and selected a variety of berries from the halved gourds that lined the wall. These berries he placed in a small leather pouch, which he tied with a cord and hung around his neck.

"Help me outside," he said at last, "and I will speak."

***

Night had fallen while they sat and talked in the god-man's cave.
An incandescent arc of stars pulsed overhead, and the people had stoked the fire at the center of the clearing to ward off unwelcome visitors.

A silence fell over the men, women, and children as Gudrun assisted the frail old man from his cave. An atmosphere of expectation filled the air.

Korth sat cross-legged at the very front of the gathering, a sneer on his ugly face.

Skarn lowered himself slowly to the packed earth.

Gudrun sat beside him and allowed the silence to continue as he looked over his tribe. He saw bright eyes, eager faces. It was not every day that the god-man spoke on behalf of the gods, foretelling the future of the people.

Only the distant ululation of an owl broke the silence.

"Skarn has consulted the gods," Gudrun declared at last, "and they have spoken."

"And what did they say?" Korth wanted to know, his tone loaded with disrespect. "Can you tell us that?"

The god-man spoke. For an old man, with a hollow chest and feeble lungs from hanging over his fire night and day, he possessed a powerful voice.

"We live in troubled times," he said. "The Ugly People drove us from our rich ancestral lands, to dwell here in the north where the soil is poor and the mammoth are few. But," he swept on, "the gods have shown me the future, and it is good. In time, when we are more in number and greater in strength, we will return to our land and take it from the Ugly People!"

A murmur of surprised delight swept through the gathering like a sudden wind.

Gudrun smiled to himself. He and Skarn had discussed this in the past, and it was clever of the god-man to mention this triumphant future now, rousing his people.

"That is all very well," Korth spoke up, "but first, to swell our numbers and make us stronger, we need meat. What did the gods say about this?"

The god-man stared at Korth, scorn in his eyes. "The gods spoke to me," he said, "and told me what should be done to bring the mammoth back."

"And what did they say?" someone else called out.

An expert orator, the god-man allowed a second or two to elapse before he spoke. "The gods said that, in order to bestow upon us the future we desire, they demand a sacrifice."

An explosion of comment animated the gathering.

***

Sacrifice?

Even Gudrun was shocked by the old man's words.

The gods had last demanded a sacrifice many moons ago, when Gudrun had been an infant. It had been deep winter, and all the mammoth had moved away, and even the rivers had frozen over so that no fish could be caught.

An ailing child, who might not have survived the winter anyway, had been given to the gods, and just two moons later the rivers had thawed, and mammoth had returned, and the tribe had eaten well until the coming of spring.

Skarn quelled the mutterings of the crowd. "We live in troubled times," he said, "and the demands of the gods are therefore great. But with sacrifice will come better times."

"How do we know you've read the coals aright?" Korth asked. "You were wrong last time, after all."

"Five times I appealed to the gods," Skarn replied, "and five times I received the same response. *Five* times! Holka of the north wind appeared in the coals, and Thurn of the south, then Palka and Rath of the east and west, and they each said the same thing. And then Bahl the god of the hunt appeared and commanded me."

Gudrun looked around the gathering. The silence was absolute as his people listened, openmouthed, to the god-man's words. Even the owl had ceased its hooting, as if in respect.

At last someone spoke up, and of course it was Korth. "And who will you sacrifice, old man? There are no sick children or old crones among us now. Why should we give up someone fit and healthy when the *god-man*," he loaded the title with contempt, "might have misread the coals?"

A crackle of comment swept like wildfire through the gathering.

Gudrun sprang to his feet and called out, "Allow Skarn to tell us what the gods have decreed!"

When his people fell silent, he sat down and nodded to the god-man.

"The gods," Skarn said, "stated that the chosen one should be taken to the Solitary Cave, and there sealed in, and during the night Bahl will come and strike the chosen one dead with a bolt to the head, just here..." Skarn lifted a frail forefinger to the center of his own forehead. "And Bahl will take the soul of the chosen one, and in return grant good fortune to the hunt, and bless the future of our people. Only this sacrifice will fill our bellies with mammoth meat!"

They sat silent, every one, staring at the old man in awe.

"And if Bahl is remiss," Korth asked, "and does not come, and spares the chosen one... What then?"

Skarn cast a withering look upon the mocker. "Then woe will befall our people, and the mammoth will stay away, and our bellies shall remain empty, and one by one we shall wither away and die."

Korth laughed aloud at this, and several others voiced their doubts.

"Why should we believe the words of an old fool who's been so wrong in the past?" Korth cried out, half-rising and staring about the gathering.

Gudrun was about to stand and exert control again, when the god-man said, "If you are so doubting of the gods, Korth, then perhaps you yourself would consent to be the chosen one and spend the night in the Solitary Cave."

This silenced Korth, and the crowd.

"Well," Gudrun said at last, relishing Korth's iscomfort, "are you man enough to accept the challenge?"

Korth was oddly quiet, staring from Gudrun to the god-man with contempt.

No one spoke. All eyes were on Korth.

At last he said, "I fear not the words of the old man, too blind to read the coals." He hesitated, then went on, "I accept the challenge, but on one condition."

Skarn leaned forward. "Name it."

"That the sacrifice be delayed for one day," Korth said. "At dawn we shall hunt, and if by sunset we have failed to return with mammoth meat then I shall gladly give myself to the Solitary Cave, and we'll see how wrong you have been when I survive."

"And," the god-man said, "if you succeed, and bring back mammoth meat? What then?"

Korth gave an ugly smile. "Then that will be proof that your words are useless, that we don't need your magic to charm the mammoths, and I will strike you dead with one thrust of my spear."

A collective gasp went up from the people.

Gudrun clutched the old man's arm and whispered, "You'd be foolish to accept such blasphemy, Skarn!"

But Skarn ignored his words. He nodded. "I accept your condition," he said. "If you succeed and bring back mammoth meat, I will give myself to your spear. Fail, and you will go to the Solitary Cave and await your fate at the hands of Bahl."

***

At dawn, as the new day touched the horizon with silver light, Gudrun led a band of twenty hunters through the forest to the plains of the north. A wind whistled in the trees, bearing the first chill bite of winter.

The men were silent. In every mind was the memory of the god-man's words, and what it would mean if they returned without mammoth meat.

They spread out, keeping only the distance of a bird's call between them, but as the day progressed not one of their number detected the scent of mammoth on the wind.

Once, toward noon, Gudrun caught the scent of a boar, then glimpsed its bulging, bristling hindquarters through the undergrowth. He raised his spear and crept forward, but something alerted the beast to his presence and it kicked off with a squeal and rushed further into the forest.

It was typical of their luck of late, and Gudrun wondered at the caprice of the gods and felt the gray caul of fate press down on his soul.

At noon they reached the northern extent of the forest and came together.

Undulating scrubland stretched away for as far as the eye could see, ending in a distant range of mountains.

"We should turn back," Lall said, "and be content to hunt boar and deer in the forest."

"We have half a day yet," Korth said, as Gudrun had expected. "We'd be fools to give up now."

Gudrun stared at the one-eyed man, tempted to ask Korth if he feared returning without mammoth meat and facing Bahl in the Solitary Cave.

"We have little time remaining if we wish to return before darkness," Lall pointed out.

All eyes turned to their leader, and Gudrun nodded toward a distant hill. "As far as that hill, and no more. We spread out and advance with the wind at our backs. Lall, climb that tree and call if you see anything."

The hunter ran off.

"The rest of you," Gudrun said, "this way."

They set off north, and Gudrun saw the lopsided expression on Korth's face, caught between suspicion and reluctant gratitude.

***

They jogged through low scrub and tall grasses, Gudrun rejoicing that they were free of the forest and able to run unhindered.

Three sharp notes on the wind stopped Gudrun in his tracks: Lall's urgent songbird call. His pulse quickening, he turned and stared at Lall's thin figure in the tree. The boy was signalling that there was a single mammoth close by, to the northwest.

Following Lall's gestures, he veered west and sprinted. He was leading the chase, with the others far behind.

Just a few heartbeats later he glimpsed the mammoth through the scrub, a dun hillock of lurching fur perhaps three spear-throws distant, and he caught the full blast of its musky scent. Driven by instinct, his heart thumping, he crouched without losing speed and ran toward the beast.

The taste of roasted, bloody mammoth meat was already filling
his mouth.

But if he killed the mammoth, he thought, Skarn the god-man would die…
and Korth would be in the ascendance.

Gudrun felt his resolve waver.

The wind changed and, before he could alter his line of approach, the
mammoth caught his scent and reacted. It veered left, panicked, its great feet
thundering across the earth.

Just as the animal was drawing away from him, it bellowed and turned
dramatically—had it caught sight of another hunter who had circled from the
rear?—and charged toward him.

He barely had time to adjust his footing and raise his spear. The
mammoth was almost upon him, a young bull with tusks as long as a fully
grown man. He saw the rage and fear in its tiny eyes, heard its bellowing roar
as it bore down on him with frightening speed.

He drew back his spear, took aim, and, with a mighty thrust, launched it
whistling through the air. Then he leapt for his life from under the animal's
pounding legs.

Gudrun lay stunned, aware that his spear had missed its target, and just
heartbeats later the other hunters reached him and slumped to the ground,
cursing and exhausted from the chase.

Korth was alone in insisting they pursue the beast. "We almost had it!
We should go on…" He was shaking in rage, and he kept his face averted from
Gudrun's gaze.

Lall pointed. "It is far away now. We would never catch it, even if we had
all day."

Someone else said, "We have a quarter's daylight left. We should start
back. I do not wish to enter the forest in darkness."

"Gudrun?" Lall asked.

Gudrun climbed to his feet and found his spear. "We return," he said,
avoiding Korth's one-eyed scowl.

He turned and led the hunters toward the forest.

***

Later, as dusk fell, he heard a sound in the forest behind him and tensed in
anticipation of the confrontation.

"Halt, Gudrun," Korth called.

He stopped and turned, slowly. Korth approached. The others hurried on,
making for home with increased speed.

"The mammoth was on top of you," Korth spat. "A child could have killed the animal!"

Gudrun held the man's enraged stare. Korth was gripping his spear with both hands, as if at any second he would lunge and run him through.

"It surprised me," Gudrun said. "It was upon me before I could prepare myself."

"You missed on purpose, so that we would return without mammoth meat and I would go to the Solitary Cave."

"I would rather have mammoth meat in my belly tonight," he said, and wondered if it were true, "even if it meant that you lived."

He adjusted his grip on his spear, readying himself for the attack.

Korth spat a gob of phlegm at his leader's feet. "I should have killed you when I had the chance, before the Ugly People did this to me!"

Gudrun stepped forward, lowering his spear and spreading his arms. He was aware of his heartbeat, and aware, too, that he was playing a dangerous game. Korth was unpredictable, and might very well act on impulse.

"Then do it now!" Gudrun said. "Go on, kill me. Take your spear and drive it through my chest and then do the same to Skarn. Do it!"

Korth took a step closer, grinding his teeth. "I *should* kill you," he hissed.

"Then kill me," Gudrun said. "Or...do you fear the alternative—a night in the Solitary Cave?"

Korth's single eye burned like a livid coal. He hesitated, then lowered his spear, and Gudrun released a pent-up breath.

"I fear nothing and no one," Korth muttered. "Not you, or the god-man, or even the gods."

He brushed past Gudrun and hurried after the others.

"Then you truly are a fool," Gudrun murmured to himself, and continued his homeward journey through the forest.

***

Gudrun led his sorry troop into the clearing, cowed by the stunned silence of his people when they realized they would go hungry again tonight.

Perhaps Skarn had looked into the future and seen that the hunters would return without mammoth meat, for he had set about sealing the Solitary Cave at the far end of the cliff face, his personal refuge when he needed time away from the tribe. Gudrun had often heard him in there, talking to himself and sometimes crying out loud like a madman.

Skarn stretched an antelope skin across the cave's narrow, sloping entrance, pinning its circumference with rocks and packing them with mud. He'd left a small space at the bottom through which Korth might crawl.

The tribe now gathered before the cave, their disappointment at the outcome of the hunt replaced by anticipation. Parents hushed their hungry children, appeasing them with roots and dried berries.

Korth was seated across the clearing with his back to the gathering, accompanied only by his woman and two young companions. He was acting, Gudrun thought, as if all the activity had nothing to do with him, despite his claims to fear no one, not even the gods.

Gudrun watched as the god-man instructed a woman to heat a gourd of honeybee wax on the fire, and while she did this, Skarn said, "The lean times will end soon, Gudrun, when Bahl has done his work."

He turned and called across the heads of the crowd to Korth. "The Cave is prepared, Korth."

Taking his time, Korth said something to his woman and climbed to his feet. He strolled through the crowd toward where Skarn and Gudrun waited, people looking up as he passed and murmuring to their neighbors.

At last Korth faced the god-man.

Skarn gestured toward the Solitary Cave, where the antelope hide was stretched as tight as a drumskin, save for the entrance flap.

"Am I expected to meet the gods without a meal in my belly?" Korth sneered.

Skarn had thought of that, and, from inside his animal skins, he pulled a small pouch which he offered to the one-eyed man.

Korth snatched the pouch and examined its contents. "Berries?" he sneered.

"It is more than many of us have eaten tonight," Skarn said. "Perhaps, had you returned with meat..."

At this, Korth called out to the crowd. "At dawn, when I have shown the god-man to be the pretender he is, *I* will lead the hunters!" He stared at Gudrun. "And we will return with meat aplenty."

He turned, clutching the pouch of berries, and approached the Solitary Cave.

The people watched in silence as he knelt and, with as much dignity as he could muster, crawled on all fours into the Cave.

Together, Skarn and the woman sealed the one-eyed man within. Skarn held the flap of skin while the woman poured flowing wax from the gourd onto the edge of the skin, sealing it to the ledge of rock.

Skarn turned and faced the crowd, his wild face even crazier in the dancing light of the fire.

"And now," he said, "only Bahl himself can enter the Solitary Cave."

***

Rather than return to their sleeping places, the people elected to pass the night before the cliff face so that, come dawn, they would be on hand to witness Bahl's work.

Skarn turned to Gudrun. "If you would care to join me on this night's vigil…"

They sat side by side, facing the Solitary Cave, wrapped in animal furs against the cold.

Gudrun considered Korth, and the fear he might be experiencing at the thought of his approaching fate. For, although the one-eyed man had poured scorn on the god-man's powers, how could he doubt the potency of the gods themselves?

Around him, one by one, the people gave in to sleep, curling within their furs and snoring gently as the night progressed. A sickle moon rose and brightened as the fires burned out and dimmed, and occasionally a solitary owl hooted as it patrolled the woodland.

Gudrun stared at the antelope skin in the meager moonlight, wondering if he would be able to detect, in some fashion, the arrival of the god Bahl.

Skarn rocked back and forth, murmuring incantations known only to himself and to those god-men who had gone before him into the spirit world.

Gudrun strained to hear a sound from within the cave—Korth's ragged breathing, which at any moment might be shut off—but he heard nothing.

In the early hours he gave in to exhaustion and lay back, folding his furs into a comfortable pillow and intending only to rest until dawn. But no sooner had he laid down his head, it seemed, than he felt Skarn's bony finger gouge his ribs.

Miraculously, the night had passed, and dawn was lighting the sky above the forest.

His people were stirring too, their usual sluggish morning languor quickened by expectation—the delicious enjoyment of misfortune visited upon a fellow man.

Skarn caught Gudrun's eye, and he helped the old man to his feet. The god-man turned his ancient head and scanned the tribe. Everyone was awake now; children were round-eyed and agog, men and women silent at the enormity of what was about to take place—or had already, perhaps, taken place.

Skarn inclined his head, and he and Gudrun approached the cave.

Gudrun strained to hear a sound from within, but all was deathly silent.

The god-man bent and scraped at the waxen seal with a chip of rock, and little by little the flap came free. At last he stood, took hold of the edge of the skin and pulled it from the entrance, revealing the interior of the cave.

His heart beating fast, Gudrun looked over the god-man's bowed shoulder and stared into the shadows.

Korth lay on his back on the floor of the cave, but whether in sleep or death, Gudrun could not tell.

Skarn limped forward, step by slow step, then knelt and examined the one-eyed man, and Gudrun saw him reach out as if to test for a pulse, then touch the man's forehead.

Skarn stood and rejoined Gudrun, then faced the gathering and called out, "Korth is dead! Bahl, god of the hunt, entered in the night and carried away his soul..."

A sound like the roar of a great waterfall issued from the gathering, along with the individual cries of those petitioning the gods, and the wailing lament of Korth's grief-stricken woman.

Skarn ordered Lall and another hunter to carry the body across the clearing to the fire. As they lifted the dead man and edged past Gudrun, he stared at the lolling head and saw the dark hole that punctured Korth's forehead.

With Skarn in attendance, murmuring prayers, the hunters laid the corpse on the fire and the people gathered round to warm themselves and watch as Korth the one-eyed burned.

***

A strange atmosphere filled the air later, as the hunters prepared themselves to leave the clearing. Gudrun could only liken it to the time, many moons ago, when the hunters had slain two bull mammoths and returned to bask in the tribe's relief and jubilation.

Except, this time, the feast of mammoth meat was but a promise.

As Gudrun was about to leave the clearing, Skarn hobbled across to him and gripped his arm.

The god-man looked into Gudrun's eyes.

"The gods have spoken," Skarn said, and Gudrun drew his arm free and led his men into the forest.

The hunters possessed the power of the gods as they ran through the trees like children. At one point, Gudrun ordered Lall to lead the way and fell back to consider his thoughts.

He knew that, imbued with renewed confidence, the hunters would bring home mammoth meat tonight, and his people would feast for the first time in many moons.

The gods have spoken, Skarn had said.

And Gudrun's position as leader of his people was secure.

But he recalled watching the god-man gather the dried berries—*poison* berries?—in his cave yesterday, and place them in the pouch he had later passed to Korth.

And in the Solitary Cave he had seen Skarn create the mark of a wound on Korth's forehead with pigment the color of blood.

Gudrun smiled to himself as he ran.

Through the god-man, the gods *had* indeed spoken.

He quickened his pace, for a hunter was signalling from up ahead that he had caught the scent of a mammoth.

Electricity

Linda Stratmann

There was thunder in the air, a headless corpse in the Grand Junction Canal, and short odds on which situation Inspector Wolfe found more disturbing. He had been alerted to the grisly discovery via the magnetic needle telegraph line, and as he made his way to the scene, he glanced up nervously at the wires trembling above him. Any moment, he thought, there would be a crackle and a bang, and electrical fluid dripping onto his head. His friend the Baron had told him that this was impossible, but Wolfe wasn't so sure. The Baron had an uncertain relationship with electricity. Several times he had sworn that he would never touch the stuff again, but before long he would be drawn back into his laboratory, from which he would emerge days later with singed eyebrows and a wild expression.

Twice in recent weeks, the discovery of a headless corpse in Paddington had alerted the attention of the new plainclothes detective division of Scotland Yard, but each time Wolfe had been called in the corpses had already been taken to the nearest mortuary and any clues well trampled. More in hope than confidence, he had asked all London police stations to ensure that, in the event of another body turning up without a head, he would be called to the scene before anything was moved. It was thanks to the prompt action of Constable Fortune of the Hermitage Street station house, that his wishes had been complied with.

Fortune had the pink new look that spoke of a youth as yet barely familiar with a razor, but he was lanky, well turned-out, intelligent, and observant. He also appeared undisturbed by the sight of the carnage in the canal. By the time Wolfe reached the towpath, Fortune had already ordered that no one should touch the body, commandeered a horse blanket and a handcart with which to carry it to wherever the inspector directed it should go, and was busy interviewing the bargeman who had found it.

It was a summer morning, the early heat and humidity auguring badly. In another few hours the gray canal water and its floating debris would be bubbling like soup and emitting eye-watering gases of decomposition. The corpse, wallowing chest-down, had been badly mangled by passing steam barges. Both legs were smashed, lying at unnatural angles, shards of blue-white bone poking through ripped flesh. Torn flaps of rough trouser and an expanse of hairy white buttock suggested that the body was male.

"You're a calm one, Constable," said Wolfe. "There's men at the Yard would be losing their breakfast about now."

"My father is a butcher, sir," said Fortune. "I grew up around a lot of carcasses, all that blood and guts; not human, of course, but you get used to the sight and smell."

"That should stand you in very good stead in the Metropolitan police," said Wolfe. "So, what have you learned?"

Fortune consulted his notebook. "I have spoken to Mr. John Dalton," he said, with a nod to the bargeman, "who informed me that he passed this place yesterday evening on his way to Paddington Basin and is certain that the body was not there then. He cannot identify the victim."

"And what do you observe?" asked Wolfe. "I know you're not a detective, but that doesn't mean you shouldn't look about you and draw conclusions." He didn't usually demand so much of constables, but there was something about Fortune's application and energy that reminded Wolfe of someone—himself, thirteen years ago, when he had first joined the force.

Fortune snapped the notebook shut. "I think the body was put in the canal under cover of darkness last night, either from a boat or from the path. There has been no rain in the last week, and the towpath is dry and hard, so I would not expect to see footmarks or cart tracks, and there are none. If he had been killed and decapitated on the towpath there would be blood, quite a lot of blood, but I have made a thorough search and there is no trace of any. So he was killed somewhere else and brought here."

"Well, we haven't had any reports of blood found elsewhere, but it's early in the day." Wolfe beckoned to the bargeman. "Let's get it out of the canal then, and take care, I want it on shore in the same state as it was in the water. We can't have anything dropping off. Fortune, while we are doing that, I want you to search the barge for bloodstains."

Both these prospects met with all the enthusiasm from Mr. Dalton that Wolfe had expected; nevertheless, the bargeman complied, and, by dexterous use of a boathook, the body was brought to the side of the canal and eased up onto the blanket. Wolfe explored the slimy pockets and found nothing.

"He's been dead a day or two, I'd say," remarked Fortune, who had returned to the towpath after a fruitless search.

"Laborer, by his clothes," said Wolfe. "But look at this." There was a length of rope loosely wound several times around the waist of the corpse, the ends knotted into the man's belt. "That's not to hold his trousers up. Someone tried

to weight the body down so it would sink and made a poor job of it. There'll
be a lump of stone or brick somewhere down there."

"Do you want me to try and get it, sir?" asked Fortune.

"Top marks for keenness, but I wouldn't recommend a dip at this time of
year." The body, which even without a head was heavy in its sodden clothing,
was lifted onto the cart and covered with the blanket.

"Someone might recognize him down at the station house," said
Fortune hopefully.

"Perhaps they will, but he's not going down there just yet," said Wolfe.
"We're taking him to a place on the Harrow Road. I'll explain on the way." He
dismissed Dalton, who grunted and returned to his barge.

Together the two policemen manhandled the cart and its blanketed
burden from the towpath up to street level, where a narrow track, Portobello
Lane, bounded the eastern corner of the new cemetery of All Souls Kensal
Green. There was a row of dingy cottages and the smell one might expect on a
summer's day when there were several families sharing one cesspit.

"The thing is," said Wolfe, "if a man goes out one night and doesn't come
back for a day or so, hardly anyone round here bothers to report it. He might
be working far off and decide to sleep in a field. If he's a bad husband who
takes what his wife earns, turns it into beer, and then beats her, the last thing
she wants is him being found and sent home."

At the end of the lane, they turned the cart west onto Harrow Road. The
old highway was busy with commercial traffic. Between low, soot-stained
dwellings could be seen the green farmlands of Chelsea, while to the south
lay the long-walled boundary of the cemetery. Fortune glanced at Wolfe,
wondering if this was their destination, but when they reached the great
arched entrance the inspector said nothing, and they walked on.

"So what do you think is especially interesting about these murders,"
asked Wolfe, "apart of course from the fact that all three victims turned
up without a head, a fact that so far has been kept hidden from the
general public?"

Fortune, seeing he was being tested, frowned with thought. "All three
were found in Paddington, and we know the first two lived here, which
suggests that the killer lives here too. The first was on the railway near
Portobello Bridge, and the second in a field just north of here. None of them
were killed where they were found."

"It's the same killer," said Wolfe, "unless we have two people going about
chopping off heads, and I sincerely hope we do not, and when someone kills
more than once you tend to find that it's the same kind of victim."

"But these victims aren't the same types, apart from being male," said Fortune. He consulted his notebook. "Danny Deane was a pickpocket, age twenty-two. Will Granby was a respectable grocer, fifty-five years old, family man, in poor health. Then there's this fellow—probable laborer."

"Exactly," said Wolfe. "Three men, all different, all without a head."

"My inspector says it's the work of a maniac," said Fortune, but his voice bore little conviction.

"Your inspector is a fine, hard-working policeman, but he has no imagination," said Wolfe.

Fortune seemed to be considering what to say to that, but wisely decided not to respond. "Do you have a theory, sir?" he asked.

"Not yet," said Wolfe, "but that is why we are here. Have you heard of Baron Frankenstein?"

"Who hasn't?" said Fortune. "That's his house up there, isn't it, the old one with the windmill." It was Fortune's darkest secret that the mere idea of a windmill filled him with horror, and he did his best to conceal a shudder. "He should have been locked away as a lunatic years ago. Do you think he did this?"

"No," said Wolfe solemnly, "he's a friend of mine and we're going to see him."

Fortune stopped pushing the cart, and for a moment was speechless.

"Hurry up, lad, we need to get there quickly, while he's still sane."

Reluctantly, Fortune began to push again, but with less energy than before. "Err...how well do you know him, sir?" he asked cautiously.

"I first met him about eight years ago. There'd been some strange goings-on round here that were hard to explain. The Baron's a very clever man, a scientist, and most importantly he's local and cheap, so we asked his advice. Ever since then he's been the man I have gone to when things get a bit peculiar. Fortunately, the Commissioner has given me *carte blanche* to call in who I like."

"You've got an interesting reputation in the force, if you don't mind my saying so, sir," said Fortune. He glanced at Wolfe, but when the inspector showed no sign of being offended, he carried on. "When you went to the detective division, there were those who said you'd been put in charge of a special department that deals with the unusual. Things that were so unusual no one could tell me what they were."

"I am certainly in charge of that department," said Wolfe, "in fact I *am* the department, because it is just me."

"Wasn't there a book about the Baron?" asked Fortune. "I've not read it myself, but I was told it caused something of a stir."

"That was about the Baron's father, Victor senior. The old Baron was a studious sort in his youth, took things very seriously, many said far too seriously. In particular, he was very interested in death."

"Was he a murderer?"

"No, rather the opposite. He experimented with the creation of life."

Fortune raised his eyebrows and looked a little pinker.

"That was not what I meant, although he was married to a very beautiful young woman. No, it was the early death of his wife which led him to brood on what it was that caused the change from life to death and whether it might be possible to change things back."

"Hmm," said Fortune, with a worried look. "I suppose we all have to endure our losses. I had a sister die of the scarlet fever, and if wishing could have made her live then she would be alive now. And there are doctors who say that you can seem to be dead but not really be dead and wake up in your coffin with rats eating your extremities, which is not a pleasant thought. But that's only *seeming* dead. Why, if someone is really dead, then they can't be made to live again, except in heaven, and that's something that no man should meddle with."

"So one might think," said Wolfe, "but the old Baron was full of fancies and too clever to be in his right mind. What might have stopped another man—morality, religion, common sense—was no obstacle to him; rather he was spurred on by the challenge, and the love of his wife."

"He didn't try to bring her back to life, did he?" said Fortune, appalled.

"No, she was too long dead by the time he thought he had the secret. He created—I'm not sure what to call it; in fact I never saw it, for all I know he might have dreamed or imagined the whole thing—a creature, like a man. Assuming the story to be true, he did it by sewing together pieces from medical dissection rooms and other less salubrious places. It's in some doubt whether all the pieces were human. But he made this thing, this man-like thing, and then he tried to bring it to life."

Fortune pondered this. "Wouldn't it have been easier to start with something smaller, like a frog?"

"I would have thought so, too," said Wolfe, "but then we're not men of science, are we? According to the book...and...err, it's best not to mention the book unless the Baron mentions it first," he added, "and don't say the name Shelley, it upsets him. According to the book, this man-thing was horribly ugly with big staring eyes, but the Baron says that isn't true. The writer just imagined all of that. After all, you don't make people's blood run cold or sell many books if you have a creature that looks normal. No, the Baron says his father tried creating it in his own image, though it's anyone's guess how close he got."

"Isn't that blasphemy, sir?" Fortune protested.

"Yes, well spotted, and a lot of other things too. Anyhow, he claimed that he succeeded in bringing it to life. I don't know how, but I think it was something to do with electricity. But next thing he knew it was going off for little walks on its own and the authorities got wind of it and started blaming it for every crime in the neighborhood, all the way from murder down to trading on the Sabbath. The old Baron, of course, he said that his creature was harmless and as innocent as the day he made it."

"Was it, sir?" asked Fortune dubiously.

"We shall never know. However, the whole episode was very upsetting, and that was when the old Baron lost his mind."

"It seems to me that he lost it some while back," said Fortune. "About the time he started playing with nature. Is this creature still about?"

"No, there was some sort of accident in the laboratory, and both the old Baron and the creature perished."

"Your friend, he's...err...not carrying on his father's work, is he?"

"No, he has devoted himself to benefitting mankind by building machines that can do the work of men and horses and inventing a cure for toothache."

"Does he have a cure for toothache?" asked Fortune, hopefully.

"He's got a sort of distillery in an outhouse where he makes this funny-smelling stuff you rub on your gums."

"And it stops your tooth from hurting?"

Wolfe grinned. "It stops everything from hurting, lad."

***

The Baron's house was both larger and older than its neighbors, a two-story stone edifice that might once have been intended as a manor house built for a gentleman whose pretensions were greater than his purse. The upper windows had long been taxed out of existence, and the whole had an incomplete, ill-proportioned look, as if there ought to have been another story, but all it had actually got was a cheap roof.

At the rear of the house there rose a windmill. The young constable contemplated it with increasing dread. It was bad enough to see the great creaking monsters from a distance, redolent with some horrible dark doom, but this was the nearest he had ever approached one, and though it was smaller and less grim than its ancestors, he still found it disturbing. It was mounted on a wooden frame that emerged from a flat section of roof and came to a point at the top. At the summit, an arrangement of eight canvas sails whirled ominously in the breeze, causing a central vertical metal pole to turn. A single triangular sail, jutting out behind like a flag, was catching the wind and swiveling the mechanism to make the most of the breeze, but in the blustery weather the wind was changing direction with a rapidity that made the whole structure rattle. A long ladder was propped against the wall of the house, and another was lashed to the side of the mill.

A figure appeared from behind the house, looking like a large ape, but in clothes, and began to swarm up the ladder onto the roof. It was dark-browed, with short hair and a beard more like fur than any human growth, and it moved with astonishing agility, scampering up to the top. Fortune didn't know whether to be repelled by it or hope that it might perform some tricks.

"Does that belong to the Baron?" he asked, apprehensively.

"Belong? No, that's his assistant, Humphrey."

"Five degrees!" said a resonant voice, and the ape-man nodded, and began to make adjustments to the sails. The owner of the voice soon appeared, a tall, well-made man in his forties. He might have been considered handsome, if he had been dressed like a gentleman, or was recently shaved, or was not bruised and bloodied about the face and hands, none of which considerations applied. He did however have the air of confidence associated with noblemen.

"Frankenstein!" called out the inspector. "I have something for you!"

"Always a pleasure to see you, Wolfe," said the Baron with a smile, "but whatever it is will have to wait. There's a storm coming!"

The sails suddenly spun round, almost dislodging Humphrey from his perch, and he just managed to hold on.

"It's life and death, I'm afraid," said Wolfe.

"Isn't it always?" said the Baron. "Come down, Humphrey, that will have to do." He turned to Wolfe and Fortune. "You'd better come in."

Fortune stared at the shrieking windmill and the old lopsided house and the mad Baron and the ape-like servant, and had half (in fact rather more than half) a mind to depart the scene as quickly as possible, resign from the police force, and take the next ship to Australia. Then there appeared in the dark cavernous gloom of the doorway the most wonderful girl he had ever seen.

She was unusually tall for a woman, but possibly not over six feet in height, which was the size she loomed in the young constable's eyes. He was not able to judge her for beauty; rather she was striking and unique. Over a plain gray gown, she wore a linen smock blotched with chemical burns, covered in pockets, and gathered about the waist by a broad leather belt, from which there hung a hook with a metal clasp and a magnifying lens. Most of the pockets were in use; one was stuffed with a pair of thick gauntlets, one was crammed with steel instruments, others contained pens, pencils, and rolls of parchment. She was holding a glass bottle, and her fingertips were stained bright blue. Long dirty-blonde hair was held back from her brow by what appeared to be a giant pair of spectacles, discs of glass in brass frames set into a leather strap. Below it was a slim face with large silver-gray eyes.

"Ah, Elizabeth, we have visitors, and I think they have brought something interesting to show us," said Frankenstein, casually, as one might have invited a student to inspect a recently excavated antiquity.

"It's a body," said Wolfe, as Elizabeth approached the cart, "as you might guess from the smell, taken from the canal this morning; but before you look at it, I must ask you all not to tell anyone else about what you see. We're keeping some details close to our chests."

"Of course," said Frankenstein. "Let's take it to the laboratory. But we won't be able to study it immediately as we have some urgent work in hand, a new experiment."

Humphrey had just descended the ladder. He came over to the cart with a peculiar loping walk, seized the shafts, and pushed. Fortune had rather hoped that closer acquaintance would make the man look more human and less like an ape in a suit, but this was not the case. He was rather less than the normal height for a man, but this was only because his legs were bowed. His shoulders and arms were powerful and his chest broad. A slightly flattened nose and scar tissue about the eyes and knuckles suggested a history of pugilism.

The open doorway did not look inviting. The porch was cluttered with broken pieces of wood and fragments of crumbling stone. Arched beams overhead had long ago been weathered to splinters. As the cart lurched toward the gloomy interior, Fortune was assisted in his determination to follow it by his loyalty to the police force and admiration of the legendary Inspector Wolfe, but mainly by his fascination with Elizabeth. He knew that he would never be able to do anything but admire her from a respectful distance, as if she were some form of exotic royalty. She was probably the same age as he, but a hundred years older in wisdom, and, more importantly, she had not yet noticed that he existed.

On the other side of the porch was a broad hallway. It would once have been very grand, even luxurious, but those days were long gone. Grimy portraits and a stained mirror hung on paneled walls, and the only light was that which, with some difficulty, seeped through leaded and smoke-blackened windows. A large wrought-iron chandelier was suspended overhead by a tangle of rusted chains. Worst of all, there was a whirring, grinding noise, which intensified in volume as they plunged farther into the house. "That's just the windmill," said Frankenstein, seeing the young policeman's frown. This was little comfort, since as far as Fortune was concerned there was no such thing as "just" a windmill.

At the back of the hall was a set of heavy double doors, which the Baron pushed open, and as he did so the horrible noise thundered more loudly than before. "More light, Humphrey!" said Frankenstein.

Once through the doors, Humphrey bent over something on a long bench. There was a fizzing crackling noise, and a sudden blaze of brilliance. Fortune blinked, and dark blotches danced before his eyes. Eventually he saw that he was in a large square room, its stone walls covered in rough shelving cluttered with bottles and porcelain jars. The bottles had things in them that looked like gobbets of overdone mutton stew, but probably weren't. The source of the light was a device consisting of two metal plates connected by pillars. A lightning bolt in miniature was flashing in the gap between the exposed ends of two rods, the tips of which were starting to glow.

The terrible grinding noise was coming from a thick, rotating vertical metal column, the top of which disappeared through a hole in the ceiling. A series of notched wheels, gleaming with oil, were causing a much larger wheel to spin rapidly, and looping coils of thick wire fed into a metal canister on a bench.

Wolfe went to uncover the body but before he could a great thunderclap sounded overhead, and the Baron rubbed his hands together. "Excellent! The time has come! My final test of the Frankenstein refillable dry-cell battery! Only I might not call it that—there are people who are prejudiced against the name. Just think," he exclaimed, "one day people will ride in electrical carriages powered by my batteries, and they will all have to come to me to refill them. I will be a rich man, Wolfe, and then I will regain my ancestral home, restore the name of Frankenstein, and buy up and burn every copy of *that book!*"

"In the meantime," said Wolfe, hopefully, gesturing toward the body.

"Not just yet, Wolfe," said the Baron with a dismissive gesture. "Humphrey!" he bellowed, "we are very close, we may soon have full charge."

"Yes, sir," grunted the man, putting on giant spectacles and a pair of gauntlets and going to inspect the canister.

There was another rumble of thunder and the hiss of rainfall. Water began to drip down the turning shaft.

Frankenstein's grubby shirt cuffs were already rolled halfway up his burly forearms, and now, with an air of great anticipation, he pushed them past his elbows. "Elizabeth, get the cables!"

Fortune was looking at Wolfe, wondering if they ought to give up on any assistance from the Baron for a day at least, when it happened. There was a sound overhead like the boom of cannon fire, and the column shuddered and stopped turning. Black smoke poured into the cellar, there was a loud popping noise, and then, with an explosive bang, the canister tore itself apart. Flying fragments of metal shattered bottles and the air was filled with an acrid chemical stench.

As the light from the fizzing lamp cut through the smoke, Fortune saw Humphrey picking himself up from the floor while the Baron stared at the remains of his project in dismay, running both hands through his hair.

"Sorry about your experiment," said Wolfe.

"It'll take days to build another!" said Frankenstein. "That infernal lightning! If I could only control it or even know when to expect it, just think what I could do!" Smoky black dust and fragments of charred wood showered down the chimney, and the Baron gasped in horror. "Oh no, the windmill! Humphrey, come with me!" He rushed out of the room, and Humphrey, tearing off his spectacles and slapping grime from his coat, followed.

Elizabeth said nothing but lifted a corner of the blanket from the body and looked at what lay on the cart. Her expression did not change, but she raised her magnifying lens and peered keenly at the remains. Seen through the thick glass, her eyes looked like great cold moons in a pale sky. Fortune might have given a substantial sum to receive even a glance of contempt from her. He had no idea whether she was Frankenstein's daughter, wife, mistress, or servant, and there was a strange place in his mind that didn't care.

With the hideous creaking of the column mercifully silenced, the policemen became aware of another noise, this one coming from somewhere deep inside the house, a low steady thumping. "Another experiment?" asked Wolfe. "It certainly isn't rats, unless they wear size ten hobnail boots."

Elizabeth gave a wintry smile. "Humphrey's work. Not to be disturbed." Her voice was calm and soft, and Fortune shivered.

Elizabeth dropped the blanket back over the body, put on her gauntlets, and began picking up pieces of broken glass and dropping them into a bucket. Fortune went to help her, ignoring a quizzically raised eyebrow from Inspector Wolfe. "Hold that," said Elizabeth, handing Fortune the bucket. In the flickering sparking gleam, his cheeks went even pinker than usual. They had just finished collecting the debris when Frankenstein and Humphrey returned, their clothes sodden with rain.

"Is the windmill damaged?" asked Elizabeth, with an anxious frown.

"Not badly, but by the time it's repaired, the storm will have gone," said the Baron. A thunderous rumble from above seemed to be mocking him. "Well," he added with a sigh, "there's nothing we can do today without the materials, so I suppose I had better take a look at this."

Wolfe glanced at Fortune as if to say that the explosion had been a spot of luck.

Frankenstein mopped his face with the edge of the blanket and uncovered the body. As he leaned forward for a closer look, he gave a little gasp of surprise. He was silent for a while, and the gleam of his face in the bright sizzling light made him look pale with shock. "What can you tell me?" he said at last.

"It's the third one like this," said Wolfe. "The first one was on the Great Western Railway line, between Portobello Bridge and the field west of Portobello Lane."

"Whereabouts exactly?" asked Frankenstein.

"He'd been under the Bristol train, so pretty much all the way along," said Wolfe. "He was so cut-up it was a while before we twigged that there wasn't a head, not even one smashed into bits. We had a look at the undersides of trains that had gone past, just in case the head had been torn off and was still stuck there, but apart from some blood and bits of tissue and bone, which were not enough to make up a head, there was nothing. Also there was something about the neck area that suggested the head had been cut off and not ripped off by a train. I think he was thrown onto the tracks, probably from the bridge, without his head."

"There were rumors all over Paddington about him being ground up in a mincer," said the Baron. "I got some very strange letters."

"Oh, the public loves a mutilated corpse," said Wolfe. "Can't get enough of 'em. But crimes like that, for some reason they always say it can't be an Englishman who did it."

"The letters I got said it couldn't be a human," said the Baron.

"Then we found another one buried in a field near Kensal New Town. No way to know how long he'd been there, and if it hadn't been for some buyers having the field surveyed, we'd never have found him at all."

"But also headless?" asked Frankenstein.

"Yes, there was no doubt about it this time, but he'd been there so long he was falling apart, and it was impossible to see how the head had been taken off."

"I suppose the cause of death was a mystery in both cases?"

"Yes," said Wolfe.

Frankenstein spent several minutes examining the severed neck, then studied the dead man's hands and pulled back a flap of trouser to view the leg. "This man was killed by being decapitated. Probably only a day or two ago. He has worked in the building trade, but not recently. There's evidence of an old fracture to the leg—scars where the bone poked through the flesh—which is the kind of injury you see when builders' laborers take a fall. He would have walked with a limp. And since the corpse is relatively fresh, we should be able to find out what his last meal was. Or drink. There's more than a whiff of cheap beer about him. Some things even canal water can't hide." The Baron rerolled his sleeves. "I'd better open him up."

Elizabeth brought a tray of knives and saws, and the Baron selected a scalpel and tested its edge on his thumb before proceeding.

Frankenstein was no surgeon, but he clearly knew his way around a corpse, and before long, he stepped back and nodded. "Yes, as I thought, the man was probably rolling drunk when he died. Last meal was a small pie and a large quantity of beer."

"I've been thinking, sir," said Fortune.

"In anyone else I'd say that might be considered dangerous, but in your case I'll let it go," said Wolfe.

"The thing is, these three murder victims—well, we've been saying how different they are, one being a young single criminal, one a respectable married man of fifty-five, and now this one a laborer who liked his drink, but apart from all being male, there is another way that they are similar." He paused.

"Go on" said Wolfe, "I'm all attention."

"A pickpocket comes into close contact with strangers in the street. The grocer was in poor health, and this man had a bad leg and was drunk. All three were more at risk than most of becoming the victims of a violent robber."

"Which, in a sense, they were," said Wolfe, thoughtfully, "a robber who took their heads. And it does mean that in all likelihood the killer didn't know any of the victims and just chose the ones that were convenient. But why did the killer take away the heads? I mean, I doubt it was so he could put them on his mantelpiece and admire them. If that was his motive, they would all have been pretty young women or even young men. No, he had some other reason. I wish I knew what it was."

The storm was back. There was a huge bang like a cannon shot, directly over their heads, and another shower of black ash down the chimney. The metal column quivered and began to turn slowly again. Deep in the house the strange thumping, which had faded, grew louder, and there was a low moaning, like wind vibrating through an organ pipe. "I don't like the sound of that," said Wolfe. "Baron, would you mind if I took a look at whatever it is that's hammering away like that?"

"I'm not sure that's advisable," said Frankenstein, an unusual edge to his voice.

"Well, now you have got me interested," said Wolfe. He hurried out into the hall and Fortune followed him.

"Inspector, I beg of you!" gasped the Baron, and rushed after the two policemen, closely followed by Humphrey and Elizabeth. After taking a moment to judge the direction of the noise, Wolfe pushed open a small door and found himself at the head of a corridor, where the pounding, louder now, echoed from rough stone walls. The only light came from fat smoky candles in iron brackets. Wolfe marched down the corridor in determined pursuit of the sound until he stood outside a door. Whatever was making the noise was on the other side of the door and appeared to be trying to escape by beating on it with feet and fists; the honking groans suggesting that there was a prisoner within who had been gagged.

Wolfe seized the handle, but the door was locked. "Who have you got in there?" he demanded.

"Inspector, it's not what you think. I can explain!" exclaimed the Baron.

Wolfe was immovable. "The best way of explaining is by opening that door."

Frankenstein clutched his bloodstained hands to his hair distractedly, and then Elizabeth laid a hand on his arm and spoke words that brought joy to Fortune's heart. "Uncle, we have no choice."

The Baron sighed. "Oh, very well, but take care, he's usually no trouble, but today he's disturbed by the storm. Please promise me you won't go inside. He senses strangers and they make him afraid."

Wolfe reluctantly agreed, and Frankenstein nodded. "Humphrey, open the door."

Humphrey scowled, but complied. As the key turned in the lock, the thumping stopped, but the moaning continued. Slowly, cautiously, he pushed the door open.

In the candlelit chamber stood the figure of a man. He appeared to be wearing a spherical helmet of polished metal. The flickering light danced off the shiny surface and picked out colored points like rainbows. It took several moments for Wolfe and Fortune to fully understand what they were seeing.

The figure had no head. The helmet was open at the front, and inside it was nothing but a jumble of wires and crackling sparks. As the chest of the thing rose and fell, so the sounds of lament emerged from a windpipe that had no throat.

Wolfe gasped. "Is that your father's creature?" he exclaimed.

The Baron sighed. "No," he said heavily, "it's Father."

Humphrey entered the room and, taking the figure gently by the elbow, led it to a bench and persuaded it to sit, then patted its shoulder, an action that clearly had a calming effect.

"They worked closely together for many years," Frankenstein explained. "Humphrey is the only one who can manage him now."

"Is he alive?" asked Fortune.

"Well, yes and no. It happened ten years ago, an explosion. I'm only thankful Elizabeth was away at school at the time. The laboratory caught fire, and the creature perished. Humphrey saved me, then he went back in to get Father. When he brought him out, we saw that his head had been destroyed, though his body was sound. I had been experimenting with electricity and was still holding the mechanical head I had been working on. We...err...put them together."

"Can he see or hear?" asked Wolfe.

"No, but he responds to unusual vibrations. That was why the thunder upset him so."

Fortune was thoughtful. He had been peering into the room and saw a laboratory table and glass-fronted cupboards well supplied with canisters and instrument boxes. "What work is being carried out here?"

"Humphrey is attempting to restore Father's speech," said Frankenstein. "In time, we hope to be able to converse with him. The new battery power may be the answer. Don't worry, he's in no pain; I have invented an elixir which alleviates all discomfort."

"He's not been wandering about trying to find his lost head, has he?" asked Wolfe. "Only—"

"Of course not! We can't allow him out. And Father would never harm anyone."

"Baron, might I ask something?" said Fortune. "When you first saw the body we brought in, you looked like you'd had a bad shock. I've been here long enough to see that not a lot would shock you. Why was that?"

Frankenstein paused. "I can't deny it—when I saw the severed neck, there was something about the cuts that reminded me of Father's work. Of course that's impossible, as he can't see."

"But someone else might work in the same way?" said Fortune. "An assistant who copied his methods? Someone loyal enough to run into a burning building and rescue him? Someone who might have wanted to replace the missing head with a human one?"

Frankenstein shook his head emphatically. "I can guess what you're thinking, but I can assure you that any material Humphrey uses in his studies is obtained legally under the provisions of the Anatomy Act."

Wolfe nodded. "And probably days old, which I'm sure is good enough for a student, but if you want a new head for a living body, I would have thought the fresher the better."

Humphrey was still standing by his master, but he had heard the conversation and turned to Wolfe with a growl. "You can't prove anything!"

"I might, if I made a proper search of this house. But for now, you need to come to the police station with us and answer some questions."

Humphrey's face contorted in alarm. He scuttled up to the door, and for a moment it looked like he was going to try and push his way past the policemen and escape, but instead he slammed it shut. They heard the key turn in the lock.

Wolfe thumped on the door. "Come on out! You're under arrest!" There was no answer. "Well, he can't stay in there forever."

"He doesn't have to," said Elizabeth. "There's another door to the rear of the house, and he has the key."

They listened carefully, and the honking moan sounded again, but more distantly.

"He's trying to get away," said Wolfe.

"Follow me," said Elizabeth. She headed back down the corridor, with the three men hard on her heels. They passed through the hall then out of the main door. Above their heads the great windmill, its sails blackened with soot, was slowly grinding in the wind. The rain had stopped, but the clouds were still dark gray and billowy. As they hurried around the side of the house, they were just in time to see Humphrey and his master emerge from a back door. The old Baron, or what was left of him, keened and stumbled, barely able to walk without the assistance of his loyal retainer. "You can't escape!" said Wolfe. "Give yourself up now!"

Humphrey looked at the thing that leant trustingly on his arm, knowing full well that he would have to abandon it if he was to have any chance of escape. Wolfe and Fortune moved toward him purposefully. It was the decision of a moment, then Humphrey's powerful arms lifted the body over his shoulder and he began to climb up the ladder toward the windmill.

Frankenstein stared up at the figures moving aloft. "Why do they always do that?" he asked, of no one in particular.

Despite the weight of his burden, Humphrey was able to scale the ladder with ease, then he scampered across the roof and began to climb up the side of the windmill. As he reached the pinnacle, there was a loud boom of thunder and a brilliant flash as a bolt of lightning like a multi-tongued snake leapt out and struck the highest point of the tower. For a brief moment all the world was one bright light, then in the dazzle they saw the sails catch fire, and a plume of black smoke, and with a scream and a howl, two figures plummeted together and crashed through the roof.

***

Next morning, Inspector Wolfe was busy at his desk when Constable Fortune arrived. "You wanted to see me, sir?"

"Yes," said Wolfe, pushing some papers aside and rubbing his eyes. "This is probably the most complicated report I have ever had to write. I think some of the details might have to get fudged in the interests of national security. But that made me think. I could really do with an assistant: some bright young constable with a strong stomach. Interested?"

Fortune blinked in surprise. "Why, yes sir!"

"Good. Your first duty would be to make a weekly visit to the Baron to collect any news he might have."

"Oh! Yes, of course, sir!"

"Are you blushing, Fortune? You'll want to watch that. Just one detail you might find handy. Miss Elizabeth has a perfect passion for windmills." Wolfe favored the young constable with a searching look. "I hope you like windmills."

Fortune considered this, then squared his shoulders, gathering together every ounce of courage he possessed. "Loved them since I was a nipper, sir!" he said.

About the Editor

MAXIM JAKUBOWSKI is a London-based former publisher, editor, and translator. He has compiled over one hundred anthologies in a variety of genres, many of which have garnered awards. He is a past winner of the Karel and Anthony awards. He broadcasts regularly on radio and TV, reviews for diverse newspapers and magazines, and has been a judge for several literary prizes. He is the author of twenty novels, the last being *The Louisiana Republic* (2018), and a series of *Sunday Times* bestselling novels under a pseudonym. He has also published five collections of his own short stories. He is currently Vice Chair of the British Crime Writers' Association. www.maximjakubowski. co.uk

About the Authors

MICHAEL BRACKEN and SANDRA MURPHY. **Michael Bracken** is the author of several books and more than 1,200 short stories, including crime fiction published in *Alfred Hitchcock's Mystery Magazine*, *Ellery Queen's Mystery Magazine*, and *The Best American Mystery Stories 2018*. **Sandra Murphy** is an extensively published non-fiction writer and the author of several short stories, including crime fiction collected in *From Hay to Eternity: Ten Tales of Crime and Deception*. This is their first collaboration. www.crimefictionwriter.com

ERIC BROWN has won the British Science Fiction Award twice for his short stories, and his novel *Helix Wars* was shortlisted for the 2012 Philip K. Dick Award. His latest books include the crime novel, set in the 1950s, *Murder Served Cold*, and the SF novel *Buying Time*. He has also written a dozen books for children and over a hundred and fifty short stories. He writes a monthly science fiction review column for the *Guardian* newspaper and lives in Cockburnspath, Scotland. www.ericbrown.co.uk

BERNIE CROSTHWAITE is a novelist, playwright, and short story writer. The three crime novels in the Ravenbridge Trilogy, *If It Bleeds*, *Body Language*, and *The Hemp House*, feature press photographer Jude Baxendale and are set in the north of England. Her plays have been performed in theatres from London to Largs, and on BBC Radio. Her short stories have also been broadcast on national radio. She was delighted that her story *The Golden Hour* was shortlisted for the CWA Short Story Dagger Award. Bernie has worked as a newspaper reporter, a tour guide, and a teacher of English and creative writing. She is very interested in art history, especially the early Renaissance, and enjoys traveling to Italy to see the real thing. She lives and works in North Yorkshire.

O'NEIL DE NOUX is a New Orleans writer with thirty-nine books published, four hundred short story sales, and a screenplay produced. He writes crime fiction, historical fiction, children's fiction, mainstream fiction, science fiction, suspense, fantasy, horror, western, literary, young adult, religious, romance, humor, and erotica. His fiction has received several awards, including the Shamus Award for Best Short Story, the Derringer Award for Best Novelette, and the 2011 Police Book of the Year. Two of his stories have appeared in the *Best American Mystery Stories* anthologies (2013 and 2007). He is a past Vice President of the Private Eye Writers of America. www.oneildenoux.com

MARTIN EDWARDS's latest novel is *Gallows Court*, a thriller set in 1930. He was awarded the CWA Dagger in the Library in 2018 for his body of work. He is consultant to the British Library's Crime Classics series, and has written sixteen contemporary whodunits, including *The Coffin Trail*, which was shortlisted for the Theakston's Prize for best crime novel of the year. His genre study *The Golden Age of Murder* won the Edgar, Agatha, H.R.F. Keating, and Macavity Awards, while *The Story of Classic Crime in 100 Books* won the Macavity Award and was nominated for four other awards. He has also won the CWA Short Story Dagger, the CWA Margery Allingham Prize, and the Poirot Award for his contribution to the crime genre. www.martinedwardsbooks.com

KATE ELLIS was born and brought up in Liverpool and studied drama in Manchester. She worked in a variety of jobs, none of which she particularly enjoyed, before discovering that writing crime fiction was what she'd wanted to do all along! Described by the *Times* as "a beguiling author who interweaves past and present," she has written twenty-three novels featuring black archaeology graduate DI Wesley Peterson and five crime novels with a supernatural twist featuring DI Joe Plantagenet. She has been shortlisted for the CWA Short Story Dagger and for the CWA Dagger in the Library. Her latest Wesley Peterson novel is *Dead Man's Lane*, and the second novel in a new trilogy set in the aftermath of the First World War, *The Boy who Lived with the Dead*, was published in December 2018. www.kateellis.co.uk

JANE FINNIS writes the Aurelia Marcella mystery series, set in Ancient Rome. The four volumes so far are *Shadows in the Night*, *A Bitter Chill*, *Buried Too Deep*, and *Danger in the Wind*. She has also written short stories for a variety of major anthologies. She was born in Yorkshire and now lives there again. www.janefinnis.com

RHYS HUGHES has lived in many different countries. He currently works as a tutor of mathematics. His fiction and articles have been published in a wide variety of books and magazines around the world, and his work has been translated into ten languages. Recent volumes include *Cloud Farming in Wales*, *World Muses*, *How Many Times*, and *The Honeymoon Gorillas*. rhyshughes.blogspot.com

ASHLEY LISTER is a prolific writer of fiction across a broad range of genres, having written more than fifty full-length titles and over a hundred short stories. Aside from regularly blogging about writing, Ashley also teaches creative writing in the northwest of England. He has recently completed a PhD in creative writing where he looked at the relationship between plot and genre in short fiction. www.ashleylister.co.uk

PAUL MAGRS lives and writes in Manchester. In a twenty-five-year writing career, he has published novels in every genre, from Literary to Gothic Mystery to Science Fiction for adults and young adults (including Doctor Who titles). His most recent books include the concluding volume in a science fiction trilogy for kids, *The Heart of Mars* (Firefly Press), and *Fellowship of Ink* (Snow Books) which continues the multi-volume saga of Brenda, the long-lost Bride of Frankenstein. 2019 sees the publication of his book on writing, reading, and creativity, *The Novel Inside You* (Snow Books). He has taught creative writing at both the University of East Anglia and Manchester Metropolitan University, and now writes full time. lifeonmagrs.blogspot.com

KEITH MORAY is a doctor and novelist. He is the author of the best-selling Inspector Torquil McKinnon mysteries, cozy Scottish crime capers set on the fictional Hebridean island of West Uist. He also writes Westerns under the pen name of Clay More and is a member of the Crime Writers' Association, International Thriller Writers, and Western Writers of America; he is a past vice president of Western Fictioneers. He lives in England within arrow shot of a ruined medieval castle, the setting for a couple of his historical crime novels. www.keithmorayauthor.com

AMY MYERS, born in Kent, UK, met her American husband Jim through her job of many years as a director of a London publishing firm. After commuting for ten years between her London office and Paris, where Jim worked, they settled in the Kentish countryside and Amy took up writing as a full-time career. Her current series, set in the 1920s, features Chef Nell Drury, but her first series reflected her commuting years and starred Auguste Didier, the half-French, half-English Victorian master chef, who appears in "Murder and the Battle of the Cucumbers." www.amymyersmd.com

SALLY SPEDDING was born near Porthcawl, Wales, with a Dutch/German background. Having trained in Sculpture, Sally won an international short story competition and was approached by an agent. Her crime thrillers begin with *Wringland*, set on the haunted Fens, published in 2001, and her eleventh, *The Nighthawk*, set in the south of France, and the first in a seven-book deal with Sharpe Books, is out now. She is also an award-winning short story writer, poet, and adjudicator. A member of the CWA, Mystery People, and Crime Cymru, Sally spends part of each year with her artist husband in the eastern Pyrénées, where timeslips occur. www.sallyspedding.com

LINDA STRATMANN started scribbling stories and poems at the age of six. By her teens, she had developed an absorbing and life-long interest in true crime, with a special fascination for the Victorian era. She has worked both as a chemist's dispenser and a civil servant. Her first published book was *Chloroform: The Quest for Oblivion* in 2003. Twelve more non-fiction books followed, including *The Secret Poisoner* and *The Marquess of Queensberry: Wilde's Nemesis*. She also writes two Victorian fiction series, the Frances Doughty mysteries, set in 1880s Bayswater, and the Mina Scarletti mysteries, set in 1870s Brighton. Linda was elected vice-chair of the Crime Writers Association in 2017. www.lindastratmann.com

LAVIE TIDHAR is the author of the Jerwood Fiction Uncovered Prize–winner and Premio Roma nominee *A Man Lies Dreaming* (2014), the World Fantasy Award–winning *Osama* (2011), and the Campbell Award–winning and Locus and Clarke Award–nominated *Central Station* (2016). His latest novels are *Unholy Land* (2018) and his first children's novel, *Candy* (2018). He is the author of many other novels, novellas, and short stories. www.lavietidhar.wordpress.com

CPSIA information can be obtained
at www.ICGtesting.com
Printed in the USA
BVHW031542050519
547395BV00001B/1/P

9 781633 539686